"I had a little incident at work," I said.

"A little incident?" Dr. Gail smiled—if you could call such a condescending facial expression a smile. "Could you explain more?"

"I destroyed a piece of office equipment. A fax machine."

The group muttered imprecations against fax machines like a Greek chorus behind a tragic hero. People understood what I was talking about. I'd had the bad fortune to tap-dance on a piece of crap in an office with a strict antiviolence policy. Then I'd had the further bad fortune to stand before a judge who clearly had it in for me. Really, it wasn't my fault, all these people could see it.

Except Dr. Gail, of course.

In the tradition of Jennifer Weiner's *In Her Shoes* and
Cara Lockwood's *I Do (But I Don't)*,
Eileen Rendahl's captivating novels meld humor and heart!

BE SURE TO READ EILEEN RENDAHL'S

Do Me, Do My Roots

"Heartwarming and hilarious, and the characters jump off the page." —*Romantic Times*

"Moving. . . . An engaging relationship drama . . . [with] a wonderful cast." —Thebestreviews.com

"Simply a winner. . . . Hilarious. . . . It makes me wish I had sisters." —*Old Book Barn Gazette*

"A warm and touching novel." —*Booklist*

Also by Eileen Rendahl

Do Me, Do My Roots

Balancing *in* High Heels

Eileen Rendahl

doWn
tOwn
press

New York   London   Toronto   Sydney

An *Original* Publication of POCKET BOOKS

 DOWNTOWN PRESS, published by Pocket Books
1230 Avenue of the Americas
New York, NY 10020

ISBN: 0-7434-7115-6

First Downtown Press trade paperback edition May 2005

10 8 7 6 5 4 3

DOWNTOWN PRESS and colophon are trademarks of Simon & Schuster, Inc.

Manufactured in the United States of America

Designed by Jaime Putorti

For information regarding special discounts for bulk purchases, please contact Simon & Schuster Special Sales at 1-800-456-6798 or business@simonandschuster.com.

Acknowledgments

Many thanks to Kenneth Bernard, Lindsay Weston, Carol Kirshnit, and Adam Weintraub for their professional expertise. Any factual errors are no reflection on these fine people, but only on my faulty understanding and my willingness to bend the facts to make them into the story I want to tell. Extra thanks to Adam for lunches where I was allowed to whine about the creative process and to Carol for long runs where I was allowed to be as snarky as I wanted to be about everything in the world and Spring Warren for long bike rides where I was allowed to worry about plot points out loud. To the lady lawyers in my life—Joni Halpern, Donna Ward, and Nora Wellman—thank you for your stories and for being the smart, determined, and very caring women that you are. Thank you, thank you, thank you to the Kéblimenos. Janice, you're a treasure and Eric (or should I say Boris?), you're not so shabby yourself. Thank you to Barbara for her beautiful garden.

Thank you to the ladies of OO-COW (Barbara, Christina, Theresa, and Jean) and the Mom Squad (Antoinette, Carol, Carolyn, Joan, and Julie) and the Sacramento Valley Rose (there's way too many of you to list!) and my two new sisters-to-be (Susanna and Jing-Jing) and my best friends (Marian and Diane) and my little ray of sunshine (Sophie). I hope you know how much your friendship and support sustain me.

Most of all, thanks to my mother who never gives up and inspires me every day with her determination and courage.

Thank you to the special men in my life. To Andy, Ted, and Alex, thank you for your patience and unwavering support and enthusiasm. To Josh and Ben, thank you for giving me a glimpse into what it's like to live around teenage boys and for making up protest slogans for strippers. Thank you to my father for, well, just for everything.

Special thanks to Sam and Joni Halpern for physical and emotional shelter during the writing of this book. There are no better people out there than you.

Much gratitude to Pam Ahearn and Micki Nuding for their patience, their guidance, their understanding, their handholding, their tolerance, and probably a whole bunch of other stuff that I never see that they do for me. You guys are great. I feel very lucky to work with you both.

In loving Memory of Frank Gordon Ullman
(December 14, 1926–October 2, 2004).
You will live on in my thoughts, my dreams,
and my heart.

"Wild women will be the first ones the Lord gonna learn how to fly."

Wild Women Never Get the Blues
by Ida Carr

"The man who gets angry at the right things and with the right people, and in the right way and at the right time and for the right length of time, is commended."

Aristotle

Balancing in High Heels

CHAPTER ONE

From *The Angry No More Manual and Workbook*
by Dr. Gail Peterson

RECOGNIZING ANGER

Do you clench your fists? Frown? Grit your teeth or breathe rapidly in and out through your nose? The first step in learning to control your anger is to recognize the signs of your own emotions before they start your Anger Train on an out-of-your-control journey. You don't have to go down the tracks into the inferno.

Helpful Hint: If you've already thrown something or hit someone, it's too late.

Alissa's Anger Workbook:

Exercise #1

List three ways you can tell that you're angry:

1. Trail of broken office equipment and furniture.
2.
3.

I fed the pages of the brief, which had to be in the judge's office by four-thirty, into the fax machine. It was ten after four. I was cutting it close, but I was going to make it. My client was counting on me to get these papers in; they meant the difference between simply continuing her probation or possibly doing jail time.

The pages flowed through one after another, and the machine began the electronic beeps and boops that said it was dialing. Then it stopped.

The digital readout said "Call Failed." No explanation; just "Call Failed."

Okay. Remain calm. The clock was ticking, but there was still time. I tapped the pages into a neat pile, put them into the machine again, and redialed. This time, the pages stopped after only three of the six pages went through. The digital readout said nothing. It was as if I hadn't even dialed.

Quarter after four. Gerald Winters came sprinting by, coffee cup in hand. "Hey, Alissa, let me know when you're done with the fax. I've got some papers to get out today."

"You might want to go to the other machine, Ger. This one seems to be malfunctioning."

He stopped. "Bummer. The other one's completely dead."

Damn! I fed the pages again and started to dial, but no numbers appeared on the readout. It didn't even beep when I pushed the buttons. The machine was plugged in; maybe it had overheated? I turned it off to reset it and then heard the slightly muffled tones of the Lone Ranger theme emanating from my purse. My cell phone. If it had been my sister, it would have been "The Ride of the Valkyries." If it had been my mother, the phone would have buzzed like an angry bee. The Lone Ranger meant it was Thomas, my husband. Well, he was nominally still my husband; we were having a bad patch.

I rustled through my bag and grabbed the phone, tucking it

between my shoulder and ear while I stacked the brief in the fax yet again and turned the machine back on. "Hey, Thomas."

"Hey, yourself, Alissa."

"What's up?" I jabbed the fax buttons. *Still* nothing! What the hell was wrong with this thing?

"I need a favor, babe."

That was a good sign. Asking for a favor implied that the askee would receive a return favor in the future. Which implied a certain amount of give-and-take. Give-and-take implied a relationship that still functioned, right? "Sure. What is it?"

"I've gotten myself into a little situation and I need to move our papers through."

I froze with my thumb on the fax machine's Send button. "What papers?"

"Our divorce papers, Alissa. Bethany's pregnant."

Bethany? He was talking to me about Bethany? Bethany, who was the source of the chlamydia that had given me PID? (That's pelvic inflammatory disease, for those unaccustomed to the acronyms of the sexually overactive and underprotected.) The PID that had landed me in the emergency room with a fever of one hundred and three degrees and nonstop vomiting, which had led me to discover my husband's infidelity, which had, in turn, led to the previously mentioned "bad patch" we were currently going through.

"Wh-what?" I croaked out. I smacked the fax machine three times hard on the side. This had worked for me in the past, and not just with fax machines. Still nothing, though.

"Bethany is pregnant, Alissa. The baby's mine. I need to do the right thing."

Now he was worried about doing the right thing? How come he didn't think about that before he started shtupping Bethany? "How is this the right thing, Thomas? We're trying to build a life here." I shook the fax machine. Just a little.

"Yes, but there's a new life coming into the world. An innocent one, Alissa."

And I was guilty? Of what? "Thomas, we need to discuss this. Let's not rush into anything."

"There's nothing to discuss, Alissa. I've made up my mind. I'm messengering over some papers, and I would appreciate it if you'd sign them and return them immediately."

"Thomas, wait!" The only response I got was a burst of static. I looked at my phone. "Call Ended."

My chest heaved. My heart beat fast and I couldn't seem to get enough air in my lungs. Thomas was leaving me. For good. For real. For Bethany.

With shaking hands, I tried to dial the judge's fax number again. I just wanted to get the stupid thing to go through so I could leave before Thomas's messenger arrived.

Nothing. Not a beep or a buzz or a blip.

A white buzz filled my mind, and suddenly the room was unbearably hot, my legs weak. I braced myself against the fax machine—the stupid, useless fax machine that couldn't send the stupid, useless papers to the stupid, useless judge so that my stupid, useless client could stay out of jail and take care of her stupid, useless children who would undoubtedly also become drug users, since the vicious cycle *never* ended!

I picked the damn fax machine up and flung it across the room.

*   *   *

"So, Alissa, tell us why you're here."

I looked around the room. Dr. Gail had a good question there. I certainly wasn't here because I wanted to be. Who would choose to spend their Tuesday evenings in a room with sour-smelling industrial-grade carpet, uncomfortable orange molded-plastic chairs arranged in a circle, and Starving Artist Sale artwork on the wall? I closed my eyes and prayed for some kind of out-of-body experience to whisk me away. Remember those Calgon commercials? I needed an industrial-sized box of the stuff.

"Alissa," Gail prompted again.

I opened my eyes and tried to smile at her, but it was hard to make my face obey. I couldn't believe a woman with 1980s Mall Bangs held my life in her hands at this moment. How could I take her seriously when every time she spoke, I was distracted by the six-inch bangs standing straight up and waving in the breeze?

After our last meeting Gail had taken me aside and confided (in an exceedingly passive-aggressive tone, I might add) that if I didn't start "sharing" more in Group, she would be forced to tell the judge that I was not participating fully in my court-mandated Anger-Management Classes. I had promised to "share" at the next meeting, managing to keep myself from pulling out a pair of scissors and chopping her bangs off at the roots only because, well, I don't carry scissors around with me.

"I had a little incident at work," I said.

"A little incident?" Gail smiled—if you could actually call such a condescending facial expression a smile. "Could you explain more?"

Gail knew it wasn't a "little" incident. "Little" incidents don't wind up with you talking to a judge, writing apologies to your colleagues, or having your ex-husband take out a protective order against you.

I cleared my throat. "I destroyed a piece of office equipment."

"What kind?" Anthony piped up. Anthony is a car salesman at a Land Rover dealership. He'd whipped a stapler at the head of another salesman whom he believed had stolen one of his commissions. He'd missed, but the other salesman had pressed charges anyway. I guess Land Rovers aren't moving quite as fast as they used to during the dot-com boom, and being a lousy throw is no excuse under the law.

"A fax machine," I answered.

Anthony nodded with great feeling. "Man, I hate those things. Won't dial half the time. Won't go through the other half. Pieces of crap."

"Yes," I said. "That was exactly it. The first time it took all the pages but didn't send them. The second time it just stopped halfway through, and then it wouldn't even dial the number."

The group muttered imprecations against fax machines like a Greek chorus behind a tragic hero. Amazing. I felt better. People understood what I was talking about. I'd just had the bad fortune to tap-dance on a piece of crap in an office with a strict antiviolence policy (funny how that had always seemed to be a good thing to me before). Then I'd had the further bad fortune to stand before a judge who clearly had it in for me. Really, it wasn't my fault, and clearly all these people could see it.

Except Gail, of course.

"Now, Alissa," she said, leaning forward in her chair, clipboard balanced in her lap, bangs jutting forward like a flying buttress. "I want you to close your eyes and concentrate on what you were feeling right then. Did you feel hot? Was your heart beating faster? Think about what you were experiencing as the fax machine malfunctioned."

I obeyed and closed my eyes. I've seen my share of reform-school movies; I know that the best way to get out alive is to cooperate. I didn't want to end up being the girl that the burly nurse wearing surgical gloves took into solitary.

"I remember feeling too warm. I wished I'd left my jacket in my office. My neck hurt, too, and I had a little headache. We were swamped at the office that day."

"Good," Gail said, as if I'd accomplished some amazing task rather than just whining. "Excellent, Alissa. Now, everyone, what are some other choices Alissa could have made right then to derail her Anger Train and remain the Engineer of her own destiny?"

Maurice's hand shot up. "Deep breathing. She could have done deep breathing." Maurice was one of our three wife-beaters. His wife had called the cops after the second time in one week that he'd stripped off all her clothes and then locked her out of the house stark naked.

"That's good, Maurice. Yes, she could have used her breathing. Anybody else?" Gail asked.

Oh, come on. I could have huffed and puffed at the fax machine until I hyperventilated, and the damn thing still wouldn't have dialed.

"Muscle relaxation." Caleb was another wife-beater, but more of your classic smack-across-the-face kind of guy. Frighteningly charming when he wasn't in your face, but apparently he had extremely strong feelings on exactly how his wife should park the car in the garage. Scary all the way around.

"Another good one. Thank you, Caleb." Gail looked around the room. "Steve, how about you?"

Steve looked up from a minute exploration of his Doc Martens. The fluorescent lights glinted off the rings in his eyebrow. Steve had taken a crowbar to another boy's car in retaliation for the other boy's flirting with Steve's girlfriend at a basketball game. "Visualization," he mumbled.

"Yes, Steve. Excellent." Gail looked back at me.

Oh, please. Like visualizing the pages traveling the phone wires to the judge's office would have gotten them there? And imagining the fat cells on my thighs shrinking will make my cellulite go away, too.

"What about walking away, folks? Could Alissa have chosen to walk away from the fax machine and come back later?"

Several heads nodded.

"*No,*" I broke in. "I couldn't. If the fax didn't get to the judge by four-thirty, we'd have missed the filing time and my client would have been in violation of her parole. It was already four-fifteen. I didn't have time to walk away."

The group stopped murmuring. None of us wanted our lawyers to miss a deadline and have us be in violation of our parole. We were all out living our regular lives with only the weekly privilege of attending Anger Management with Gail the Good Witch because we had lawyers who didn't miss deadlines.

These people knew how important that fax was. I had them on my side again. Of course, my haircut was also much better than Gail's, and this was L.A., where such things matter.

"Okay. That's reasonable. You couldn't walk away," Gail agreed. "But the other techniques might have helped. What happened next, Alissa?" she prompted.

I took a deep breath. "Well, I was trying to get the fax to dial again when my cell phone rang."

"Who was on the phone, Alissa? How did the call make you feel?" Gail asked.

"It was Thomas on the phone. My ex." I closed my eyes again and saw his handsome face. How had I felt? Betrayed? Humiliated? Undercut? I started breathing hard just thinking about that call, just thinking about Thomas. "He wasn't quite my ex yet. That's why he called." I swallowed hard.

"Go ahead, Alissa. What happened next?"

"The stupid fax *still* wouldn't dial. I kept punching the buttons, but it just sat there. It didn't even bleep at me—like I wasn't even worth the effort. Thomas said he was messenger-ing some papers over that I needed to sign right away. He needed the final divorce papers in. He and Bethany needed to get married. She was pregnant." My eyeballs felt hot and I couldn't get enough air in. My throat seemed to have closed up. I breathed harder. My fingernails dug into the palms of my hand.

"And how did that make you feel?" Gail asked. "Remember to use 'I' statements."

How did it make me *feel?* I took a slow, deep breath in through my nose and then let it out slowly through my mouth. "I felt frustrated that the fax machine wouldn't work."

"Good, Alissa. Go on."

"I felt annoyed with Thomas for disturbing me at work."

"Is that all?" Gail leaned forward in her chair. "Really try to remember. What did you say to Thomas?"

Thomas had sounded so calm, so reasonable. He always did. It was just his behavior that was so damn unreasonable. It is simply not reasonable to screw around on your wife, give her a sexually transmitted disease that may or may not completely foul up her reproductive system, and then six months later expect her to expedite your paperwork so you can marry your pregnant girlfriend. I was thirty years old and living in a mildewy garden apartment, crying over him every night and unable to even get bleeped by a damn fax machine.

The very unreasonableness of it all swept over me like a giant tidal wave, lifting me up on its giant curl to new heights of indignation and incredulity.

Bethany is vapid and phony. She wears false eyelashes and her skirts are too tight and too short and . . . and . . . Thomas loved her better than he loved me.

Of course I was angry! Who *wouldn't* be angry? So angry, in fact, that you might just take the useless fax machine, rip it out of the wall, throw it on the floor, and stomp on it.

"How did you *feel*, Alissa?" Gail prodded.

"*How do you think I felt, Gail? You're the therapist. I felt like it wasn't freaking fair!* I FELT CHEATED AND ABUSED AND PISSED OFF! THAT'S HOW I FELT!"

"Alissa, put the chair down!"

I looked around.

I'm not sure how it happened, but somehow I'd ended up in the middle of the circle with my orange chair up over my head. Gail was on the floor behind her chair, bangs quivering with fright. Anthony and Maurice were both cowering. So was Chad, the third member of our wife-beating trio. Steve and Liang, the little Asian woman who had slammed a fellow office worker in the back of the head with a three-ring binder over a coffeemaker dispute (only *one* scoop per cup and use *cold* water), were the only ones sitting up straight. Steve gave me a little smile, the first I'd ever seen from him. Liang winked.

I remembered my prayer for an out-of-body experience.

Maybe I should have wished for a pony.

"So did you throw the chair?"

"No, Marsha. Of course I didn't throw the chair. What kind of person do you think I am?" I couldn't believe my sister had even asked. Didn't she know me at all?

"I'm not sure anymore, Alissa. A few months ago, I wouldn't have said you were the kind of person to rip a fax machine out of the wall and try to use it as a trampoline," Marsha observed. "Although you always were an overachiever. I suppose if you were going to start displacing your anger on inanimate objects, no one should have expected you to do it halfway."

She had a point, and not just about the overachiever thing. I hadn't thought I was the kind of person to rip a fax machine out of the wall and stomp the bejeezus out of it, either. Maybe I was the one who didn't know me at all. "Normal" people knew where the boundaries were, where the lines were that you weren't supposed to cross.

I remembered the horrified looks on my colleagues' faces when I finally came back to myself and looked around from atop the fax machine. People stood frozen, coffee mugs halfway to lips, pens poised in the air, mouths open in shock, dismay, and maybe, in a few cases, gleeful anticipation of imminent fall from glory. Clearly they didn't know me so well, either.

So I was wrong about what kind of person I was and I had been wrong about Thomas. I'd thought he was the man of my dreams, my life partner, my helpmeet. What else was I wrong about? What else didn't I know? Maybe I'd walk out the door tomorrow and the grass would be purple and the sky would be pink. Maybe two plus two would no longer equal four, which, while it would have the benefit of explaining why my checking account never balances, would still be very confusing. Maybe up was down and red was blue and horizontal stripes didn't make me look fat. Maybe everything I'd counted on was just a house of cards ready to collapse beneath me. Maybe it had already collapsed. I felt off-balance, unstable, as if the very ground beneath me had become treacherous. Like I'd been walking a tightrope all along and had only just now realized how precarious my situation was.

My breath started to come hard and fast as my mind raced over the possibilities, over the millions of missteps I could make every day. There were dozens of things that I could be wrong, wrong, wrong about. How to plead a case. How to write a brief. What shoes to wear with my new Prada knockoff skirt. I began to shake.

It was hard enough to balance on the line each day; not knowing where it was made it damn near impossible.

"Please, Marsha. Don't joke. I don't know what to do. I'm frightened. Tell me what to do."

"Come home," my sister said without a second's hesitation. "Come home where I can take care of you."

It was so quintessentially Marsha. The bossiness. The conviction. The love. Marsha's nearly ten years older than I am. In the years between our births, there were at least three miscarriages and one heartbreakingly stillborn baby boy that my mother still lights a Yahrzeit candle for every year. By the time I came along, Marsha was old enough to help take care of me. As far as she is concerned, I was her baby then and I still am now.

I've been fighting it since I could draw breath, so you can understand how surprised I was when I said, "Okay."

What with quitting my job at the public defender's office and setting things up back home, it took close to six months to actually get my stuff in a moving van and up I-5 from Los Angeles, but I did finally find my way back to San Jose. Thank you, Dionne Warwick.

I pulled into the driveway of my new condo and walked into the front courtyard entrance. When I first looked at it, family in tow, my mother had said it felt like a prison. My sister had clapped her hands together and said it would hold a beautiful container garden that she immediately began to sketch out for me. Sometimes I think she actually channels Martha Stewart.

I set Snowball's cat carrier down and opened the door. He did not emerge. I peeked inside. He looked back at me with a disdainful look in his slightly crossed blue eyes. Supposedly, he is a flame point Siamese. I asked the woman at the no-kill shelter where I got him what a classy cat like that would have been doing there. She only shrugged. Whatever he is, I like the way he remains haughty despite having landed on hard times.

I fished a brand-new feather-and-fur covered catnip mouse out of my bag and dragged it in front of the carrier in an enticing manner.

Nothing.

I peeked in.

Snowball yawned.

"Come on, little man. It's time to come out. This is home now."

I opened a tin of Fancy Feast Flaked Tuna, his favorite, and set it a few feet from the carrier. He gave me an owlish blink.

"Hiding won't help. You might as well come out and face it." I know that's true; I'd tried it briefly after Thomas dumped me. I moved into my bed with several Costco-sized boxes of Little Debbie snack cakes and a lot of ice cream. Hiding does not change your reality. It will, however, add ten stubborn pounds to your thighs and bring your secretary knocking on your door to see why you haven't been to work in close to a week.

I created a trail of Pounce Treats from the carrier door to

the Fancy Feast tin and walked away. A watched cat is, in my experience, damned unlikely to do anything but stare at you with kitty disdain.

I dialed my cell phone. Kathleen answered on the first ring.

Kathleen has been my best friend since third grade, when we both ended up in the infirmary at Girl Scout camp. She'd marched through a veritable hedge of poison ivy that had left her skin a topographical map of ooze. I'd turned my ankle trying to catch crawdads in the creek. I was lucky not to be covered with leeches. She was lucky not to go into anaphylactic shock. I spent the afternoon putting calamine lotion on her bony little back, and she fetched ice for my ankle. Since then she's been Ethel to my Lucy (except she's prettier than me), Shirley to my Laverne (except she's the blond one to my brunette), and occasionally Tonto to my Lone Ranger (without the ugly racial overtones).

Moving away to L.A. and moving back, one of us having babies and one having an eighty-hour-a-week job, one of us having a good marriage and one having a not-so-good one—none of it had really changed us. I'd studied for the bar while she studied Dr. Spock. I whined to her about the political structure at the public defender's office while she complained about playgroup management (remarkably similar when you come right down to it). I'd flown back to San Jose to be her maid of honor. She'd flown down to L.A. and held my hand when Thomas dumped me. Through all of it, we'd both managed to think what the other one was doing was important.

"I'm baaacckk," I crooned into my phone.

She rewarded me with an immediate high-pitched squeal.

She's always been a screamer. "We'll be there in fifteen minutes." She hung up without even saying good-bye.

I called my mother and then my sister. The movers were due with my stuff in about an hour. I sat down cross-legged on the concrete of the new courtyard and leaned back against the pink stucco wall. It was chilly and rough beneath my back, not yet warmed by the weak spring sunlight.

The courtyard smelled dusty and looked desolate with only a few dead, decaying leaves that must have come over from a neighbor's tree. A sharp crescent of waxing moon was just visible in the day-lit sky above the spot my sister insisted was perfect for bougainvillea. It was mine now. Mine to neglect or mine to make something of. I guess we'd just have to see.

Snowball emerged from the carrier, stopping to eat each Pounce Treat on his way to the tuna, which he then devoured. He leaped on the mouse, rolled around with it a few times, growled, and trotted off with it in his mouth. He likes to play hard to get, but I know how to get my man in the end.

Provided he's furry and neutered.

Kathleen got there first, with Hayley and Jason stumbling behind her, their thumbs frantically working the buttons on their Game Boys.

"Don't judge me" were the first words out of her mouth, almost before I could hug her. "The GameBoys will keep them busy for hours so I can actually help you, instead of yelling at them to stop doing whatever they're doing the whole time."

She set a cooler down next to me and started pulling out peanut butter and grape jelly sandwiches (crusts cut off and then sandwiches cut into triangles) and grapes (washed). Then she opened a charming tangerine-colored net tote bag that matched her sandals and pulled out little bags of potato chips (fattening) and chocolate chip cookies (even more fattening and lucious with the chocolate chips gone slightly melty).

"Thank you," I said through the crumbs. I hadn't realized how hungry I was.

"You're welcome. It's nice to receive some appreciation." She glanced pointedly at Jason.

He rolled his eyes. I was impressed; Jason was only in first grade. I hadn't learned to roll my eyes like that until junior high, at least. Then again, I learned it from Kathleen. Maybe it was genetic.

"You didn't make her carry hers in a bandanna," he said, wrinkling his freckle-covered nose.

I arched a brow at Kathleen.

She blushed. "I read this article in some magazine about packing lunches your kids would love. They had apparently not met my kids. Not only would Jason not eat the Hippie Lunch, he wouldn't even carry it to school."

"Hippie Lunch?" I grabbed a handful of grapes, and they burst on my tongue as I bit into them. I am so lucky to live in a place where the fruit is this good and migrant labor is so cheap. I feel guilty about this often, but it doesn't stop me from eating fruit.

"An apple, some string cheese, homemade fig bars, and organic juice, all wrapped in a red bandanna. It was darling!" she cooed.

"It was lame," Jason said.

"It was packed in a bandanna," I said.

They both nodded.

"You have no idea of the scrutiny I'm under every day with this stuff," Kathleen said. "One time last fall I let Jason get hot lunch. Then the next day in the quad when I picked him up, Jenny Wilson's mother came up and in this really loud voice announced that Jenny had told her that Jason had only eaten the cookies and had thrown out the rest of the lunch."

"Oh," I said. What else was there to say?

"I was so embarrassed! She said she only told me because she 'thought I should know,' but I know she just wanted everyone to know that I wasn't giving Jason a proper lunch."

I grabbed another bunch of grapes. "Why would she want to do that?"

"I don't know. Maybe because I nixed her idea of having the Little League party at the pizza place and suggested a cookout at the park instead, and everybody said afterward how much better it was."

Clearly, Kathleen needed to get out more. Or maybe Jenny Wilson's mother did. All I knew was that somebody needed a big dose of perspective.

The sound of my mother's voice wafted over the courtyard door. "Marsha, put that in my walker. I can push it."

Judging from the sounds, they were quite close.

"I don't need you to push it for me, Mom. I've got it," Marsha's voice answered.

"But it will fit right here," Mom protested.

"It fits right in my arms."

"Why won't you let me help?"

"Why won't you walk to the door?" It pleased me to hear Marsha's composure snap a little.

Just listening to them made me want to bean Mom over the head with whatever Marsha was carrying. It must have been heavy, since last time I was home, Marsha gave me a little speech about letting Mom do everything she could do and not coddling her. Apparently carrying things for Mom was damaging to her self-esteem, and I needed to be more sensitive to that fact. I took pity on Marsha and went and opened the courtyard door.

Mom wheeled through with her pausing step, shoved the walker aside, and lurched into my arms. Marsha peeked at us from around the gigantic plant in her arms.

"What the hell is that?" I asked.

"A hollyhock for your courtyard," Marsha said, marching in. "And you're welcome."

Having my mother, my sister, Kathleen, and her two kids all in my house with movers trying to place what little I'd opted to bring with me wasn't the pure hell I'd expected. It was more like purgatory. I knew it would end eventually, I just didn't know exactly when.

By eleven o'clock that night my dishes and kitchenware were put away in places where I would probably never find them again, courtesy of my mother. My books had been organized on shelves by color and size. Hayley's only four and can't read yet, so I couldn't expect her and Jason to organize books by category. About one quarter of my clothing was precisely lined up in one of my closets, while the other closet was stuffed with the things Kathleen thought I shouldn't have bothered to move. She'd also tactfully mentioned a new show on the Learning Channel called "What Not to Wear" and jotted down when it aired.

I couldn't wait for them to stop helping me and go home.

You would think that the stupefying drive would have given me my solitude fix for the day, but apparently I was turning into a solitude junkie. Pretty soon I'd be ducking furtively into isolation booths and lying about where I was going.

I shooed them out the door with a promise to walk with Kathleen the next morning, showered, and then collapsed with wet hair on my freshly made bed with its precise, crisp hospital corners (thank you, Marsha). The ceiling fan whirred a lullaby above me. I fell asleep faster and more completely than I had in months. Until about two A.M.

In my dream I stood on the edge of a cliff. Mist swirled around me. The sounds of my pursuers drifted up out of the fog behind me. I didn't know who they were, how many they were, or even why they were after me. I just knew they were coming. The only escape was over the precipice, and I flung myself into the air. The ground rushed toward me. Right before I hit, my eyes flew open as if by electronic switch.

For a heart-stopping thirty seconds of emotional vertigo, I had no clue where I was. My bed was on the wrong wall, the shadows on the ceiling ran the wrong way, unfamiliar noises (the neighbor's dog growling softly and traffic from Lawrence Expressway) made me jump. My eyes felt like I'd spent a day at the beach—hot and gritty. I went downstairs to get a drink of water.

Once I made it to the kitchen, the French doors to the courtyard beckoned me outside. My hollyhock rustled its leaves at me, almost like a greeting. In the silver light of the moon, its showy pink flowers lost their color and blended in with the leaves. How like Marsha to buy me something with big pink flowers. I am so *not* about pink. It was just like when she used to tape bows to my bald head when I was six months old.

Snowball sauntered out and crawled into my lap, settling into a steady purr. I buried my nose in his white fur. The moonlight softened the courtyard's hard edges turning everything a soft gray with shadows hiding within shadows. I felt like hiding in the shadows a little more myself, where the moonlight made everything seem mysterious and full of possibilities.

Because let's face it—these days I needed all the possibilities I could get.

CHAPTER TWO

From *The Angry No More Manual and Workbook*
By Dr. Gail Peterson

NO STUFFING ALLOWED

Lashing out indiscriminately doesn't work, but neither does pretending you were never angry in the first place. The key to derailing your Anger Train is to control it without it controlling you. You can master your passion without being the slave of reason.

Alissa's Anger Workbook:

Exercise #2

List three ways of dealing with anger that don't entail hitting anyone or throwing anything. How have these techniques worked for you?

1. Deep breathing. Nearly hyperventilated.
2. Visualization. Fell asleep.
3. Breaking office equipment. Highly satisfying, but not so good for life plan.

"So when are you going to start sleeping around?" Kathleen asked.

"Excuse me?" I came to a standstill.

We were walking the track at the community college. Kathleen had on pink terry-cloth shorts with a matching zip-front jacket. Her blond hair was up in a high ponytail that swung from side to side as she marched forcefully along. I'd thrown on black bike shorts with a giant T-shirt that someone had given Thomas when he'd donated blood. Kath had winced when I showed up at her door.

Think Uma Thurman and Janeane Garafalo in *The Truth About Cats and Dogs.* Think Betty and Veronica if Veronica was short and Betty was flat-chested. That's Kathleen and me.

"Oh, please," Kathleen said over her shoulder, not waiting for me to catch up. "It's what women our age who get divorced do. It's part of the recovery process. You know, reclaiming your sexuality, feeling attractive again. A little sluttiness can go a long way toward that."

"Kathleen, you have to stop watching *Oprah.*" I jogged to her side.

She shrugged. "What else am I supposed to do while I'm folding laundry? Watch the Golf Channel?"

I conceded the point.

"Besides, it's not an Oprah thing," she continued, still marching like a mad marionette. "Rhonda Kranowski got divorced last year and went through at least half a dozen guys in about four months. She said it was the best sex of her life."

"Who the hell is Rhonda Kranowski?"

"Deanna Kranowski's mother."

"And she is?"

"A little girl who was in Jason's class last year." I'd never been afraid of Kathleen's elbows before, but she was swinging them so hard right now I suspected they could go through steel. "Though I suppose you could do the New Age thing instead."

"What New Age thing?"

"Worshipping ancient goddesses. Carol Epstein—she has a little boy at the same preschool that Hayley goes to—did that."

"What exactly did she do?"

"Oh, she started wearing a lot of crystals and hand-woven things and reading tarot cards and stuff. She got a bumper sticker that said 'Ankh If You Love Isis.'"

"I don't think I can do that."

"Why not?"

"For starters, because I hate bumper stickers even more than those yellow window signs that say 'Baby on Board.' Even more than stuffed Garfields with suction-cup feet."

"You don't have to get a bumper sticker, you moron. That was just an example."

"An example of what?" I asked.

"Of something to do while you're getting over it. Of moving on. Seriously, Lissa, you're not the only person to have a marriage dissolve on them." Pump, pump, pump went Kathleen's elbows.

"Actually, I was beginning to wonder if you knew anybody who wasn't divorced."

Kathleen stopped marching. "Fewer and fewer, every year that goes by. Shit happens. People get divorced. Life goes on. Don't you think you've spent enough time moping over Thomas? He wasn't even that great of a husband."

I whirled to face her, hands on my hips. "What's that supposed to mean?"

"Even leaving aside issues of fidelity and condom usage, he

wasn't exactly a stellar life mate, now, was he?" Her hands went to her hips as well.

I'd whined to Kath about Thomas countless times in telephone conversations and e-mails, but I suppose it's the difference between saying that you're fat and having your girlfriend *tell* you that you're fat. I was the only one who got to say that Thomas was a lousy husband.

We stood there, nose to nose, glaring at each other until Kath cracked up and shoved my shoulder. She turned and went on walking. "I personally think I'd choose sluthood. It sounds like more fun."

I trotted after her again.

"I have the perfect candidate for your first step on the road to life as a fallen woman, too," she said. I was glad that she was starting to sound a little winded.

"Kath, I don't want to be fixed up." Had we sped up? Why had my heart started pounding like that?

"Why not? Because you're doing such a great job of lining up dates on your own? Or because you're just too scared?"

She had a point. Thomas had already remarried and started a family. I'd yet to go for coffee with someone. It wasn't as if I hadn't considered her idea; a good orgasm could be a real tension reliever. It would, however, require another person. Therein lies the rub. Or I guess the lack of a rub.

Sex was one of the things Thomas and I really had going for us. The man had had an extremely talented set of hips. His hands and mouth were none too shabby, either. Even now, after everything that had happened and all the months that had passed, I still missed his touch. I'd wake up sometimes aching for him, reaching for him before I realized that he wasn't there.

I'd thought the heat between us had meant something. Like we were soul mates or fated to be together. If two people's bodies could do that together, surely their minds and souls had to be somehow entwined as well? Hard to believe I was such an idealistic idiot, isn't it?

But while Thomas and I were racking up some steamy minutes between the sheets, he was also getting his accounts serviced personally by Bethany. All that heat and passion hadn't meant much to Thomas, and I apparently couldn't tell the difference between good technique and true love.

Then there was the whole control thing. I'd worked so hard to keep things together since the chair incident, and sex (at least, the good kind) was so out of control. It would have to be a heck of an orgasm to make it worth the risk.

"I just haven't met anyone who interested me," I said primly.

Kathleen sighed. "You've been so shut down that Rob Lowe could walk in and sit in your lap and you wouldn't be interested."

I questioned the fairness of bringing up junior high crushes, but it would only devolve into the same argument we'd been having since we were fifteen over whether Kirk Cameron was cuter than Rob Lowe. History has shown me to be the winner on that one, but Kath is so damn stubborn she won't concede. "I haven't shut down."

She snorted. "Please. In half the conversations we've had in the last six months, your voice has been flatter than the library recording that calls to tell me my books are overdue."

"I'm just trying to stay centered. I'm trying to stay calm."

"There's calm, Alissa, and then there's dead."

I got home, showered, and came downstairs to survey my new office. Unfortunately, my professional life was as much of a shambles as my personal one. After my little leave of absence from the public defender's office had ended, I was clearly derailed from the fast track. I didn't get the plum assignments anymore. If a case came along that might put me in contact with someone who could help me later on or get me a little attention, it went to another associate.

The current blanks on my professional dance card were worrisome. So worrisome that I actually considered opening the bank statement lying on my desk to see what my checking account balance was in reality, rather than the sort of fuzzy general number I kept in the back of my mind. Thank goodness the phone rang and distracted me. I'll do almost anything to keep from facing bank statements, even when I do have money.

"Ms. Alissa Lindley?" the voice at the other end of the phone said. "This is the court clerk down at City of San Jose?"

"Mmmm," I said in response. I mean, if she wasn't sure she was the court clerk, how was I to be?

"We have a case for you if you have the time right now?"

I'd signed up to be rotated in when the public defender's office got overloaded, hoping I'd get a few clients, and here I was being presented with an opportunity almost immediately.

I opened my PDA just so the clerk could hear the beep and not think I was just sitting around on a Tuesday morning waiting for her call. I hate to look easy. It's bad enough being cheap. Just as I thought, the only thing on my schedule for the day was dinner at my mother's around six-thirty. "Sure, I've got the time. I'll be right down." No sense in playing too hard to get, either.

I changed out of my sweats and into a gray knee-length skirt and a white fitted blouse with a black V-neck sweater over it. I put on my new BCBG boots (stretchy, black, high on the calf, medium heel) for good luck and hit the road. I know I shouldn't have bought them with my financial status so uncertain, but they were on sale at Nordstrom. Could you have resisted?

I thought not.

I headed down Interstate 280 toward the Guadalupe Parkway exit in San Jose. A wine-colored BMW slipped into my lane without a look or a signal. I breathed deeply in through my nose for a count of five and out through my mouth for a count of ten, just like my stress-relief tape advised. Then I watched as the bonehead pulled the same maneuver in front of someone else. Apparently the breathing thing worked a little. I still wanted to pound the asshole's face in, but I was completely sure I could do it without my left eyelid twitching.

I parked my Volvo in the giant parking complex across from the courthouse and walked over West Hedding Street on the big pedestrian walkway.

Inside the courthouse the heels of my boots tapped on the linoleum floor when I headed for the bathroom. It's good to enter a new courtroom confident that you have no lipstick on your teeth and that your hair doesn't look like it's been styled by small vicious animals.

On my way I passed two men who had just come out of

the courtroom to my left. One was probably in his mid-fifties with silver hair and a beautifully tailored navy blue suit. The wool looked so soft and smooth that I wanted to rest my cheek against it. Luckily, those weren't the boundaries I had trouble with. The other guy was probably in his early forties, and either he'd gained a lot of weight recently or he'd bought his suit in both an unfortunate shade of brown and a size too small. They didn't spare me a glance.

Back in L.A. I would probably have run into three people I knew by now and would have known every politically motivated move they'd made in the past five years. In San Jose I didn't know anybody and they didn't know me. This had both good points and bad. On the one hand, no one was likely to run screaming if I approached a photocopier or a fax. On the other hand, no one owed me any favors, either. Overall, I guess it was a wash.

Inside, the bathroom looked like the model that all those Pottery Barn bathrooms are based on, except, well, actually old. A few of the checkerboard floor tiles were missing and a lot of them were cracked. Some of the fixtures had been replaced and didn't match. The mirrors had that foggy look that they get when they've been around a long time. It was relatively clean, though, and everything worked.

I could relate. I wasn't quite as bright and shiny as I used to be, but I was still clean and serviceable. So why was my heart racing and my mouth as dry as a desert?

I took a deep breath in and let it out, trying to still the butterflies in my stomach. *I would be fine.* So I hadn't actually been in a courtroom in quite a few months. It was like riding a bicycle: it would all come back to me. I just had to get past this first moment of fear as I pushed off and started to pedal.

The first Gail-sanctioned coping strategy was to ask someone else if the anxiety was appropriate. That wouldn't work; no one else was here to ask.

Okay. Second step. How was my coping strategy working? Well, hiding in the bathroom in the courthouse was better than my kitchen, but it wasn't exactly the high road to success, either.

I left my temporary refuge and made my way to Courtroom 218.

It was a typical afternoon in a typical courtroom. There were drunks and homeless people and some tough-looking kids working hard at continuing to look tough in a tough situation. There was also one guy curled up in a ball in his chair, who occasionally meowed like a cat or hissed when someone walked too close to him. I hoped he wouldn't lick himself.

I stared at the file jacket and then back at the person the clerk indicated was to be my client. Her name was Sheila Montrose. "But the jacket says burglary," I stated flatly.

"It is a burglary," the clerk answered.

"But that person is female." Not just female. Defiantly female. Outrageously female. Splendidly female. Sheila filled out a prison jumpsuit in a way that had every man who wasn't blind or insane slicking his hair back and checking his breath. I think the one blind guy in the room was even sucking in his gut and straightening his cuffs. She was that gorgeous. Not even Ru Paul could pull off a prison jumpsuit the way this babe did.

Granted, I've only been a defense attorney for five or six years now, but burglars are always male, almost always young, and nearly always junkies. They are not the brightest bulbs in the crime chandelier nor are they the biggest fish in the felonious food chain. They are opportunists taking the path of least resistance between them and their next fix. The charming cat burglar who looks like Cary Grant or Pierce Brosnan (depending on how old you like your movies) is a movie thing, not a reality thing.

A burglar who looked like a *Sports Illustrated* swimsuit model was definitely not a reality thing. It was more of an Internet fantasy-site kind of thing.

But a client is a client and I needed some of those. Since no one knew me here in San Jose, I might have to take on a few weirdo cases until I'd networked my way in.

Then also, a person in need of defense is simply that: a person in need of defense. Even if just looking at her made me feel every one of my thirty years and the gravitational pull on my not-so-slender body, Sheila definitely needed defense. She could even be innocent. Have I mentioned that burglars are pretty much NEVER EVER female?

I introduced myself, and the deputy showed us to a conference room where Sheila and I could confer in private. He'd puffed his chest up so big that the wild array of communication devices and weaponry attached to his body stuck out like quills on a porcupine. Sheila didn't seem to notice.

Interesting girl. What she had noticed, as we walked out of the crowded courtroom, was a slack-jawed young man with a blue Mohawk and multiple piercings. He'd slumped to one side, looking skinny and frail in the big orange jumpsuit. Every once in a while, he twitched.

Before I could stop her, Sheila put a hand on his shoulder. He started, bared his teeth, at her and growled deep in his throat. Great. All we needed was for Cat Man to hiss and climb up a curtain with Mohawk Boy in growling pursuit, while Deputy Porcupine smacked people over the head with his billy club. I really didn't want to get knocked ass over teakettle by a couple of guys who'd taken enough drugs to be confused about what genus they belonged in.

Before I could pull Sheila away, she had knelt down next to Mohawk Boy so they were face-to-face. "I didn't mean to startle you, sweetie," she'd said.

I waited for him to bite her, but the kid with the Mohawk just stared at her.

"There's something icky in your 'do," Sheila said with great earnestness. "Can I get it out for you? I promise to be real gentle."

Mohawk Boy nodded, eyes glued to Sheila's face, mouth slack open.

Sheila stood back up and, with pert nose squinched, worked a dead fly out of whatever glop made hair stand up that tall. She gave a little shiver of disgust but had her face back under control before she knelt back down. "Can I throw it out?" she asked.

Mohawk Boy nodded.

Sheila flicked it into a trash can as we walked out of the room after the deputy.

Cat Man yowled loudly, then settled into a steady purr as we left. For some reason, that made me feel a little afraid.

"What would you have done if he'd said you couldn't throw the fly out?" I asked.

Sheila shrugged. "Given it back to him. It was like, totally his fly, you know."

Totally his fly. Hard to argue with that.

If you're talking to your defense lawyer, chances are you're not having a good day. Usually something fairly cataclysmic (like being arrested) has occurred. Even when cataclysmic occurrences (like being arrested) become commonplace in some people's lives, it's still not a good day. Sheila was bizarrely perky for someone having the kind of day that requires you to talk to your defense attorney.

"It's like really cool of you to come down and help me out this way," Sheila announced, looking around the room as if she expected unicorns to come prancing in.

"It's like really my job, Sheila. You seem like a nice girl, but you should recognize that I'm not here as a favor." Sheesh, this girl made me feel so old. I had less than a decade on her in human years. Maybe I'd converted to dog years? The past year had certainly felt like seven years.

She ducked her head, and blond hair escaped from her barrette and fell across her face. I'm not sure if I've ever seen someone pull off charming so well in a prison jumpsuit. Helpless? Yes. Naïve? Absolutely. Innocent, even? Of course. Given the number of sociopaths that cross my path, I've seen innocent done to a T. It's easy for sociopaths; they really *think* they're innocent. But not charming. As near as I can remember, never charming.

"I know. I know," she was saying. "But it's still cool of you to be this nice."

I sighed. I have good instincts and my heart is in the right place and I spend my working life fighting for truth and justice, but I'm actually not a very nice person. Just ask my mother. "So tell me your side of the story, Sheila. How did this all come about?"

Sheila became completely absorbed in examining her hair for split ends. People have a hard time looking you in the eye when they're lying, so split-end contemplation is not uncommon. People lie, prevaricate, and misrepresent all the time. They're just not very good at it. Sheila really sucked at it. "I'm not really sure."

I looked through the police report that started her file, finding solace in the familiar format.

FROM THE SAN JOSE POLICE DEPARTMENT
DAILY BULLETIN:

VIOLATION: Unlawful incarceration, Burglary

LOCATION: Burton and Finney Accountancy Limited

CRIME/INJURY/WEAPON: Between the hours of 1800 and 1900, the suspects clad in gray and/or brown trench coats open to reveal assorted lingerie entered the victim's office. Suspects did not break or force their way in. Victim invited them in despite not knowing their identities. Suspects then strapped victim to a rolling office chair with duct tape and examined and photocopied several client files. Victim is unsure of which files were examined and photocopied as every time they were going to open the filing cabinet the "redhead with the big jugs would lean over and I would forget to look anywhere else." After retrieving the information they sought, suspects left victim taped to the chair. Victim was discovered by his cleaning lady at approximately 1930 hours.

VICTIM AND/OR WITNESS: Carl Burton, 2123 Mockingbird Lane, San Jose, CA.

SUSPECT(S): Three women (two Caucasian, one Asian). Victim was unclear on height, weight, and eye color of suspects. He remembers hair color as one redhead, one brunette, one blonde, their legs as long and their breasts as large. One of the Caucasian suspects may have a butterfly tattoo on her right hip.

"So you and your friends tied a guy to a chair and stole some files?"

"Well, sort of." My client stared at me with eyes that were blue and clear and wide and round. "We more duct-taped him than tied him. Isn't duct tape just the most amazing thing? Did you know you can remove warts with it?"

I took yet another deep breath for a count of five. "So you and your friends duct-taped a guy to a chair and then lap-danced financial information from him?"

Sheila frowned, but just a little, and in a very dainty fashion. "Mainly, Helena did. I felt kind of bad that Lily and I just watched Helena do all the work. I mean, we helped tape him down and looked through the files and everything, but Helena did the hard part alone."

"So you feel remorse about assaulting Mr. Burton?"

"Well, no. Not really. We had to do it. We had to help Joey."

"Joey?" I flipped quickly through the few pages of information. Nowhere could I find a mention of someone named Joey. "Who's Joey?"

"He's a little boy who goes to the preschool where I teach."

"Preschool?" Generally speaking, I do not ask my clients only single-word questions nor do I suffer from echolalia. Most of the time, I put together complete, cogent sentences that reflect my thoughtfulness and my understanding of the law. At least I hadn't resorted to curling up into fetal position under the table and sucking my thumb. Yet.

"Li'l Dudes 'n Dudettes," Sheila said, beaming and proud. "It's a great place. It's the best daycare center I've ever worked at. Totally primo."

I smiled back at her. You really couldn't help it; she just demanded it. Something about that wide open face, the heavy-lidded eyes and that pouting mouth . . . "And you also work at . . ."—I looked down at the papers again—". . . the Crescent Moon?"

Sheila leaned back in her chair. "Being a daycare teacher just doesn't pay the bills in Silicon Valley. I dance at the Crescent Moon three or four nights a week to make the extra cash I need to pay my rent. And my car payment. And food. All that stuff." She giggled. "I think what I get at Li'l Dudes 'n

Dudettes would like basically keep me in gas and not much else."

"Let's back up a second. How about we start at the beginning and work our way along? I'll try not to interrupt this first time through, but I'll warn you, I'm going to want you to run through your story more than once. How about we start with Joey?"

She brightened. Literally brightened. It was as if more sunshine suddenly glinted off her hair, which was really strange since we were in a room with no windows. Freaky, I know, but I swear it's what happened. "Cool! That'll work great."

I decided to be thankful that she didn't call me "dude." I hate being called "dude."

"Joey is just the sweetest kid and he's as cute as a bug, too. Jet-black hair and big blue eyes with just about the longest lashes you've ever seen. The other teachers always say those long lashes are such a waste on a boy, but I don't think so. After all, a girl can wear mascara and nobody'll make fun of her, but a guy just doesn't have that option. Not even this close to San Francisco."

My pen was poised over my pad of paper, ready to take notes, but the discourse on Joey's eyelashes stunned me for a second or two.

"I don't know where he gets those lashes from. His dad sure didn't pass them on. I'm not sure if Malcolm Palmer even has eyebrows, much less eyelashes."

"So Malcolm Palmer is Joey's father?"

Sheila looked at me as if I'd asked her if two plus two was really four. "Yes, but he's not a very good father. If he was a good father, he wouldn't have been eight months behind in his child support payments. If he hadn't been eight months behind in his child support payments, his ex-wife wouldn't have been six months behind in tuition payments at Li'l Dudes 'n Dudettes. If she hadn't been six months behind in tuition payments, Joey wouldn't be getting kicked out of Li'l Dudes 'n Dudettes, and my heart wouldn't have broken for him."

"Okay," I said. This was a common story. It takes months for the system to catch up with deadbeat dads. Meanwhile the divorced moms are left holding the bag, and the bag has no money in it. I wasn't entirely clear on how this led Sheila and her friends to lap-dance files from Carl Burton, but I was beginning to guess the connection.

"See, Joey has Asperger's syndrome, which is not nearly as funny as it sounds. He has all these weird little quirks, but at Li'l Dudes 'n Dudettes, we'd found a place where he fit in. He actually made friends and went out on the playground during free-play time to swing on the swings and play tag, instead of sitting in the room endlessly sorting all the wooden blocks by color and shrieking whenever another kid messed them up or attacking other kids with pencils when they touched his drawing. Susan said he'd been doing better at home, too. He's actually talking to her instead of just repeating phrases from videos and TV."

Oh, great. Not just a mom left to shoulder the burden of rearing a child alone, unable to count on the child's father for financial support, but a mom left to shoulder the burden of a child with a disability.

My heart wrenched as I imagined the poor woman who

had brought her child so far, and had done it without any assistance from a father that I was already starting to hate, just to have all that progress undone by the fact that the system wouldn't make her husband live up to his legal obligations. Though there's a system set up to deal with these things, the truth is that the system doesn't begin to help until you're in such dire straits that having a bunch of strippers lap-dance financial information from your ex-husband's accountant probably seems like a golden opportunity.

"Then Susan told me why she was taking Joey out, and it went from being a total bummer to being so just totally unfair that I was still mad about it when I got to the Crescent Moon that night."

Well, sure. I didn't even know these people, and I was mad.

"So anyway, we were all putting on our makeup and doing our hair and getting dressed—it always makes me laugh that we put so much effort into getting dressed to get undressed, but there you have it—and I was just so darn mad, I couldn't stop spouting off about this guy who'd made a fortune in the dot-com craze and was now like totally welshing on his ex-wife and little boy so he'd have to drop out of the school where he was doing so great and was so happy.

"After I was done ranting, Lily said I should just forget it, that's just the way the world was, and that we couldn't do anything about it. Then Helena said that maybe there *was* something we could do.

"And that's how we ended up in our very best stripper outfits and some old Halloween masks at Malcolm Palmer's accountant's office, trying to find out where he'd hidden the profits from the sale of his company, so his ex-wife could get somebody to attach his bank accounts and pay his back child support."

I was representing a daycare teacher/stripper/vigilante. I had never heard of a daycare teacher/stripper/vigilante, and wondered what kind of precedents I was going to find in the law books. Assuming I could remember what color my law books were and find them on my shelves. "And they arrested you for burglary? Did you take anything?" I asked.

Sheila shook her head vigorously. "No. I told the policeman we didn't take anything, so how could it have been burglary?"

Told the policeman? I put my head in my hands. I really didn't want to believe what I had just heard. "Did the policeman tell you that you didn't have to talk to him without a lawyer?"

"Oh, yeah, he told me all that stuff about my right to remain silent." Sheila smiled as if expecting a gold star on her spelling homework.

"So why did you keep talking to him, Sheila? Why didn't you ask for a lawyer right then?" Had they threatened her? Coerced her? Refused counsel even though she'd asked? I was grasping at straws, but I couldn't leave anything left unasked.

She twiddled her hair some more. "Well, the other policeman was so nice that other time, I didn't want to seem, you know, like ungrateful or anything."

"Other policeman? Other time?"

"Yeah. Doug something. He replaced my taillight for me."

"A police officer replaced your taillight? When?"

"After they took my picture and stuff."

"You're telling me that a police officer stopped you on the road, brought you to the police station, took your picture, and then changed your taillight?"

If what I was putting together was even close to the truth, she would be walking out these doors a free woman in just minutes.

Sheila nodded vigorously.

Bingo!

CHAPTER THREE

From *The Angry No More Manual and Workbook*
by Dr. Gail Peterson

IS YOUR ANGER APPROPRIATE?

Are you really reacting to the situation at hand? Or are you reacting to something else? Is what is happening triggering memories of other upsetting episodes in your life? Have you blown the present situation out of proportion?

Before you react, take a little reality check. Make sure the speed of your Anger Train is appropriate to what is actually happening around you.

Alissa's Anger Workbook:

Exercise #3

Rate the last few things that have made you angry, with 10 being most angry and 0 being not being angry at all.

1. Getting cut off in traffic: 6
2. Meeting client's arresting officer: 2
3. Lying, cheating, diseased spouse: 10

Do you feel those levels are appropriate? Why?

1. Yes. The guy was a dickhead. What's so hard about signaling before a lane change?
2. No. But it wasn't my fault. His eyes distracted me. Otherwise I would have been furious.
3. Yes. Do I really need to elaborate?

"Sheila, could we back up and cover that other trip to the police station a little more fully? The one where they fixed your car for you and took your picture." The scent of opportunity filled the room; I was sure I'd be getting my client off without even a bail hearing.

"Oh, sure. It's not really backing up, though. It's more going forward. It happened a few days after we went to Malcolm Palmer's. One of the taillights on my Tracker must have gone out and I hadn't realized it. So I was heading over to the gym when this officer pulled me over. I kind of think I'd seen him before, like maybe over at the Juiced Up 2 Go where I get my smoothies, but maybe I'm wrong. I told him he looked familiar and he didn't say anything."

"So after he pulled you over, what happened?"

Sheila sighed. "Let's see. He had me get out of the car and he checked me for weapons. . . ."

I nearly choked. "He frisked you? Because of a taillight?" This police officer was so going down.

Sheila thought for a second. "He more sort of patted me than frisked me."

I wrote as fast as I could.

"Then he had me follow him down to the police station and he took my picture a bunch of times."

"You mean your mug shot."

"I don't think so." Sheila shook her head. "I think mug shots are just supposed to be of your face, and these were more whole-body things."

I hadn't known I could write any faster.

When she reached the end of her story, which was just a

few seconds later since not much more happened besides Officer Dougie changing her taillight for her, she nailed me again with those big blue eyes and said, "What do we do now?"

I stood up, picked up my notebook and my attaché case, and said, "We're going to go back into that courtroom and get every shred of evidence that this Detective Rodriguez has gathered against you thrown out as inadmissible, and then you're going to go back to the jail to gather up your things and go home."

"Really?"

"Yep. And then sometime later this week, we should talk about your harassment case against the police department." Oh, yeah. This felt good. This felt right. I knew without doubt each step I should take next. I hadn't been sure I could walk this line again, the one where everything was in balance, but here I was, like an acrobat on the high wire. I knew just where the line was and just how to walk it, even in heels.

Things went pretty much as I had planned from there. I had a little chat with the overworked underling assistant district attorney. She agreed to throw out the case, although she wouldn't comment on the police officer's behavior.

We had just headed into the hallway when Sheila pointed and said, "There he is. The cop who arrested me."

There must have been half a dozen men standing in the hall. "Which one?"

"Khaki slacks. Dark blue blazer. Light blue shirt. Red tie."

"Give me a break, Sheila." At least four of them wore khaki slacks and dark blue blazers. Dressing is so easy when you're a man.

"Yeah. I see what you mean. Second guy from the left."

I marched. Sheila trailed behind me. I tapped Mr. Second from the Left on the shoulder. "Excuse me, Detective, ah, Rodriguez?" I had to check the paperwork to find the name.

He turned.

Wow.

There's just something about cops and firefighters. Probably a latent hero-worship thing I haven't had beaten out of me yet. Even when they're not actually that good looking, they come off as cute. Even when they're not in uniform, they're cute. But this guy was way more than cute. He was . . . "wow." Dark hair. Some gray flecks, but not much. Cocoa-colored skin. Cocoa with lots of milk. Green eyes. Square jaw. Shoulders that looked like they could hold up collapsing buildings. I didn't dare let my eyes drop to his chest. I was only eye level with his second button, so I had to crick my neck up. At least I wouldn't look like I had a double chin that way.

"Yes?" Those pale green eyes bored into mine. Okay, they didn't actually bore. They more just looked, but in a really intense way.

"My name is Alissa Lindley. I'm representing Sheila Montrose."

His brows arched, but all he said was "Oh."

"The case has been dismissed."

Again, all he graced me with was "Oh."

"I'm sure you're not surprised."

He kept his face blank and didn't even bother with an "oh" this time. He kind of just stared at me, as if maybe I'd said something shocking or rude. It was more than a little unnerving.

"I can't believe you arrested her on the basis of some Polaroids that should never have been taken, much less passed around the police station." I could just imagine the scene now. All the "boys" gathered around a desk leering at Sheila's photos, and Rodriguez finally noticing the butterfly tattoo on her hip and the fact that she'd been picked up for the taillight infraction just a few blocks from Carl Burton's office. It was so typical it didn't even warrant indignation; I might as well rage about why the line at the women's room was ten times longer than the men's room.

"What precisely do you feel I was 'getting away' with, Ms. Lindley? Besides keeping your client from duct-taping innocent citizens to their office furniture?"

Oooh. His voice was deep. Smooth. Not down to Barry White cartoonish levels, more sort of Lyle Lovett-y. The kind of voice that made you need to press your knees together.

"Shall we begin with dragging my client down to the police station without representation?"

He raised his hands as if to fend me off. "Hey. I invited Ms. Montrose to accompany me and she did so willingly. Happily, I might even say."

I could just imagine it. Sheila skipping along beside the detective with butterflies dancing around her head and woodland creatures cavorting at her feet.

"You're lucky I'm not suing your department for sexual harassment. Although that may change in the near future."

That shut him up for a second. Rodriguez had a funny look on his face, like he'd bitten into an apple and found half a worm. If I didn't miss my guess, he didn't like his fellow detective's little photo session with Sheila any better than I did. What had they been thinking, anyway? Taking cheesecake photos of a suspect in custody is simply idiotic. I suppose the answer is that they *weren't* thinking—at least, not with their big heads.

Though that hadn't stopped him from using the photos as evidence against Sheila. Evidence that any judge with a lick of sense would throw out in a New York minute, which was partly why the D.A. had dismissed the charges.

"Arresting someone on the basis of a butterfly tattoo on their right hip? Do you know anyone under thirty who doesn't have a tattoo these days? Would you care to hazard a guess how many of those are butterflies? Geez, it wouldn't even have to be real one. I could go down to the corner drugstore and come back with a tattoo on my hip that would be gone after I took my next shower."

"The victim picked your client out of a photo lineup."

"The same victim who couldn't describe much besides his attackers' cup sizes? The one who didn't even know which files they'd looked at?"

That eyebrow quirked up again. "Ms. Lindley, I'm not going to argue the merits of the evidence I gathered with you. But I will tell you this." He leaned down toward me, almost whispering in my ear. He smelled good. Like laundry day with the dryers on high. "I'm not done with Ms. Montrose and company." He shifted to look at Sheila, who still hovered behind me.

Of course he did. Who would look at me with a Sheila around?

"Do you hear that, Ms. Montrose? I'm watching now."

"That's fine with us, Detective." I lifted my chin to look him straight in the eyes, before I turned on my heel (thank God for lucky boots that don't let your ankles wobble). "Right now you can watch my client waltz right out of this courthouse."

If only it had been that easy. We had to wait around for thirty minutes until a deputy could take her back over to the jail to collect her clothes and belongings. Then I hung around to make sure she had a way home, and that none of the deputies who were drooling over her would take that step over the line like the cops had already.

Finally, despite the signs every six inches in fifteen different languages that told everyone to pay for parking before they returned to their car, and the gigantic red sign that said PAY HERE on the parking garage booth where you were supposed to pay, I got stuck behind a woman who hadn't noticed any of these things and simply stopped her Honda Accord at the exit and wouldn't budge. I went to my special calm place, deep inside.

I only emerged from my imaginary tropical grotto, redolent of jasmine and full of bird song, when someone blared their horn behind me. The Accord was gone; my path out of the garage was clear.

Do I even need to describe the traffic at rush hour around San Jose? The way people around here drive, I am continually stunned that the highways are not littered with bodies. I breathed in for counts of five and out for counts of ten so many times, I nearly passed out.

And traveling these roads was almost surreal. All the names and intersections were familiar, but the area has changed so much since I grew up that it was nearly unrecognizable. Malls have gone up that weren't there before. Ones that were there have been torn down. Schools are gone. Major landmarks have disappeared, and brand-new ones loom up with no warning whatsoever.

I'd come back to be safe and familiar, like putting on a favorite pair of jeans that are broken in just right. Instead, I had on a brand-new pair that I wasn't sure would ever look as good or feel as easy.

I was so grateful to walk in the door of my condo that I nearly kissed the floor tiles. The message light was blinking and a surge of hope ran through me. I was not a social leper!

"Message sent today at four-fifteen P.M.," my voice mail informed me.

"Alissa, this is your mother. Bring a bottle of something with you tonight. Something red," my mother's voice continued. "Chianti would be nice."

Shit. Shit, shit, shit. I'd completely forgotten dinner at my mother's at six-thirty. It was past six-fifteen now. I'd be late, but not too late. I started changing clothes as the next message played.

"Lissa, It's Kath. Call."

I grabbed the phone and called her. I'd change clothes while we talked.

"I told Rob I was thinking about going back to school last night," Kathleen said.

"And what did he say?"

"He said something along the lines of 'that's how baseball managers make their money.'"

"What?" I stopped with one boot in my hand. Had I missed something? That happened to me sometimes these days. I meant to pay attention, then suddenly found myself lost in my own thoughts. Then I had to scramble to cover up that I'd missed something important. I blamed the Prozac.

Kathleen sighed. "The Diamondbacks were playing the Giants. Shinjo was on first threatening to steal. Ortiz kept raising and lowering his bat, so Schilling didn't know if he'd bunt or not. I guess it was some kind of testament to great baseball management."

"So he didn't say anything about you going back to school?" I took off the other boot, cradled the phone with my neck, and rolled off my pantyhose. I sighed with relief.

"Don't get sad about it." Kathleen laughed. "We talked about it eventually."

I decided not to enlighten her as to why I'd sighed; Kathleen wouldn't know the pleasures and horrors of control-top pantyhose. First of all, she didn't need control-tops even after two children, and secondly, these days, she didn't wear pantyhose except to weddings and funerals. "So what did he say?"

Kathleen didn't answer right away. "Kath?" I prompted. I unbuttoned my skirt and laid it across the bed next to my jacket.

"He said he thought I should do whatever made me happy," she said in a flat tone.

"That's good, right?"

"Sure."

After another few seconds of silence I said, "Kath?"

"Yeah?"

"Wasn't that good? I mean, he said go ahead and do it, right?"

"It's just . . . well . . . " Kathleen sighed, a great big gusty one. "He didn't even ask what I wanted to study. Then when I asked him if he wanted to know, he said something about not realizing I'd gotten that far with 'this one .'"

"This one what?"

"That's exactly what *I* said! I know I've started a few things I haven't finished . . . or I guess really started before I abandoned them. But that doesn't mean he doesn't have to take me seriously, does it?" she wailed.

I hung up my skirt. "Of course not."

"It's not like I didn't really want to do those other things."

I bit back my sigh this time. I didn't really blame Rob. Since Hayley had started preschool last year, Kathleen had come up with three plans to go back to school and eight possible jobs for which she wanted to apply. So far she hadn't done more than download applications from the Internet and start looking at what kind of daycare, if any, she would need.

That's when she would freeze up.

"I can't bear the thought that someone else might get to spend more time with Hayley and Jason than I do! No one can take care of them the way I do!"

"Of course they can't."

Hayley was four and Jason was six. They were everything Kath had ever wanted and they were wonderful kids. Bright and cute and funny, and it's not just that I'm biased because they're my best friend's kids. They really are terrific. "Lots of kids go to daycare, Kathleen."

"Lots of kids go to bed hungry every night. Lots of kids are sexually abused. Lots of kids never eat their vegetables. Just not my kids."

"I don't think you can equate three days of after-school care a week with raping children, and I've seen Jason eat three peas and have you call it eating his vegetables."

"You are such a lawyer," she hissed.

"Yep," I said, yanking on my jeans and giving a silent Hosanna to stretch denim. I love being a lawyer. My mother claims that I came out of the womb arguing, which in our family would be normal, so it doesn't surprise me. Most of my family memories consist of relatives pounding their fists on dining room tables and yelling at each other about everything from politics to art theory. By second grade I myself had successfully sent two student rabbis applying for jobs at our temple back to the Yeshiva in tears by debating their sermons with them. (If you're going to ask a rhetorical question of a congregation, make sure it's really a rhetorical question and that the seven-year-old in the back doesn't know the answer.) By fifth grade I had changed our elementary school's hot-lunch policy of serving whatever the hell they wanted regardless of what was on the preprinted menus by staging a Cold Lunch Only strike. By junior high and high school I was regularly protesting and debating everything from apartheid to the Equal Rights Amendment. Lawyering is in my blood.

"I might not be able to keep Hayley in daycare anyway. I had to pick her up early from preschool today," Kathleen said.

"Why? Was she sick?"

"Nope. Tantruming."

"Hayley? Threw a tantrum at school? What about?" Hayley was about as close to a fairy princess as a little girl could get. She's tiny, like Kathleen, and she has her blond curls and huge brown eyes and a voice so high that sometimes only dogs can hear it. The only time I'd ever seen her throw a tantrum was over a year ago at Michaela Hirsch's wedding, and that was because she'd eaten half a bowl of sugar cubes before anyone noticed. Mother Teresa might throw a tantrum on that sugar high.

"Penises," Kathleen said. "She threw a tantrum about penises."

"Because she didn't have one?" I wondered if Rob made enough money as a software engineer to have Hayley in analysis for the rest of her life.

"Because she wanted to see one."

"Any one in particular?" I asked.

Kathleen sighed again. "You know how Hayley kind of attaches to people?"

"Mmmhmm." It was hard to miss how Hayley attaches to people. The last time I'd been over for dinner, I'd had to pry her fingers off my leg to leave.

"Well, she's decided this little boy at preschool is her best friend, and she wants to be his Bathroom Buddy."

"What's wrong with that?"

"I'm getting to it. Stop interrupting. You're always in such a rush."

"I am not," I said, even though I was.

"You are, too. Now shut up."

I didn't say anything.

"Alissa?" Kathleen finally said.

"I'm listening and not rushing or interrupting or being lawyerish, even though I'm supposed to be at my mother's in five minutes with a bottle of wine I haven't purchased yet," I answered while buttoning a ribbed cotton cardigan over my tank top. It was always wise to dress in layers when going to my mother's apartment. I never knew whether I'd be hot or cold or both, depending on how her temperature was swinging.

"They have a rule that Bathroom Buddies have to be the same gender. Apparently Hayley doesn't want the rule to apply to her. When I got there she was lying on the floor, kicking her heels and screaming that she'd seen plenty of penises and she didn't see why she couldn't see Joey's."

"Ouch."

"I'm just relieved they didn't call Child Protective Services."

"Kath, they wouldn't! They know better."

"Still . . ."

I looked at my watch. "Kath, I've got to go. Do you want to walk tomorrow?"

"Can't. First I have to figure out how to get Silly Putty out of the carpet in the living room and then I'm having lunch with my mother. It'll take me most of the morning just to decide what to wear."

"Oh." I stayed silent for a second. "Wanna meet for margaritas tomorrow night?"

She laughed. "Maybe."

"Why do you do this to yourself when you know she's going to drive you crazy?"

"She's my mother. Look, not seeing her has occurred to me many, many times. Usually when I'm sitting across from her. Not allowing the kids to have Silly Putty has also occurred to me, but I keep buying it even though I also keep having to find new ways to get it out of things."

"Fine. Torture yourself, then. Just try to get along."

She laughed. "Alissa, after all this time, you must realize that there is no getting along with my mother. There's only getting out of her way."

CHAPTER FOUR

From *The Angry No More Manual and Workbook*
by Dr. Gail Peterson

SPECIAL TRIGGERS

Are there certain situations that make you particularly angry? Certain people that always upset you? Do they always upset you in the same way? Being aware of what can start your Anger Train in motion is the first step in making sure it stays in the station!

Alissa's Anger Workbook:

Exercise #4

List three of your special anger triggers:

1. My mother trying to dress me.
2. My sister trying to boss me around.
3. Police officers trying to arrest my clients.

I rang the bell and then slid my key in the lock to let myself in. Mom was expecting me and I didn't want to make her trudge all the way to the door just to open it. The knob turned from the other side before I could pull my keys out, and the door opened to reveal a woman who looked vaguely familiar, but I couldn't place.

Damn that Prozac.

"Alissa," my mother's voice called from down the hall. "You remember Virginia, don't you?"

I didn't, but smiled anyway.

Virginia smiled back. It creased her soft wrinkled face in a nice way. She touched her white hair and said, "I've let my hair go natural. Maybe that's why you don't recognize me."

I smiled wider and nodded, desperately racing through the possibilities of where I might have met Virginia.

"Virginia's husband was your father's roommate during his second hospital stay. You remember Harold, don't you?" my mother's voice sang out again.

It all clicked into place. The two of them had lain around watching westerns on TNT and swapping World War II stories. I slid past Virginia, who didn't quite seem to register the need of stepping aside to let me in. My mother's apartment is a shotgun affair with a long narrow hallway before it widens into a dining room and living room.

"How is Harold?" I asked.

"He passed last month."

"I'm so sorry." Although I had to wonder why she made him sound like a kidney stone.

Virginia patted my shoulder. "Thank you, dear. I understand you've had troubles of your own."

I shuddered to think about exactly how my mother would have explained my recent "troubles."

My mother clomped around the corner, leaning heavily on her walker. She wore khaki slacks and a light blue top that picked up the lights in her bright blue eyes. "Don't slouch, Alissa. You don't want to end up all bent over like Virginia and me." The two of them let out wild brays of laughter, as if my mother had said something funny.

"You look nice, Mom," I said. "Is that a new top?"

She pulled herself up as best she could without letting go of her walker to display it. It was like every other one of her tops: wide waistband, pointed collar, made from something that had never grown outside, but a good color for her. She had been trying to get me to wear tops like that since I was in junior high. I have always refused. In fact, I have refused to the point of not leaving my room for forty-eight hours when I was thirteen. They make me look just like my mom, and I'm afraid I'm turning into her fast enough already.

"Virginia and I got it today at Ross's. It was only $9.95."

"Really? It suits you," I said. Shopping with Virginia at Ross's. That was new.

"C'mon, c'mon," my mother urged as she executed a careful three-point turn with the walker. "Marsha's already here."

Virginia followed me, clumping along with a four-footed cane, nattily decorated with little crocheted bands that matched her outfit. "I like your cane," I said.

She smiled. "Gives me something to do to pass the time, dear."

I envisioned rooms full of women sitting around, crocheting outfits for their quad canes while waiting to die, now that their men were gone. Could there by anything more depressing? On the other hand, whom did it benefit not to accessorize? Would it be better for them to sit around waiting to die without matching cane covers?

I traveled the rest of the way down the barrel of the shotgun directly to the source of much ammunition—my mother's dining room table. My sister, Marsha, sat there with her husband, David, and their sons, Andrew and Terry. Marsha and I have this running joke about which of us is what. We laugh about who the pretty daughter is and who the smart daughter is, and who the dutiful daughter is and who the ambitious daughter is. It puts the sibling rivalry crap out there on the table to look at, which seems to take some of the poison out of it.

In case you haven't guessed, I would be smart and ambitious. Marsha scored pretty and dutiful. She barely wears makeup and only recently succumbed to wearing contact lenses. It's not like she's stupid, either, so she has not always been the easiest big sister to have. Hence the need for getting the poison out of the sibling crap.

She's a psychologist. She has a reasonably good-looking (if somewhat tight-assed) husband who has stayed with her for seventeen years of wedded bliss and not dumped her at the first sign of trouble, and two great kids that she conceived and delivered with nary a varicose vein or hemorrhoid.

Marsha has it all and does it all and does it better than anyone. At least, she does it better than me. Her house is immaculate. She dresses impeccably. Her children are gorgeous and bright and always clean. I couldn't even manage to have it all in the first place, and what I *did* have I couldn't hold on to, so I guess I'm not much competition.

Marsha jumped up and grabbed me in a hug, pressing my face into her chest. Did I mention that she's four inches taller than me and weighs about the same amount?

"Hey, sweetie, how's it going?" Marsha said. "Don't let me forget. I have some plants for you in the car. Sweet alyssum. It'll make a nice border. Remember that raised bed thing I sketched for you? I have some time tomorrow; I could come over and we could start on it."

"Thanks. I'm fine except for the waffle pattern you're leaving on my face. I'm not sure about tomorrow. I have a new client," I mumbled into her textured sweater. She released me. It was a nice sweater. A boatneck thing in black and white with floaty sleeves. I wondered if it would fit me. Probably not. I inherited my mother's bust line. Marsha got my dad's. I mean that literally: She barely has nipples.

Andrew stood up. I still haven't adjusted to him being taller than me. I know he's fourteen now, but he'd been shorter than me for twelve of those fourteen years, and I hadn't gotten used to the new Andrew. His brother was two years older than him, and I hadn't adjusted to the manly Terry yet, either. He let me hug him, but I could tell it was painful for him so I didn't prolong it. Nothing like having a too-bosomy aunt be a too-clingy aunt to boot. I should know; I have several that are both.

"Hey, Thing Two," I said. "I think you might have become Thing Two times Two."

My mother, who was headed back to the kitchen, called out over her shoulder, "Don't you think Andrew has grown again, Alissa?"

"I dunno, Grams," Andrew smirked. "Maybe you just shrunk."

It would have been funnier if it wasn't true.

Terry, born with charm that would allow him to sell shit to cows some day, followed his brother with an equally awkward squeeze. "How's my favorite aunt?"

"I'm your only aunt and I'm fine, darling. How are you?"

"He's dating Smashley," Andrew threw in.

Terry turned red and then punched his brother.

"Smashley Wu?" I looked to Marsha for confirmation. She nodded and then gave the boys one of her squinty-eyed looks capable of stopping a charging lion in its path.

Smashley Wu (aka Ashley Wu) had been pursuing Terry since they ended up in the same table group in third grade. She'd pursued him with all the wiles available to an eight-year-old girl, chasing him around the playground at recess and bonking him over the head with her books. Hence the family pet name for her. "What happened? Can she finally outrun you?"

"Nah," Terry mumbled.

"She grew boobs," Andrew said, helpfully.

Terry punched him again. I looked over at Marsha again, who once more nodded confirmation. I'm just not sure if she was confirming Smashley's new boobs or Terry's interest in them. I found both equally shocking, since I remembered Terry being interested in breasts only as a food source and Smashley as being about as developed as Gwyneth Paltrow.

David came over and gave me a brother-in-law-ish squeeze. "How's it going, Alissa?"

"Not bad," I said, following my mother into the kitchen with the wine. "I got my first new client today."

"Interesting case?" David asked.

"Does it pay well?" Mom asked.

"How nice," Virginia said.

"What's for dinner, Grams? It smells great," Andrew said.

They all spoke at once.

"Spaghetti," Mom called from the kitchenette, answering Andrew.

"Red sauce?" he asked with a hopeful lilt to his voice.

"Of course. And cake for dessert."

"Your icing or store-bought?"

"Do you really think I would use store-bought when baking for my grandsons?"

My mother's icing is spectacular and impossible to duplicate because there is no actual recipe. It's really more like a glaze that drips down and hardens. Marsha has tried about a thousand times and can never do it, and if she can't, what chance do the rest of us have?

"Can I help?" I asked.

"No." Quick and curt.

Time was, she would have had me make the salad or had Marsha make the garlic bread, but since the hip replacement that left her barely mobile, Mother had eschewed pretty much all assistance in domestic matters.

I admired it, but it also made me crazy. With my help, dinner could be on the table in fifteen minutes. Without, it would take thirty. Where's the rush? you ask. As well you might. It was one of the questions my Anger Management instructor kept asking me, too. "Decelerate, Alissa, and your Anger Train might never reach the station," Gail would say.

"Couldn't I at least chop something for the salad?"

"It already has tomatoes, cucumbers, and green onions. What more could you possibly want to put in it?"

She set the plates on the ledge between the kitchenette and the dining room, then made her way around with her walker. She picked the plates up from the ledge and set them on the table.

Andrew looked up from inspecting a scab on his arm. "Want me to set the table, Grandma?"

"That would be lovely, dear. What's that on your arm?"

He shrugged. "I fell off my skateboard and scraped my arm. No biggie."

She grabbed his arm and twisted it around to look at the scrape.

"Ouch, Grams, you're hurting me," Andrew whined.

"Hold still." She peered up at him again, bending his arm into an even more unnatural angle. "That's going to need some ointment. Marsha, did you clean this out when it happened?"

"Oh, I bet she thought it would be more interesting to see if it could get infected," I said.

Mom looked at me, amazed. "Why would she do that?"

My mother doesn't have much of a sense of humor about certain things. Open wounds on her grandchildren would pretty much top that list.

"She's joking, Grams," Terry said helpfully.

"Marsha, get me the ointment." There are few things in life that give my mother more pleasure than putting antibiotic ointment on a wound. It did no good to tell Mom that Marsha had washed his arm, put on ointment, and kept an eye on it. It wouldn't be done right until Mom did it herself.

I started putting out the plates while Andrew waited for his ointment. Three on one of the long sides, two on the other long side, and one on each end. I ended up with one more plate in my hand. "Mom, there's one too many dishes here."

"No, there's not. I counted. We're eight." She was still inspecting Andrew's scrape and didn't bother looking up at me.

I looked around the room and counted seven. "Is someone else coming?"

"No." Even without her facing me, I knew she was getting pissed. I could tell by her shoulders, the funny way she has of tensing when she feels argumentative.

"Then we're seven, Mom. Not eight."

She turned in her chair. "Alissa, there's David, Marsha, Terry and Andrew. That makes four. Then there's you and Virginia. That's six. Then me. That's eight."

"Mom, you're just one person. Not two."

She froze, just for an instant, and then turned back to Andrew saying, "I'm sorry. You're right. We're seven."

She didn't turn fast enough for me to miss the quick rush of tears to her eyes. I looked at the plate in my hand, the one that was for my father. He'd been dead for six months, and she was still setting a place for him at the table. I made as little noise as possible as I put it back in the kitchen.

Virginia hobbled over and put her hand on my mother's shoulder. "I still prop Harold's pillows up just the way he liked them at night before I go to bed."

Virginia had just raised herself about ten points in my estimation. I might make a little outfit for her quad cane myself.

Over dinner my mother began to describe infected wounds she'd known and loved. Body fluids have always been dinner conversation at our table; it's one of the disadvantages of having a nurse for a mother, even a retired one.

"It was so deep, I could see the tendons in his finger," she said with relish before taking a bite of garlic bread. The time my father had cut himself while trying to fix the washing machine was one of her all-time favorites, undoubtedly on her top-ten list. I think number one belonged to the young man impaled on a bar from his own bike. She used to tell that one every time my sister or I whined that all the other girls had boys' bikes, that we were the only ones who had to have dorky girls' bikes.

"Grandma," Andrew whined, looking longingly at his plate of spaghetti. "I'm eating here."

"Of course you are, dear." She beamed at him. Watching a grandchild eat made her almost as happy as putting ointment on something nasty.

"Seriously, Mom, do you think you could change the subject until the boys are done eating? That is, assuming that you want them to eat?" Dial "M" for Marsha and Manipulation.

Mom looked sheepish, but only for a second. She's completely incorrigible and I suspected that before dessert was done, she'd return to the topic and finish the story, but at least we wouldn't have to hear tendon descriptions while trying to slurp up spaghetti covered in red sauce. I tried to remember how many times she'd launched into a description that matched our food, but all the injuries and entrées blurred.

I figured that it wouldn't hurt to help her out with a change of conversation topic. "So, Virginia, I'm sorry. I can't remember when exactly your husband was my dad's roommate."

"It was your father's first pacemaker," Mom broke in.

At least three years ago, after the open-heart surgery, but before the pacemaker with the defibrillator (the same model Vice President Cheney had, mind you, and didn't that make us proud).

"So you and Mom have kept in touch all that time?" I asked. Something sharp hit my shin. Hard. "Ouch!"

I glared around the table. Marsha looked excessively innocent and I mouthed "What's up?" at her as Virginia said, "Heavens no! Your mother called me right after Harold passed."

Marsha mimed locking her mouth and throwing away the key. It reminded me of when our Uncle Stan brought us Aunt Sharon's costume jewelry after she died. Marsha had practically broken my tibia by the time I figured out I wasn't supposed to tell him that Aunt Sharon had already given Marsha her diamond earrings and I had her tennis bracelet. I was only seventeen; how was I to know she had given us all her good stuff so Stan's third wife wouldn't get it? He was only on Wife Number Two at that point, but we all knew there'd be a Number Three. Probably even Number Two did. Still, I don't think it was any reason to give me a lump on my shin the size of a grapefruit. Marsha kicks like a mule.

She still thinks having changed my diapers gives her the right to do things like that, and unbelievably, I allow it.

"Oh, how nice," I said quickly. Marsha gave me a barely

perceptible nod of approval, but I drew my legs under my chair anyway, just in case.

When I'm being totally honest, I suppose I even encourage Marsha. She was the one I'd called and sobbed to because I didn't know what to do, after all. It had felt like such a load off my shoulders. Somebody to take care of me, like a warm, safe cocoon I never had to leave. So now that I was here being taken care of, why did I sometimes feel like I couldn't breathe?

The fact that my mother kept the apartment heated to a balmy eighty degrees or so didn't help. I unbuttoned my cardigan and fanned it to cool off a little.

"Are you warm, Alissa?" Mom asked.

"A little."

Virginia said, "Have you tried soy, dear? I've heard it helps quite a bit with the hot flashes."

"I am not having hot flashes. I am only thirty." I stood up and stacked my dishes. Every woman at the table leaped up and tried to make sure her stack of dishes was highest, but I won. My triumphant march to the kitchen was marred somewhat by slopping spaghetti sauce on to my tank top.

"Is Aunt Flo still visiting regularly, dear?" Virginia whispered to me as she set her stack next to mine. Minus five points for Virginia, which isn't bad, really. Some of my mother's other friends have existed in negative numbers since I was twelve and started to grow breasts. "I mean, with your troubles, does that cut down on how often you, uh, have your little visitor?"

"She's never been regular," my mother said. "Always been all over the map."

This was beginning to remind me of the first time I was fitted for a bra. All the little old ladies at Macy's discussing my somewhat embarrassing secondary sex characteristics with my mother as if I weren't in the room, standing there half-naked and humiliated. "Can we change the topic?" I asked.

"Hey, Alissa," David said. "Would you give Marsha a ride home? The boys and I need to get back. They both have homework and I have some work to do tonight. I have an early meeting tomorrow."

"No problem." I scrubbed at the spaghetti stain with a wet paper towel. Marsha's house was less than a ten-minute drive from mine. Mom's apartment was within twenty. Maybe we'd just knitted my cocoon a little too tight. Maybe that was my problem.

"Alissa, dab. Don't rub. You'll rub the stain into the fabric." Marsha grabbed the paper towel out of my hands and began patting my tank top. As far as I could tell, she just smeared the sauce around.

"Grandma, can I have a piece of cake to take home?" Andrew asked.

"Of course, dear. Take the whole thing." She waved distractedly at the cake. "Alissa, take that top off. You can wear mine home."

"I don't want your top, Mom, but I do want a piece of cake." I tried to pull away from Marsha's hands, but she glared at me. I leaned back against the counter with a sigh.

"It's no problem, dear. I'll wash it and give it back to you later this week." Mom started working her arms out of her sleeves. Andrew grabbed the cake and turned to face the wall, half-naked grandmas being more than any fourteen-year-old should have to face. "You said you liked this one. You can keep it if you want."

"I said it suited you. I didn't say that I liked it and I certainly didn't say I wanted it." I wrested my tank top out of Marsha's hands. "Andrew, put that cake down."

He looked at me shrewdly. "Fine. You can have a piece, but I have dibs on the middle." A lot of the chocolate icing drips down the middle of the cake (my mother always makes a bundt) and pools there. It's like eating a candy bar.

"The hell you do! And since when is it your cake to divvy up?" I snapped.

"Watch your language, Alissa," my mother said.

"It's mine since Grandma gave it to me," Andrew said.

I scowled at both of them. "Fine. One piece, but I get half the middle, Andrew."

"Thank you, Aunt Alissa," Andrew said with fake sweetness.

I smiled at him. Who could not? He was gorgeous. And he was ours. "Who's the best auntie?"

He leaned down to kiss my cheek. "You are."

I got my piece of cake, although I didn't get to eat it, too, since Marsha and I were doing the dishes. Andrew and Terry and David headed for the door and Virginia decided to decamp with them. While Mom ushered them all out, I asked Marsha, "So what was with the hush-hush act at dinner?"

Marsha gave me a blank stare.

"You know? With Virginia?" I handed her the saucepan to wipe.

"Oh." Marsha looked around to make sure Mom wasn't near. "Mom's reading the obituaries."

"So? She's always read the obituaries. She reads the lists of plane crash victims, too. She likes to try to guess which ones are Jewish."

"Yeah, well, now she's calling them up and inviting them over for dinner." Marsha set the saucepan on the stovetop, and I gave her some salad plates to put in the dishwasher.

"All the Jewish ones?"

"No. They're not all Jewish."

"So just ones she knows, right? Like Virginia?"

"Do you really think she knew Virginia? Their husbands shared a hospital room for two nights three years ago! I can't believe she even recognizes their names. She must keep a list somewhere." She handed a dish back to me. "Get that sauce off. Mom's dishwasher doesn't work worth a damn."

"So there have been others?"

Marsha nodded. "Virginia's the best of the lot."

"Why?"

"Oh, one was too bossy. Another was too cheap."

I closed my eyes. "I meant, has Mom said why she's doing it?"

"Oh." Marsha started wiping wineglasses. "She says all her friends are married. She feels like a fifth wheel when she's with them."

I knew how she felt. After Thomas dumped me and the inevitable splitting up of the friends took place, it was hard to go anywhere even with the ones I had retained custody of. The rhythm was off. The extra plate was always there, even if it was only in your head. "So she's choosing her friends through the obituary column?"

"She says at least she'll have something in common with them."

My mother came back into the kitchen. "Alissa, are you sure you won't leave that top here and wear mine home? What size is the one you're wearing? Is it dry clean only?"

Thirty years of resistance melted away in the face of that extra plate. I went home in a polyester knit top with a pointed collar.

I let myself into the courtyard, lugging the sweet alyssum Marsha had gotten me and a grocery bag full of leftovers in orange and yellow Tupperware containers that my mother has kept meticulously sine the 1970s, all neatly marked with masking tape labels.

I set everything down on the kitchen counter. I had quite the collection: my mother's clothes and food, my sisters plants, my nephew's cake. I wasn't entirely sure whose life I was leading, but it sure didn't seem to be mine.

"Want to go for a walk?" Kathleen asked over the phone the next day.

I glanced at my watch. It was only one-thirty. "I thought you were having lunch with your mother."

"Yes, well, plans change. Meet me at the track in thirty minutes."

Kathleen's lunch with her mother had not gone well. She was still outraged after six laps. "I swear, Alissa, I have become so beige I can't even see myself anymore!"

"That's not true, Kathleen. You're a beautiful, vibrant, intelligent woman. People look at you wherever you go."

"It's like I've camouflaged myself. I have a tan minivan with a taupe interior. I had on a beige skirt with a brown cardigan and calfskin boots. I came out of that restaurant, got in my car, flipped down the vanity mirror, and I COULDN'T EVEN SEE MYSELF!" she wailed.

"It was just the angle, Kath. That and having lunch with your mother. She makes everyone look beige." True enough. Kathleen's mother was a bona fide Beauty Queen. She had wiggled down runways in bathing suits and heels, twirled batons, talked gravely about her hopes for world peace, and padded her bra while other women burned theirs. She is now in her mid-fifties and looks like she could be Kathleen's sister rather than her mother. I suspect that she owes some of it to plastic surgery, but not much.

"You should have seen the way she flirted with that waiter. It was so disgusting I couldn't eat."

I wondered how disgusting something would have to be to make me unable to eat. Even watching Kathleen's mother having wild monkey sex with the waiter might not have done it. I have a very healthy appetite. When some women get depressed, they can't eat. They shed pounds the way Snowball sheds fur in the summertime. I, on the other hand, can't cram food in my mouth fast enough. I remember one time when my sister called in the last days of my father's illness. By the time we got off the phone, I'd eaten half a loaf of bread. I don't think I even chewed it. I just knocked the carbs back like pills.

"She can't help flirting," I said. "It's the way she's always gotten along. You can't expect her to change it now. Besides, she doesn't want to change it. She likes it like that."

"Why would a woman of her age and station need to prove that she is attractive badly enough to flirt with a waiter?" Kathleen's voice climbed a register or two. Pretty soon she'd sound just like Hayley. "Why does she go nowhere without mascara and a matching outfit? Why does she still order the grilled chicken salad, no cheese, and dressing on the side?"

"What'd you get?" I asked, resisting the urge to point out that her ponytail scrunchee matched her shorts, and her socks had the same blue trim as her T-shirt.

"I ordered the Reuben." I could hear the satisfaction in her voice. "Mother said it was like ordering a plate of fat."

I smiled. "Did you eat every last bite of it?"

"No. I told you. I barely touched it."

"Kath, it doesn't count if you don't eat it. Spite-ordering isn't enough. You must actually spite-eat it to annoy your mother."

"I walked out right after our meals arrived."

"Oh, Kath."

"That's when I got into the van and couldn't see myself in the mirror."

"I'm sorry."

She let out a gusty sigh that could have wiped out half of Topeka. "It's okay. How was dinner at your mom's?"

I snorted.

"That good?"

"My mother is picking new friends from the obituary column, and I got spaghetti sauce on my favorite silk tank top and ended up wearing one of her tops home."

This was shocking enough to stop Kathleen in her tracks. "One of *those* tops?"

"Yes," I confirmed. "It didn't seem worth it to argue."

She shook her head. "You have changed, haven't you?" We walked a little while in silence and then she said, "So, better than my lunch, but still not all that great."

"That's a pretty good summation."

"At least you have something to sum up."

"You have plenty happening in your life, Kath."

"Oh, sure. Thursday I'm driving for the first grade field trip to the science center, and this Saturday is my turn as Snack Mom for the soccer team. Whoop-de-doo."

She sounded so desolate and glum, it nearly broke my heart. "Kath . . ."

"Don't." She stopped me before I could start, which was good, because I wasn't sure what to say besides tired clichés about children being our most important resource. "You of all people shouldn't have to be comforting me about this," she said.

My face got so hot so fast, I wondered if I *was* starting to have hot flashes. How could she fling out backhanded pity like that, when I'd been doing such a good job of remembering that this wasn't about me? "What is that supposed to mean?"

"Nothing," she said a little too quickly. "Did I tell you that Hayley's goldfish is swimming upside down?"

"Kathleen, I'm fine with the whole kid thing. So I can't have any. Big deal. It's not the only path to happiness. Right?"

"You don't know that you can't have any. You don't know that for sure, Alissa."

I snorted. "Right. And Kath?"

"Yes?" She sounded wary.

"If a goldfish is swimming upside down, it probably isn't actually swimming anymore."

"That's what you think. Come over for dinner tonight and you'll see. In fact, come early and help me shop."

I let it drop, but through my shower and getting dressed, Kath's comments rankled. I'm not sure there's anything I hate more than being pitied.

I looked at the Breakfast of Champions I'd set before myself: black coffee, four hundred milligrams of ibuprofen, twenty milligrams of Prozac, and dry toast.

And I thought about the blanks in my life. I thought about Kathleen asking me the difference between calm and dead. I thought about the fact that the things I related to most these days seemed to be architectural. Did I really want to be a courtyard or, worse yet, the bathroom in the courthouse? Or did I want to be an actual person?

I cut the Prozac tablet in half.

The phone rang and I grabbed it up so fast that I clunked it against my head.

Sheila's breathy sweet voice came down the line. "Hi, Alissa."

"Hello, Sheila. What can I do for you?"

"Remember how you made me promise not to talk to the police officers anymore without you there?"

"I certainly do."

"Well, Detective Rodriguez came by my house this morning."

"And . . ."

"Well, I'm down at the police station. Do you think you could come?"

CHAPTER FIVE

From *The Angry No More Manual and Workbook*
by Dr. Gail Peterson

DOES THAT OTHER PERSON DESERVE YOUR ANGER?

Sometimes the people around you can't behave any differently regardless of whether it angers you or not. Take a moment and put yourself in the other person's shoes. Try to evaluate the situation from their perspective. Maybe they have a good reason for what they're doing, even if it shovels coal into the furnace of your Anger Train's engine.

Alissa's Anger Workbook:

Exercise #5

Think about things that have made you angry recently. Could those people have behaved differently? Answer yes or no.

1. My mother. Apparently not.
2. Sheila. Probably not.
3. Rodriguez. Definitely not.

I told the uniformed officer behind the bulletproof glass that I was there to see Detective Rodriguez. He ushered me back through the rabbit warren of cubicles immediately. Rodriguez looked even better today than he had at the courthouse. He had on a dark blue banded-collar shirt and charcoal-gray slacks. A sport coat was draped over the back of his chair.

"Detective Rodriguez, I can't believe you're doing this again."

"Hello, Ms. Lindley." I wondered what size a shirt would have to be to go around that chest. His top two buttons were undone and I could see just the top of a ribbed T-shirt underneath. I love those. I didn't see any chest hair, but that didn't mean there wasn't any. I could go either way on the chest hair issue. I tried to imagine him both with and without.

Jesus, couldn't they control the heat in these buildings? The place was a sauna. I set my briefcase down and took off my sweater. I'd put on a front-slit, straight-cut skirt that ended just above the knee with a hip-hugging grommet belt, a ribbed twinset, and my favorite Via Spiga ruched pumps. "Where is my client?"

"In an interview room." He stayed leaned back in his office chair, all relaxed and casual. Not a nerve showing on the man.

"Why?"

For an answer, he tossed a police report my way. I read it through. While I read, he did the hands behind the head thing. I stole a quick look at him over the top of the police report. Nope, it wasn't just me being paranoid—he was watching. He didn't take his eyes off me the whole time I was reading.

FROM THE SAN JOSE POLICE DEPARTMENT
DAILY BULLETIN:

VIOLATION: Malicious Mischief, Vandalism

CRIME/INJURY/WEAPON: At approximately 1630

hours, the suspect reached into the driver side window of the victim's BMW Z3 and tore the directional from the steering column. Suspect then handed the victim his directional saying that she had done it because he hadn't been using it anyway.

VICTIM AND/OR WITNESS: Darryl Miller, 9728 Drake Avenue, Sunnyvale, CA.

SUSPECT(S): Female caucasian. Approximately 5'10" in height, 125 pounds. Possibly blonde. Butterfly tattoo on right hip. Wearing pink thong.

"You've brought her in here on the basis of her butterfly tattoo again? I thought we'd covered this ground before, Detective."

He shrugged and his shoulder muscles rippled. His eyes never left me. I was glad I'd worn the sleeveless version of the turtleneck. "I thought we'd try it again," he said. "It was so much fun the first time."

"Yeah, just a barrel of laughs. May I speak to my client now?"

He stood up and headed through the maze of cubicles toward a hallway. The way his butt looked in those slacks, I would have followed if he'd thrown open the door to a cage of lions and sauntered in.

No lions on the other side of the door, though. Just Sheila making origami cranes out of paper from a legal pad that was sitting in front of her. I shook my head and looked over at Rodriguez, who shrugged, then left us alone, pulling the door quietly shut behind him as he left.

"Sheila, what happened?"

"Do you want me to start at the beginning again?"

"Absolutely."

"Okay," she said, all eager and ready to go. "I've been thinking about it while I was waiting for you, and I'm pretty sure that I know where it began this time!"

I sat down across from her and got out my legal pad to take notes. "That's great, Sheila. Good job."

She beamed at me. "See, there's these dancers' meetings at the Crescent Moon. They're pretty bogus. It's mainly time for us girls to bitch about not getting enough stage time or not getting good hours. Nothing ever changes, but we get together and bitch anyway and we're required to be there."

"Okay."

"Well, once I finally left my house for work, I was like ten minutes later than I should have been. Greg wanted to . . . well, I mean, he needed to . . . well, uh . . . Never mind. Anyway, I really was in a hurry to make it to the meeting, and I was kind of ticked off that I had to spend like one of my only nights off at this stupid meeting, and I was kind of annoyed with myself for being late because of letting Greg talk me into . . . well, uh . . . you know . . . and I think that's why I followed the dude in the Beamer. I mean, I like totally didn't have time for it. I was totally late, but I was kind of pissed about being late. But I mean, it's not like people don't cut you off in traffic like a million times a day around here. It's like an every-minute occurrence."

Thank heavens. We were finally getting to the actual story about the car and the directional.

"So you just decided to follow this gentleman in the BMW because he cut you off?"

"I think so. I mean, he almost clipped the front of my Tracker, and it just really bugged me. Why couldn't he like signal or something? I'd have let him in. I thought maybe somebody should tell him that, so I totally followed him. He kept zigging and zagging in and out of traffic. Never signaled once. I didn't change lanes that many times, and you know, all those lane changes didn't even put him too far ahead of me. I was just a few seconds behind him when he pulled into the mall parking lot."

"Which mall?" I asked without looking up from my legal pad.

"That little strip mall at the corners of Henderson and El Camino."

"Go on," I said.

"Okay. So I walked right up to his little Z3 and knocked on the window. Before he rolled it down, I knew he wasn't looking at my face. I was wearing jeans and this great wraparound lace top I just got. It has these really pretty scalloped edges and bell sleeves, but it leaves your tummy bare and shows a lot of cleavage. He was checking out the butterfly tattoo on my hip and trying to figure out if my jeans were really cut as low as they looked. I mean, my jeans are not Britney or Shakira low, but they are low."

"Mmm-hmmm," I murmured.

"He still wasn't looking at my face when I bent over to talk to him. Then he was checking out my tits so thoroughly that he didn't even notice when I reached in and pulled the little stick thingie you signal with off the steering column. I was glad it snapped off as easy as it did. I was afraid I wouldn't be able to get it off."

"You just snapped the directional off? And he did nothing to stop you?" My mouth gaped open. Generally something I try not to do during meetings with clients, but Sheila kept managing to knock me back on my keister.

"I told you, he wasn't looking at my hands. Or my face. He did notice when I dropped the stickie thing in his lap, though. You should have seen the look on his face when I told him I'd done it because he wasn't using it anyway."

"And he still just sat there?" I asked.

"Yeah, well, by then I was walking away. I figured he'd be more likely to be able to tell the cops the color of my thong than the color of my eyes."

True enough. "Sheila, wait right here. I need to talk to Detective Rodriguez."

He was still at his desk. He was also still way too good looking. "Is my client under arrest, Detective?" I know. I'm such a smooth operator.

"No." He shook his head. "Once again your client happily accompanied me to the station."

"Of course she did. She probably needs her brakes checked. So why is she here?"

"I wanted to ask her a few questions about this incident and she said she wouldn't talk to me without her lawyer, so we ended up down here." He smiled. "Would she be interested in standing in a lineup?"

I seethed. "She would not."

He did that leaning back in his chair with his hands behind his head thing again, a smile playing at the edges of his lips. "Then I guess she can go if she wants to."

"She wants to."

I hustled Sheila out of the police station and to my Volvo. "Should I take you home?"

She checked her watch. "Nah. My shift at Li'l Dudes starts in forty-five minutes. I'll be early, but you might as well drop me there. I'll get Bridget or somebody to take me back home afterward."

I struggled to find the right words to say as she flipped through the pile of CDs scattered around my car. "You can't keep doing things like this, Sheila. Rodriguez doesn't need any more ammunition right now. He's already trying to intimidate us."

"I know." She flipped over my Waifs' CD to read the song list on the back.

"So you're going to cut this out, right?"

She nodded, but I didn't feel terribly assured.

"And the other women? You'll tell them to cut it out, too, right?"

Sheila turned the full force of her baby blues on me. "I can only control my own actions, Alissa. I can't control anyone else's behavior but my own."

The words sounded foreign coming out of her mouth. "Where'd you hear that?"

"From Helena."

"Helena?"

"Yeah, Helena down at the club."

"Maybe I should have a chat with Helena, too, then. And what was the other woman's name?"

"Lily," Sheila said.

"With Lily, too. Can you set that up?" I asked as I pulled into the parking lot of Li'l Dudes 'n Dudettes Child Care and Preschool.

"Sure," she said. And then she was gone.

Marsha would simply love to give up some of the things she does. She spends so much time doing so many things for so many people, the poor thing is wrung out at the end of the week. The problem is that nobody else will do the things she does as well as she does them. Or at least, they won't do them precisely her way, and that she cannot endure.

For instance, I had purchased a lovely scarlet flowering bougainvillea for the courtyard and plunked it down just where I wanted it. The last time Marsha had stopped by, she had laboriously shifted it to the spot she originally had chosen for it. I spent a half hour grunting, shoving, and dragging until I got it back to where I'd originally put it.

This isn't anything new. I remember when I was given the unenviable chore of ironing my father's handkerchiefs. Marsha would actually come home from college on the weekends and re-iron the stack I'd done because they weren't folded in perfect squares the way Daddy liked them. I eventually stopped ironing them at all. I mean, why bother, right? I had other ways of earning my father's approval.

So I knew I was in real trouble when Marsha happily relinquished driving my mother to Colma to visit my father's grave once a month without a fuss. In case you're unfamiliar with Colma, it's pretty much the place to go to get buried in northern California. A million people can't be wrong, can they? Somewhere in the early 1900s the forward-thinking members of San Francisco's board of supervisors realized that they were going to run out of room for people who were still living, and decided that they could at least move out the ones who weren't.

That was great, but San Franciscans who were breathing when the rules went into effect still kept making that transition to not breathing, and they had to go somewhere else, too. For some reason, they all decided to go to Colma. Now Colma is the only incorporated city in America where the dead actually outnumber the living.

I suspected that any chore Marsha would hand off that fast had to be bad. This was confirmed when she hissed at me that at least I hadn't had to go choose the goddamn plots with them in the first place. Marsha never swears.

I knocked at my mother's door precisely at noon. I am by nature a punctual person. Of course, this is not enough to satisfy my mother. She is ultrapunctual, even early. Her new slowness was driving her crazy, and she had apparently decided to compensate by being even earlier. She opened the door almost before I could knock. A twinge of guilt ran through me when I saw that she'd dragged a dining-room chair down the long hallway. A paperback lay next to it. I wondered how long it took her to get that chair there and how long she'd been sitting there. I didn't ask, though; my mother hates being pitied even more than I do.

The day was cool by California standards, down in the

mid-sixties. Even so, by the time my mother had clomped her way to my father's grave, her face had turned red and a fine sheen of sweat shone on her forehead. Watching her make the effort to lift and move the walker and drag her right foot behind her was almost as excruciating as walking slowly enough for her to keep up.

I looked at where my father's marker would be in six months and the mound that covered his casket. I still couldn't quite believe he was under there, despite having thrown a shovelful of dirt on it myself after the casket was lowered (Jewish funerals are brutal). He'd been the core of our family for so long. The three of us—my sister and mother and I—had danced around him like attendants on a king. Now sometimes it felt like we were twirling about with no purpose at all.

He had been regal, too. Not in a snotty way, mind you, but in that kind of benevolent ruler way, passing down wisdom and judgments as if from a lofty place we couldn't quite attain. Long after Marsha and I figured out that he was just faking it half the time, that he had no more access to some higher form of logic than we did, the pattern of our dance had been set and we couldn't seem to change the way our feet followed the steps.

What I missed most was his sense of humor—dry and fast and occasionally wicked, but never mean. He was still making jokes when he could barely get enough air in his lungs to talk. Three nights before he died, the hospice nurse on duty had come in to introduce herself. "I'm Cindy and I'll be with you tonight," she'd said.

"Which side of the bed do you like?" my father had gasped out without missing a beat.

Oh, it's not like he was the perfect father, mind you. He was the master of the backhanded compliment: Your hair looks so much better this way, or that dress is much more becoming than the one you wore yesterday. Petty things that can make an adolescent girl freeze in her tracks, but honestly don't matter much in the end.

In the end he had been my daddy and he was gone. When he'd first gotten sick, we'd all assumed he could be fixed. It hadn't occurred to any of us that the doctors wouldn't make him well. Having him gone and my mother alone was just one more thing in my life that made me feel out of whack. Sometimes I was relieved I hadn't had to face him after screwing up so drastically, though. If he was watching from some afterlife, at least I didn't have to directly confront the quiet, exasperated way he had of looking away from us when we'd displeased him.

I clenched my jaw against the heat in back of my eyes. He was gone. Crying wouldn't bring him back. Nothing would.

My mother lifted her chin to let the breeze blow across her face and cool her a little. She leaned heavily on the bars of the walker and stretched. Her hair ruffled a little in the wind. "Your father wanted to be in the sun," she said. "I thought a little shade might have been nice. I love a nice shade tree."

"Why didn't Daddy want to be in the shade?"

"He said it's too hard to keep grass growing in the shade. It dies too easy, requires too much fertilizer. He said he didn't want people dumping chicken shit on his head for all eternity." Mom pulled herself straighter yet. "I had to admit he had a point, but honestly, a little shade would have helped a lot on a day like today."

"It was nice of you to compromise like that, Mom."

"I didn't, really. It was your sister who cast the deciding vote. Marsha thought that the two of you would probably rather stand in the sun than the shade."

"You chose this spot because Marsha thought we would like it better?" That just seemed wrong, especially since I really didn't care where we stood.

"Seriously, Alissa, by the time I'm here I won't give a fig whether it's sunny or shady, now will I?"

After the cemetery I stalked my mother through Safeway. She has become so frustrated with people doing things for her that she has taken to smacking their hands away, so I was reduced to lurking behind endcaps spying on my mother as she toddled through the aisles.

I darted out from behind the day-old bread display to rescue her when she managed to wedge herself in the milk cooler trying to get to the gallons on the bottom shelf that were on sale, and pretended to just happen to show up in the cookie aisle at the same time she did and thus was able to reach the reduced-fat vanilla wafers off the top shelf for her.

I carried her groceries up to the apartment for her and got most of them put away in the time it took her to go to the bathroom. "Anything else I can do for you, Mom?"

Her shoulders came up. "I'm fine, Alissa. I am perfectly capable of doing things for myself."

It took me a second to figure out why Mom's tone sounded

so familiar. She sounded just like me. Every once in a while Hayley will say something in such precise mimicry of Kathleen that it'll just crack me up. It's not nearly so funny when you hear your own words and attitude coming out of your mother's mouth. I've spent a huge amount of energy trying not to turn into my mother, and I'm not just talking polyester tops with pointed collars. For thirty years I've been trying to convince Mom and Marsha to let me do things for myself, that I am competent to lead my life without their help. Now here was Mom, insisting that she didn't need any help when she so clearly did.

I thought of her trapped like a hamster in a wheel in the milk freezer at Safeway, her little feet pawing along without ever moving her forward, and the longing on her face as she looked up at the vanilla wafers just out of her reach on the top shelf. Sure, she was just fine on her own. Just like I was.

Riiiiggghhht.

Kathleen and I stood side by side in Hayley's room. I'd come for dinner and to see Goldie the goldfish do her "new trick." Our heads tilted at identical angles as we watched Goldie swimming around her bowl, in and out of her little castle, over her pink and blue gravel, upside down, while Hayley danced around us in circles singing "Goldie's swimming upside down" to the tune of "London Bridge Is Falling Down."

"She's swimming upside down," I said, my firm grasp of the obvious refusing to slip.

"Yep," Kathleen agreed.

"Why, do you suppose?" I tried tilting my head the other way.

Kathleen's head slowly made the arc to the new tilt. "I have no idea."

"Maybe it's a tidal thing. Maybe when the moon changes, she'll start swimming right side up again," I suggested.

Kathleen shot me a look from the corner of her eye. "She's in a two-gallon fishbowl. I doubt there's room for a tide."

Hayley stopped dancing. "Do you think she could have sprained her fin? Do they make fish splints?"

"No, I don't think fish can sprain their fins," I said. "I don't think they have bones there."

Hayley frowned. "Then why, Mama?"

Kathleen kissed her forehead. "Maybe she's just enjoying swimming a different way. Go see if your brother is done with his homework so we can go to the store and pick your dinner."

As Hayley skipped out of the room, I wondered what it would be like to skip everywhere I went. It looked like such a happy way to go places. If I tried, I'd probably slip on the linoleum in the courthouse and break a leg.

"So what would possess a fish to suddenly start swimming upside down? Do you think she got bored and decided to see if a different perspective would make it more interesting?" I asked.

"I dunno. She's got the little castle, the fake plant, the pink and blue gravel, the top-of-the-line fish food, and clean water. What else does a goldfish need?"

I shook my head. "That's one ungrateful fish."

"I wonder what the human version of swimming upside

down might be." Kathleen headed out of the room. "Come on. Let's go to the store."

Kathleen and I took Hayley and Jason to pick out a video *(Ice Age)* and dinner (mac 'n cheese, baby carrots, and chocolate chip cookie dough ice cream) to share with the babysitter.

As we walked out of the Albertsons into the parking lot, a gray-haired woman in a long blue skirt and striped blouse leaped out from the cart return and yelled, "Jesus loves you!"

Her leathery skin and the pile of belongings beside her made it look like she'd spent some time living rough.

"Thank you," I said, handed her a dollar, and kept walking. Kathleen shot furtive glances over her shoulder. She's really been in the suburbs too long.

"The Lord is your saviour," the gray-haired woman called after us.

"Somebody should do something about that," Kathleen said, clearly uncomfortable.

"What do you suggest? Fines and prison sentences for unwanted religious solicitations?" It's not that I'm so comfortable with the homeless, I'm just used to it. To the reality of it and the hopelessness of it, as well. Only someone who hadn't been around the problem much would think something could be done about it.

"I'm not heartless. I was thinking more about getting her some kind of help."

"What? Like a twelve-step program for religious fanatics? What would they do at the third step? Promise *not* to give everything over to a higher power?"

"A lot of those people just need a little help," she said primly as she put the groceries into the back of her minivan. Hayley and Jason had already climbed into their seats. "We pay tons of taxes. There ought to be some money somewhere for that."

"A lot of those people don't want help." I'd learned this the hard way at the PD's office. "A lot of those people are living just the way they want."

Kathleen scowled. "Nobody would want to live on the street and beg for food."

"It's more complicated than that, Kath. Trust me, you can't let it get to you. If you do, it will overwhelm you."

"So you don't do anything?"

"What would you have me do? Give her the key to my condo? Invite her to move in?"

Kath chewed her lip. "No. But I don't think nothing is the right choice either."

"I gave her a buck. You want me to go back and give her twenty?"

"Forget it," she said and climbed into her van.

I should have remembered Kathleen's comment about there being someone she'd like me to meet and been suspicious of her dinner invitation, especially when it became an evening out instead of a family dinner in. She had ambushed me.

We'd walked into the Fish Market at Henderson and El Camino, and Rob strode over to shake the hand of a man sitting alone at a table for four.

I stopped and glared at Kathleen. "You set me up, didn't you? Even after I told you not to. You're not my best friend anymore."

She gave me one of her smug Mona Lisa smiles and said,

"You know what they say: The best way to get over one man is to get under another. And who do you think you're going to replace me with? Your sister?"

"I was thinking of Snowball."

She strolled to the table, not even glancing to see if I was following. I was tempted not to but did anyway, seething the whole time.

His name was Kirk and he was drop-dead gorgeous. What was Kath thinking?

He pushed the bread basket away from him. "I'm trying to watch my carbs, and only get them from places and at times that really fuel me. I put on five pounds over the winter and I'm really feeling it on the hills."

I couldn't imagine this guy losing any weight. He was all lean muscle already. You could see his muscles ripple through his lightweight V-neck sweater and his linen slacks. He was like a greyhound, all corded sinew, coiled to spring.

"Kirk's a triathlete," Rob said, helping himself to two pieces of bread. The only time Rob participated in three sports at once was with a remote control in his hand, and even then one of them was likely to be bowling.

I tried to get another look at Kirk without looking like I was looking. Honestly, the man was amazing and it wasn't just the bod. Chiseled cheeks and just-tousled-enough hair and the longest eyelashes I've ever seen on a man. I tried to come up with something to say. Something witty, clever about weight loss or triathlete stuff.

"Oh, how tri-ing," I said. My laugh rang out alone. Kath and Rob and Kirk just looked at me blank-faced.

I watched the lightbulb go on over Kirk's head, though. He covered as fast as he could. "Oh, I get it now. Tri-ing and tri-athlete. Ha ha."

I wanted to crawl under my seat. "Will you all excuse me for a second?" I headed for the ladies' room. Maybe if I splashed cold water on my face, I'd eventually stop blushing.

"Hey, wait up." Kath was behind me. "I'll come with you."

I banged through the women's room door with her in hot pursuit. At the sink I splashed cool water on my still-hot red face. "What were you thinking? That guy is totally out of my league."

"No, he's not." She put a little lipstick on.

"Yes, he is." I applied Kath's lipstick to my lower lip and then pressed my lips together to spread the color around. "He looks like one of those guys in a Calvin Klein underwear ad."

"So he's handsome. Big deal. That color's totally wrong for you. Try this one." Kathleen rummaged in her bag for another lipstick.

"I'm not dressed for this, either." I'd put on jeans and a cream-colored ribbed turtleneck and pulled my hair back into a ponytail. It was just supposed to be dinner at Kathleen's, after all. Thank God I'd worn my little rock star ankle boots and a leather jacket.

"You look adorable, like you're not even trying." She handed me another lipstick. "This one's definitely a better color for you. More mauve, less of a pink."

"How many of these do you have in there?"

"Three, and no teasing. You can't benefit from my lipstick stock and ridicule it at the same time. It's against the rules."

I grinned. "What rules?" I asked as we left the bathroom.

"The ones that say you should sit your ass down at the table and be yourself, and stop obsessing about whether this guy is in your league or not."

I decided this guy was so completely out of my league that there was nothing I could do about it anyway, so I might as well be myself. I found myself spouting off on why I like M. Night Shymalan movies and why I hate books by John Updike and my personal conspiracy theories on Jon-Benet Ramsay and the California energy crisis. Before I knew it, we'd finished our coffee and were headed for the door.

Kirk offered to walk me to my car after dinner.

"I'd like to call you some time if I could," he said.

"You've got to be kidding," I said.

He winced. "Ouch. I guess I misread you even worse than I usually misread people. I thought maybe there was something there. Sorry." He started to walk away, his incredibly tight glutes getting ready to disappear into the sunset.

"No!" I grabbed his arm. People turned to look at us. I realized I might have been a little louder than I mean to be. Was I willing to let an ass that looked like it could crack walnuts between its cheeks get away that easily?

He shook his head. "I went on too long about my weight problems, didn't I? Obsessing about your weight is a total turnoff, I know. The last woman I dated said she couldn't stand hearing me talk about my body anymore. Or was it the conversation about aluminum bikes versus carbon fiber bikes that bored you so out of your skull that you wanted to run from the table screaming?"

I laughed. "Neither. I just was surprised that you were interested in me. I mean, I didn't think you—"

"Please! You're like a breath of fresh air. Nobody I hang around with talks about books or movies or politics anymore. They just want to talk about their time on their last marathon or what new sports drink they're trying. And your smile. I just love your smile." He smiled.

Could this really be happening? Could I get the great-looking guy by being a good conversationalist and having a pretty face? Did this mean that all the lies my mother ever told me about men were going to suddenly come true?

I thought about all those muscles. I thought about all those muscles pressed up against me. I thought about all those muscles pressed up against my completely muscle-free stomach and my ten extra pounds. It was like imagining Arnold Schwarzenegger pressed up against Roseanne Barr. Eeewwww.

On the other hand, I could maybe push the bread basket away a little faster.

I smiled my apparently mesmerizing smile and handed him my card.

Imagine. He wasn't even fuzzy or neutered.

CHAPTER SIX

From *The Angry No More Manual and Workbook*
by Dr. Gail Peterson

TAKING RESPONSIBILITY FOR YOUR ANGER

No one can make you angry. No one can decide for you how to feel. The only person who can make you angry is you.

Alissa's Anger Workbook:

Exercise #6

Think about how you can take responsibility for your own Anger Train instead of blaming others. List how you helped make yourself angry in some of your last few anger bouts.

1. By believing in him.
2. By believing in love.
3. By believing in truth.

"So, Mr. Chardlin, tell me your side of the story." I'd gotten another call from a court clerk that morning, another new client. Yay, me!

Mr. Chardlin leaned back in his chair in the interview room and regarded me with great suspicion. "How old are you?"

I hesitated. I generally prefer not to divulge personal information to clients. On the other hand, most people feel more comfortable and more forthcoming if they know your credentials and background. "I'm thirty. I've been a defense lawyer for nearly six years."

He grunted. "You got any brothers or sisters?"

"I don't see how that's relevant to my credentials," I replied, sounding stiff even to myself.

"I got a brother. A little brother." Chardlin rocked back in his chair. "A little brother who's been a pain in my backside pretty much since he was born."

"I take it this brother is the other Mr. Chardlin, whose window you allegedly broke."

"Put an alleged rock through it," he said, smacking his lips as if he could still taste the sweetness of his revenge.

It took a while to get the whole story, but it seemed that the younger Mr. Chardlin had convinced my client to allow him to change the oil in my Mr. Chardlin's new truck. Chardlin the Younger promised he'd do it better and cheaper than the dealer. Besides, who would my Chardlin rather give his money to? Some big corporation or his chronically unemployed little brother?

Unfortunately, little brother forgot to put the plug back in.

"You know what happens when all the oil runs out of your engine?" Mr. Chardlin asked me.

I am pretty much of the school of thought that believes in putting the key in the car and turning it on. If it goes, life is good. I get my oil changed every three thousand miles because my daddy told me to, along with that thing about slowing down before the curve.

"Nothing good, I imagine," I said.

"Your engine seizes," Mr. Chardlin told me.

"That doesn't sound good."

He shook his head. "Five thousand dollars I'm out, and the little bastard wouldn't even talk to me. I knew he was in there. I could see the lights on and his piece-of-shit car was in the driveway. Didn't leave the plug out of his own engine, of course."

"So you were just trying to get him to talk to you?"

"Yeah," Chardlin said, eyes brightening. "Yeah. I was just trying to get his attention."

"With a rock."

"He's a hardheaded guy, Ms. Lindley."

We all know a few of those.

As we waited our turn to come before the judge, I calculated it had been nearly four months since I'd actually stood in a courtroom. I swallowed hard. Would I remember what to say? Would I remember how to say it?

Write it down. That's what my dad always told me. Write it down and you won't forget.

I dug through my briefcase and found some index cards stuck in a side pocket, then jotted down what I wanted to say in appropriate lawyerese. They called Mr. Chardlin's name. We went up to the table.

"How do you plead, Mr. Chardlin?" Judge Holt asked.

"M-m-my client p-p-pleads n-n-not guilty," I stammered.

Mr. Chardlin whirled around and stared at me, then smacked himself in the forehead. The judge stared at me, too. He was about sixty years old and had the eyebrows of a

Jack Russell terrier. They quivered. "He d-d-d-oes?" he asked.

My face flamed red. "Yes," I squeaked.

He turned his eyebrows on my buddy the D.A. "Any bail suggestions, Ms. Ferguson?"

Before she could speak, I jumped in. "Mr. Chardlin is a l-l-local businessman with a family. He is n-n-n-not a flight risk. This matter is largely a d-d-domestic dispute that I think can be settled out of court. I'm asking that Mr. Chardlin be re-leased . . . be released . . . " Oh, my God. What did I want him released on? I couldn't remember the words. I grabbed my index cards. Where was it? Where was the one? There it was! "On his own r-r-recognizance!"

Sweat trickled down my back and my stomach heaved. How could I forget "own recognizance"? I took a deep breath in and let it out slowly, aware that even the court clerk had stopped what she was doing to stare at me.

"Maybe you should practice that in the mirror a few times before we come back," Mr. Chardlin whispered to me.

After helping Mr. Chardlin arrange to go home, I dragged myself out of the courthouse to my car, plugged Shemekia Copeland into the CD player, and let her voice wash over me as she begged the devil to leave her alone.

I swung through the grocery store for a few things and managed to keep it to a gallon of milk, a pound of coffee, a bag of prewashed lettuce, a can of tuna fish, and six cans of Fancy Feast. I resisted the ice-cream aisle and the cookie aisle. Going walking with Kathleen was firming things up. I didn't need to let my former best friend, Little Debbie, undo everything I was working for.

Back in the car I didn't pay much attention to the cheesy radio hosts until the male news anchor said, "So, Charlotte, I understand an area man got a visit he didn't want to refuse."

The female news anchor replied, "That's right, Alan. Carl Burton, a San Jose accountant, was accosted in his office by three half-naked women demanding information on a client's financial status."

"I knew the dating scene was tough out there, but I didn't realize it was that tough!" Alan said with a plastic laugh.

I cringed.

I got back to the condo, parked the car in my designated covered spot, pulled my bags of groceries from the trunk, and headed to the door, grabbing my mail as I walked by my box. I tossed everything on the kitchen counter and sorted through the mail: a book of coupons, a phone bill, two credit card offers, and a square ivory envelope. I picked up the square one and looked at the return address. All the air sucked out of my lungs. It was from Thomas.

My first instinct was to scream "fuck you fuck you fuck you" at it. Thomas and I didn't have the kind of chummy divorce where you promised to "keep in touch with each other" and "still be friends." As breakups go, ours was pretty bad. It certainly felt like it generated as much gossip and rumor as Nicole and Tom's, went as public as Diana and Charles's, and made me look as ridiculous as Burt and Loni. As far as I'm concerned, it was damn near as tragic as Ann and Henry's.

Ann Boleyn has the edge on me because she actually died, and I just wanted to for a while.

I counted to ten while doing deep breathing, and then I opened the envelope. Mr. and Mrs. Thomas Lindley (hey, wasn't that me?) were pleased to announce the birth of their baby girl. I lost all sensation in my face. I was cold from my head to my feet. My lips felt like ice.

They had included a picture. How thoughtful. The kid didn't even have the decency to be ugly; she looked like the Gerber baby. Bethany had put one of those little pink headband bows on the baby's little round head, and even that looked cute. I wasn't even going to get the satisfaction of making fun of some cone-headed, red-faced, screaming creature.

I looked around my living room, decorated in Early Divorced Minimalist, the stacks of untidy papers in my office, and the dishes in the sink. It was as if Thomas were standing there, handsome and square-jawed as ever, and gloating. The sting of his betrayal felt like it had just happened yesterday, and anger twisted around inside me like a malignancy.

Would I ever let this go? Maybe when my fallopian tube started functioning again, which would be pretty much never. Why *should* I let go of it, anyway? Six months of court-mandated anger-management courses aside, that picture really made me want to break something.

I looked around for some food to shove in my face, but the kitchen was filled with vegetables and fruit. There was not one sugary, white-floury bit of comfort food to be had. I didn't even have a loaf of bread handy.

I looked at the clock. Kathleen was due to pick me up any minute to drag me along to Andrea Rappaport's bridal shower. How was I possibly going to get through a bridal shower tonight? Or ever again, for that matter?

Andrea had been part of our "gang" in high school. Not really close enough to stay in constant contact with, but close enough to exchange Christmas cards with each year. And now that I was back in town, close enough to be invited to buy her lingerie and show up at her shower. I needed to change fast or Kathleen would pick my outfit for me.

I looked in my closet, seriously uninspired. Boots and an A-line skirt would mean no pantyhose. That seemed like a plus. I grabbed the black-and-white printed skirt off its hanger. Black sweater? Supposed to be slimming and still in its dry-cleaner bag, so there shouldn't be much white cat hair on it.

I barely had the sweater pulled over my head when the doorbell rang, signaling Kathleen's arrival. I dug my trenchcoat out of the closet and stepped out into the fine drizzle that was now falling outside.

We got in Kathleen's minivan. Kathleen always likes to drive; it's a control thing. She claims she gets carsick if she's not driving. I know better, largely because I get some of my control jollies from driving a car with a manual transmission and a stick shift.

She buckled her seat belt, started the van, pulled her makeup bag out of her purse and set it in her lap, and then started to back up.

This didn't give me a warm, fuzzy safe feeling. "You're going to do your makeup while you drive?"

"I was running late and didn't have time to put it on."

"Do you want me to drive?" I asked.

"I can do almost all my makeup while driving these days. Everything except the eyeliner. I can only do that if I get a really long red light."

"You can't really count on that. Let's just take my car," I said.

"No. You don't have a lighted vanity mirror on the passenger side."

I really wasn't sure if that was true or not. I really *really* wasn't sure if Kathleen knew if it was true or not. I really really REALLY didn't want to ride in a car being driven by a person putting on mascara. "Go inside and do your makeup before we leave."

"We'll be even later then."

"So leave off the makeup."

She stopped rummaging in her bag and pulled out a bottle of tinted moisturizer. "Why don't you take off your panties?"

"*What?*"

"I'd feel as naked without eyeliner as you would walking around without any underwear on. Would you go to this party without underwear?"

Oh. "No. Of course not."

"Well, I won't go without eyeliner. So, will you buckle up or what? Make up your mind."

I buckled up and she pulled away from the curb. "I got a card from Thomas today," I said with feigned nonchalance. I wanted to see if having him send me a birth announcement was as weird as it seemed to me. It must have been, since Kathleen jumped, stuck the mascara wand into her tear duct, and yelped.

"Why?" she asked when she stopped cursing.

"To tell me that Bethany had a baby girl."

"The rat bastard," she breathed.

We drove along in silence. Finally Kathleen put her mascara away and said, "I'm sorry, Alissa."

"Yep. Me, too."

She pulled into the restaurant parking lot.

"I can't believe you talked me into this," I hissed at Kathleen as we walked into the restaurant.

"Oh, stop whining and try to enjoy yourself," she hissed back as the maître d' led us back to a private room. At least fifteen women in varying shades of black and beige were gathered there.

"Do you sometimes feel like you're only dressed appropriately when you're completely anonymous?" I whispered.

"You feel like you're dressed appropriately? I never feel like I'm dressed appropriately," Kathleen whispered back.

"Well, you look fine today. In fact, you look like everyone else here. You blend right in."

"Maybe the witch who cursed me on the day of my birth finally died."

This was Andrea's first wedding and she was enjoying all the trimmings. Showers, parties, dress fittings—the whole enchilada.

Andrea is attractive, smart, and funny. She's also the chief technical officer for one of the few Internet start-ups that didn't go under in the last few years. From what I could glean from Kathleen, Andrea basically stopped working eighteen hour days and decided she'd better hitch up and start reproducing before the alarm on her biological clock told her she was out of time altogether.

If you think all this makes her atypical, you haven't been spending a lot of time around Silicon Valley. Andrea's more typical than Kathleen is. Although I, as the slightly embittered divorcée, may be more typical yet.

Come to think of it, that may be why Kathleen insisted that I go. She claimed it would do me good to get out and see people who weren't related to me or facing possible prison time, but I think she just wanted me there so she wouldn't have to keep fielding questions about what she "does." Far be it from me to say she's defensive about her choice to stay at home with her kids, but her lower lip occasionally trembles when she answers that one.

Human shield or charity case, I was there and decided Kathleen was right. I might as well try to enjoy myself. I grabbed a drink from the tray at the door. It was a giant yellow thing in a martini glass.

Kathleen squealed, "Oooh! Lemon Drops! Yummy!"

It tasted like lemon Jell-O and hit the back of my head like a straight shot of tequila. I can't swear to it, but I really think it was the Lemon Drop that made it seem perfectly normal for Andrea to come running up to hug me while wearing a Pepto Bismol–pink name tag in the shape of a penis.

"Alissa, I'm so glad you could come! I'm sorry we haven't had a chance to get together before this. It's just been so crazy with the wedding and everything."

"You look great, Andrea." None of us had that great crease-free skin we took for granted in high school, but she did look fabulous.

Andrea rolled her eyes. "The Atkins Diet. I've been on it for six months to fit into my dress. The day after the wedding, I'm eating an entire loaf of bread for breakfast. Until then I'm not touching anything but meat and cheese." She grabbed my hand and pulled me over to a table where a pink penis with my name on it awaited.

"What do you think?" I whispered to Kathleen as I pinned it to my top. "I think it goes with my eyes."

Kim Broward sailed over. "Alissa! I can't believe it's you!"

The hair on the back of my neck stood up. Remember the girl in junior high who'd pal around with you just to torment you? That would be Kim. At least, that was Kim after her parents started making real money. Before that, she'd just been one of us. Then her father made partner at the law firm. Kim's mother opened a boutique downtown that sold five-hundred-dollar linen jackets, and Kim started wearing clothes with designer labels and going on family ski vacations to Vail. It was supposedly in Vail that she skied into a tree and had to have that nose job to fix her face. I actually bought that one hook, line, and sinker until Kathleen pointed out that if you had skied into a tree hard enough to break your nose, you probably would have hurt something else as well. I had been too jealous of Kim's new nose and new life to put that one together.

The one time I spent the night at Kim's after her family had moved into their Country Club home, Kim had taken me to the club the next day to go swimming, then started a rumor with the kids around the pool that I had tried to French kiss her the night before. I had called my mother to pick me up early and drove away with the rich boys' taunts of "Lissa the Lesbo" still ringing in my ears.

All in all at fifteen, Kim and her new lifestyle had left me green with envy and red with fury. I tried to maintain color equilibrium while Kim kissed the air somewhere near my left cheek.

"Alissa, it's so wonderful to see you."

"Mmmmm." I don't like to lie and Kathleen had begged me not to be rude. Plus, I was annoyed that Kim had apparently not aged since high school. Where the hell were her crow's-feet? Isn't there some point when inner ugliness should start to show?

"I heard all about you and Thomas," Kim brayed. She'd always been a bit horsey. Plastic surgery can't remove all of that.

I shot a look at Kathleen, who gave me her best "who me?" look in return.

"It's such a shame! You two looked like you were just going to conquer the world! And now I hear you're totally kaput. What happened?"

"I guess appearances can be deceiving." Otherwise Kim would be twisted up like an old hag from a fairy tale.

"And I'm so sorry about your father," Kim went on. You mean the one who wasn't good enough to socialize with your father after he went up a tax bracket or two, I thought.

"So hard to lose a husband and a father in just one month," Kim said.

Gee, and I thought I wasn't in a party mood when Kathleen picked me up. Maybe Kim would start talking about starving orphans next.

Before things could go any further, Andrea's maid of honor clapped her hands and the games began. The silhouette of a naked man had been drawn on a huge sheet of butcher paper. A head shot of Andrea's groom-to-be had been pasted on. Apparently we were to be blindfolded, spun around, and, in an X-rated version of Pin the Tail on the Donkey, we were to replace the missing member on Andrea's fiancé with our nametags.

I got myself another Lemon Drop.

After the rousing game of "Pin the Dick on Rick" (I am not the one who made that up, so don't blame me), we lowered hot dogs that dangled from long strings off our back belt loops into water bottles. That one required two Lemon Drops to get me to participate, but damned if I didn't win. Apparently, being nearly unable to stand is an advantage in hot dog dangling. Also apparently, my wild war whoop of victory was enough to convince Shelly, the maid of honor, that it was time to have the food served.

I dug into my grilled salmon with gusto, ignoring Kathleen's looks of concern. I did allow her to pour me a glass of water instead of a glass of wine, but I kept a firm grip on my cocktail.

"So how many of you have been married?" Shelly asked the group.

I raised my hand. Kathleen trod on my foot. "She didn't ask if we were still married or even happily married," I whispered.

"You know what she meant," Kathleen whispered back.

Shelly was still talking. "So what advice do you ladies have for the bride? What's the key to a happy marriage?"

"Consistent condom usage!" I yelled, raising my Lemon Drop high.

Kathleen barely gave me time to grab my name tag off Rick and shove it in my trenchcoat pocket before she dragged me out of there and drove me home.

I woke the next morning with a pounding head and a tongue coated in lemon-flavored fuzz. I showered until the hot water turned cold, drank a nonfat latte, and ate a piece of toast with peanut butter and sliced bananas. I shook open *The San Jose Daily News* and nearly aspirated a piece of banana when I found the article in the Metro section.

TWO TATTOOS?
by Joel Shapiro

Two Bay Area men have recently reported being accosted by women wearing not much more than a butterfly tattoo on their right hips. Carl Burton of San Jose claims a group of scantily clad women, one of whom had a butterfly tattoo, broke into his accounting office and demanded information on his financial status.

Darryl Miller of Sunnyvale claims that a young woman in extremely low-cut jeans ripped the directional lever off the steering wheel of his BMW. "She made some sort of crack about me not needing it and then just handed it to me," said Miller. Miller, who according to witnesses had entered the parking lot without signaling the turn, claims he has no idea why the woman singled him out in the parking lot.

Other witnesses were able only to report that the woman wore pink thong panties.

Police sources say that while a pattern is emerging, they are not ready to see the two incidents as a trend.

This required another latte.

By the time I sat down at my desk, I felt human. Maybe not a highly evolved human, but a tool-user nonetheless. The first tool I employed was my telephone.

"Sheila?" I said when she answered her cell phone. "That little talk? We need to have it today."

We set up a time for a heart-to-heart with her and her fellow strippers, and then I finally got down to work. I had plans for Mr. Chardlin that involved getting him to pay for his brother's window and having the assault charge reduced to vandalism, but just in case, I started a brief that called into question everything about the damn rock from its geological origins to its actual existence.

My morning slid happily away. I took a break at eleven-thirty. In the interest of getting my mother out more so she might not need to scan the obituaries for potential new friends to entertain her, I called to invite her to a concert. She and Dad had been regular attendees of chamber music and symphony orchestra concerts. A little culture in the form of something other than yogurt wouldn't hurt me any, either. At least not much.

The Peninsula Orchestra was having an evening of Handel, and tickets were still available. I expected an enthusiastic acceptance of my oh-so-generous offer.

"I'm sorry, dear. I can't. I have my class that night."

"You're taking a class?" My mother has never been one of those ladies who raced off to do tai chi or watercolor painting or conversational French lessons. My mother stayed home and waited hand and foot on my father. She didn't even have a bridge club. "What class are you taking?"

"A computer course at the Senior Center. It's called . . ." There was a pause and the sound of paper rustling. "It's called Introduction to Windows." She pronounced this like someone sounding out words in a foreign language.

"Mom, you don't even own a computer."

"But I might want to. Everything these days is www this and www that."

It sounded so reasonable, I couldn't quite put my finger on what was bothering me. Maybe she wanted to search the Internet for recipes. Maybe she wanted to shop for shoes. Maybe other people used the Internet for more productive things than I did. "So you want to surf the Web, Mom?"

"Who said anything about surfing? The class isn't even close to the ocean."

I rubbed my thumb against the crease in my forehead where my headache was starting. "Sorry. I must have misunderstood. So what prompted this sudden interest in computers?"

She sighed. "Your sister thought it would be good for me to get out of the house and suggested I check into the courses at the Senior Center. The line-dancing class just didn't seem like an option."

I snorted. I couldn't help it; she'd caught me off guard.

Then she said, "Besides, I never really liked that chamber orchestra stuff anyway. That was your father."

"Mom, you and Dad had season tickets to the chamber orchestra since I was eight."

"It's just one of the little things you do in a marriage, dear."

As if I wouldn't know about things like that. I'd made plenty of compromises for Thomas. Hadn't I? "Like the cemetery plots?"

She sighed. "Alissa, enough."

I dropped the subject.

At four-thirty I was sitting on a high swiveling stool in the unnatural twilight of the Crescent Moon Gentlemen's Club. Very classy joint. Not. It did have a great sign outside, though: a sliver of a moon that flashed back and forth from left to right. Underneath it the silhouette of a long-haired, wasp-waisted, and overly endowed woman (kind of a dead ringer for Sheila) swung from one side of a pole to another. Flash. Moon on the left, girl on the right. Flash. Moon on the right, girl on the left.

Inside, over on the stage, a girl in a string bikini twirled around the big pole at center stage. She shimmied halfway up and then—while hanging upside down by her legs—undid her top and let it drop to the floor. The three men sitting up at the stage's edge didn't even change their facial expressions.

Personally, I don't think it's much of a striptease when you're barely dressed to start. I was, however, impressed with how strong her legs must be and mentioned as much.

"Yeah," Sheila said. "Melinda does really good pole work."

A guy with a face like a hatchet blade and a scar that skimmed his right cheekbone sauntered through the bar and looked me up and down like I might be a prospective dancer. His gaze lingered on my chest and crotch for longer than is deemed socially acceptable in most circles. Of course, this wasn't exactly my usual social circle; maybe he was actually just being polite—like a dog sniffing another dog's ass. Either way, he barely took in my face.

He turned to Sheila and, with a head jerk toward me, said in a thick accent, "Who's the bird in the suit?"

I snorted. I mean, really. Who did this guy think he was? The Ukrainian Ernest Borgnine? "Who's the Russian Mafioso?" I asked.

He whirled around, glaring at Sheila. "What did you tell her?"

"Nothing. Honest, Gregory." Sheila eyes were round blue saucers. "What's to tell, anyway?"

I wished I'd kept my mouth shut. He couldn't seriously be Russian Mafia, could he? I took a harder look. On second thought my guess was his uncle in Sacramento could get me a damned good deal on a used car if I wasn't too fussy about paperwork. Not a good sign at all. "It was a joke," I said.

He looked at me through eyes narrowed to squints. I'm sure he meant to look tough and not like he was pretending to be Asian. Chances were, he actually was kind of tough. But I'm a defense attorney. My regular clientele isn't exactly the PTA or the ladies' garden club. I've represented drug dealers, gang members, stone-cold killers, and people who had to check the all-of-the-above box.

This guy was strictly small potatoes—though that didn't mean he couldn't be a nasty piece of work. It also didn't mean that he couldn't be dangerous to Sheila. As he left, he gave a practically obligatory smack to Sheila's ass.

"He has a tail, you know," Lily whispered to me. Lily would be the Asian member of Sheila's little gang of Do-Gooders with Décolletage. She was tall, slender, with a straight fall of black glossy hair halfway down her back. She was wearing khaki capris and a white sleeveless turtleneck. In that outfit I'd look like I was on my way to do laundry. She looked glamorous.

But what she'd said surprised me. Maybe I'd misunderstood, though. "Do you mean a story? Or do you mean . . . ?"

"I mean a tail. Like a cat has a tail," she said.

"It's actually called a vestigial caudal appendage," Helena said, as if that would be helpful.

Helena was definitely the ringleader of our Gorgeous Gang. She would be the redhead of Mr. Burton's fuzzy memory. The way these girls were built, though, I was surprised he'd even re-membered their hair color.

"It's nothing like a cat's tail. More like a piggy, really." Sheila flushed, then rushed to cover what she had just said. "It's hardly even noticeable. I don't know why you guys make such a big deal out of it."

"Because it's really weird, Sheila," Lily broke in. "It's weird and kind of sinister, too."

"It's not sinister! His family was poor. They didn't have good health care in the Ukraine. They couldn't afford to do surgery for something that was just cosmetic."

"Cosmetic?" Lily laughed. "A mole is cosmetic. A big nose is cosmetic. A tail is something else entirely."

I looked at Sheila. She was blushing. Here was a woman who undressed in front of crowds of men several times a week and let them slide money into her panties (such as they were), and a little piece of tail made her blush. Then I put it together with the ass slap. "That's Greg, isn't it? You're dating him, aren't you?"

Helena rolled her eyes. "Don't even try to talk to her about it. It's useless. We've all tried."

Sheila examined the ends of her hair with great intent, and I decided, for the moment, not to waste my breath on her social life. "Let's talk about your recent extracurricular activities."

"You mean like band or French club?" Points to Lily for sarcasm.

"No, Lily." Helena put her hand on Lily's arm. "I think she's talking about Malcolm Palmer."

Lily looked blank. Uh-oh, it wasn't sarcasm. Very scary. Then the little lightbulb went on over Lily's head. The wattage may not have been high, but at least the circuit connected. "Oh."

"Ladies, I understand the temptation. There are always times that we want to take matters into our own hands, but you can't do this. It won't end well for anyone." If I'd had on glasses, I would have looked over the top of them at the girls. That's the kind of voice I used.

"It already doesn't end well." Helena was smoothing a rough spot on one of her nails. She couldn't have looked more unconcerned if she'd tried. "That's why we did it in the first place. You think things would have ended up well for the little Palmer boy if we hadn't gotten involved?"

I couldn't believe she was challenging me so nonchalantly when I'd used my best Reasonable Lawyer Voice. "That's not the point, Helena. You have to rely on the system to deal with these situations. There are agencies in place precisely to help with deadbeat dads."

"But the system doesn't work," Lily broke in, her hands flying in excitement. "And people like Joey don't have anyone to stand up for them. I mean, unless the mother can afford to pay a lawyer to help her, she really has nobody to take her side, and who can afford a lawyer these days?"

"I know that. But all you're going to do is make trouble for yourselves. You especially have to lay off now that Sheila's caught the attention of the police. And now there's this." I slapped today's *San Jose Daily News* down on the bar and pointed at the "Two Tattoos" article.

"This isn't how to handle things that piss you off, ladies. Even when you know you're right."

Lily swiveled in her chair and looked straight at me. "What is the right way, Alissa? Tell us."

"Yeah, Alissa. What should we do instead?" Helena asked. "Have a bake sale? Or a car wash?"

I didn't know what to say. Sure, there are departments that deal with enforcing child-support payments, but they are understaffed and overwhelmed. Ditto with Legal Aid. In some ways you were better off getting legal assistance if you were on welfare than if you were a typical working woman with a couple of kids to support. It was easy to make too much money to qualify for federal assistance, but still not make enough to be able to afford a lawyer to help you navigate the shark-filled waters of the legal system. "I don't know, Lily. I just know this isn't it."

Helena smiled. "Don't knock it until you've tried it, Alissa. Did Sheila tell you what happened after we sent copies of those files to Joey's mother?"

I shook my head.

"The auditors found tens of thousands of hidden dollars based on that information. The guy was a total scumbag. He sucked the life out of the programmers that worked for him and then laid them off the second the code was written. He owed money to his first employees who actually developed the system that he sold, to the firm that backed him in the first place, to his ex-wife, to his mortgage company, to his credit card companies, to nearly everybody on the planet. Now he has to pay. What's so wrong about that?"

I didn't have an answer.

*   *   *

I walked out the doors of the club feeling low. I'd expected to waltz in, explain the error of their ways to the confused and not-too-bright strippers, have them extol my genius and thank me for my help, and then waltz back out, secure in my intellectual and ethical superiority. Instead I ended up in a debate trying to support a legal system that I wasn't so sure I believed in wholeheartedly anymore. Plus, their butts were higher than mine.

Then I saw Detective Rodriguez, big as life, crammed into the front seat of a white Ford Taurus. I hesitated, but only for a step. There is nothing more satisfying than knocking the wind out of someone else after you've had it knocked out of yourself. I strode up to his car window and knocked.

"Detective Rodriguez, what brings you here?" I asked pleasantly. "Out for an evening's entertainment?"

He smiled. Darn. Still completely wow. I had been hoping it had just been one of those flukey things. "Nah," he said. "Not my style. I'm more the dinner-and-a-movie type."

"How nice for you and your dates. Why exactly are you here, then?"

"Just thought I'd stop by and check on our little Ms. Montrose."

"And is there a reason for this? Or is it just part of the police department's agenda to denigrate, humiliate, and unlawfully incarcerate my client?" I asked with a smile. More likely he knew they were up to something, and figured his occasional presence might prevent whatever it was from actually happening. I hoped he was right. I certainly wasn't doing a great job of convincing them to lay off.

He smiled wider. "Just curiosity on my part, I guess."

"You know what that did to the cat."

"Is that a threat?"

"Oh, please, Detective. What on earth would I be able to threaten you with, besides yet another one of the dozens of lawsuits against the police department that are old hat by now?" I tossed my hair back and walked away. My butt might not be as high as Sheila's and her friends', but I can still give it a good shake.

CHAPTER SEVEN

From *The Angry No More Manual and Workbook*
by Dr. Gail Peterson

MASKING OTHER EMOTIONS

Are you sure you're angry? Some of us have been angry for so long that feeling anger seems safer than feeling fearful, anxious, or even happy.

Alissa's Anger Workbook:

Exercise #7.

What might you be feeling instead of angry?

1. Frightened.
2. Anxious.
3. Horny.

"So how goes the road to sluthood?" Kathleen asked. We were going around the track again. And again. And again and again.

"Paved with good intentions," I said.

"I was just wondering if Kirk had called yet. He seemed like he really liked you."

"He left a voice mail." It had been waiting for me when I got home from the Crescent Moon the night before.

"Did you call him?"

"Kathleen, I don't want to go out with someone who's that much better looking than me. It's just asking for heartbreak."

"You're such a pessimist. Can't the glass be half full just once?"

"If it's important to you, of course it can be half full. But I'll still be thirsty when it's empty, one way or the other."

"You're impossible."

"You're meddlesome."

"I'm bored."

"Then do something."

"I am. I'm meddling with your life." She shook her head. "God, I don't miss the whole dating scene, though. The awful will-he-call/won't-he-call thing. Waiting by the phone while trying to seem like you're not waiting by the phone. Trying to figure out what you've done wrong or even if you have done anything wrong. At least with Rob, I always know."

"You're lucky to have Rob." I actually meant this. True, he was kind of a computer geek, but he was a reasonably cute computer geek and he adored Kathleen.

"I suppose."

"You suppose?"

She snorted. "Do you know what he did last night? We were kissing, and Rob's always been a great kisser. It's one of the things I've always loved about him—that he kisses so well and he can do it for hours."

"So what was wrong with that?"

"Nothing, that was still the good part. But then he grabbed my face to pull me against him and kiss me hard, and then his thumbs were on my nose."

"Your nose?" Had it been so long since I had had sex that I'd forgotten that the nose was a major erogenous zone?

"Yes. My nose. He pinched it."

"Why? What was he doing?"

"He said I had a little whitehead on the tip of my nose, and it would just take a second to squeeze it."

"Right *then?*"

"He said it would only take a second."

"And?"

"He was right. But apparently that's how long it takes me to go from Primal, Passionate Tiger Woman into Tired, Dried-Up-Like-a-Raisin Woman. So I rolled back over to my side of the bed and went to sleep."

"That's it?"

"That was it. That was the end of the passion. What happened to it? What happened to the magic, the craziness, the way we couldn't keep our hands off each other?"

"Kathleen, you've been married for eight years. You have two kids. What do you think happened to it?"

"I think it died, is what I think." Kathleen stomped along. "I think I may be the most boring woman on the earth and that I'm sick of talking about it. You're sure you don't want to call Kirk back?"

"I'm not sure I'm ready."

Kathleen began to cluck like a chicken.

"Stop it. I am not a chicken," I said.

"Oh, really? Let's see. You won't call a guy that's interested in you because he's too good looking." She clucked louder.

"Seriously, Kathleen, cut it out. People are looking."

Kathleen bent her arms and began flapping them like wings. "What's to see?" she asked. "There's nobody here but us chickens."

"So, Alissa, what can I do for you?" Dr. Kinder asked. I loved her name. I thought it was a great name for a doctor who was willing to hand out prescriptions for antidepressants as if they were candy. I'd mentioned the two big D's that had happened in my life that year—death and divorce—and she'd had that prescription pad out faster than Clint Eastwood's Magnum in *Dirty Harry*.

"I need a new Prozac prescription," I said.

Dr. Kinder flipped through my chart. I swear I've only been her patient for about three minutes. I've never even been in the office before. I picked her name off a list of preferred providers when I moved, yet my chart is like two inches thick. What the hell is in those things, and where does it come from? Are they talking to my friends, family, coworkers? Are the insurance companies performing covert surveillance on me and reporting back to my physician?

"The prescription you have shouldn't have run out yet. Why do you need a new one?"

"I'd like a lower dosage." I'd cut the tablets in half for a while and it felt like time to cut them back a little more, but cutting them in quarters looked impossible.

"Lower? Most people want to raise it."

"Well, I want off of it."

Dr. Kinder closed my chart and looked up at me from her little rolly stool. She had curly brown hair pulled off her face with one of those plastic tortoiseshell flexibands and absolutely no makeup on her big brown eyes. "Off? Entirely? Right now?"

"Eventually. But a sooner eventually rather than a later one."

Her face stayed impassive, but I had the impression I was being weighed and measured behind those big puppy dog eyes. "Is there a reason? Are you experiencing some sort of side effect that's bothering you? There are other antidepressants—Selexa, Welbutrin, Paxil, Zoloft, to name a few. You could try one of those, if that's the case."

"No. No unpleasant side effects." Actually, there were a lot of pleasant ones. Less PMS, for one. Not as hungry, for another. I'd already lost five of the pounds I'd packed on after Thomas dumped me. It could be those daily walks with Kathleen, but the Prozac didn't hurt. "I just want off. I think it's time. I want . . . I mean, I need to be on my own now."

She nodded slowly. "Are you sure you're ready?"

Sure? Hell, no. Did I need to try? Absolutely.

Luckily, I'm an excellent liar. It's essential in my profession and has made my personal life smoother on many occasions, as well. I think a too-strong attachment to the absolute truth is foolish. I mean, how many of your friends really want to know if those pants make their butts look big or if that dress makes them look fat? They're looking for a compassionate reply, not a truthful one. On the other hand, if they have spinach between their teeth or toilet paper on their shoe, instant and complete honesty is required. This particular occasion struck me as more of a big-butt question than a tooth-spinach moment, so I went with my gut and lied. "Yes. I'm sure," I said.

"All right, then." She scribbled something on her pad and handed it over to me. "Here's a scrip for the lower dosage and a schedule to phase it out. Call me instantly if you want to go back to the higher dosage. Okay? And good luck, Alissa."

"Thanks," I said. I walked out of the office feeling a little like I'd just gotten a "Get Out of Jail Free" card.

I went home and put on my lucky suit, a navy blue silk that I wore with a conservative white shell and my grandmother's pearls, the ones my dad had given me for my sixteenth birthday and that Marsha still coveted. After three tries I gave up putting on eyeliner and lipstick. My hands were shaking too much. Somehow I'd made it to several judges' short lists for appointed work. In the past few days I'd picked up a middle-aged man who tried to settle a dispute over a property line with his neighbor by use of a machete, and a young man who had used a rock-climbing hammer to liberate several purses left in cars at a parking lot. Today was the day Machete Man came before the judge.

I threw my jacket over my arm and headed to the courthouse, stopping only to try to untwist my pantyhose, which had developed a life of their own. I had spent the past few days scurrying between my client, the ADA (Lisa Ferguson again, who was beginning to think I was stalking her), and Machete Man's neighbor's attorney, and I had a deal in place. I just needed the judge's approval. So why was I panting like a race-horse?

Well, duh.

This was it. My first real step back onto the tightwire act that used to be my life. I'd fallen before, publicly and humiliatingly. What if there wasn't any net this time?

I breathed in for ten and out for five about seventy times while I watched the dial over the elevator stick on three and not move for an interminable amount of time. This gave my pantyhose plenty of time to twist up again. I made a mental note to never ever buy them at the outlet mall again. The wait in the actual courtroom was worse. By the time it was my turn to get up before the judge, the left leg of my pantyhose was as tight as a tourniquet. I went forward to present my deal-in-the-making and requested to approach the bench in a shaky voice.

Judge Brock—a massive African-American woman who I'm pretty sure could kick my ass both physically and intellectually—motioned me forward. She peered down at me. "Before you begin, Ms. Lindley, will you do me a favor?"

"Yes, Your Honor," I squeaked, trying to wiggle my leg free of my hose's death grip.

"Put your hands behind your back."

I looked up at her, surprised. "My hands? Behind my back?"

"Yes, Ms. Lindley. Your hands behind your back. I don't know how else I can be expected to hear what you're saying. The trembling is very distracting."

When it was all over, I slumped down on one of the benches outside the courtroom next to a woman weeping gently into a cell phone.

"Well, that went well," Lisa Ferguson said above me.

I sat up and gave her a weak smile.

She was right. It had gone well, despite the humiliation factor of the judge making me put my hands behind my back. My client had been put in anger-management classes (hey, they worked for me) and entered into supervised arbitration to decide whether or not his neighbor's new driveway crossed his property line or not.

"Thanks," I said.

She smiled. "I was talking to some friends in L.A. and your name came up."

My weak smile got weaker. "Oh?"

Lisa Ferguson leaned down and whispered, "I once pulled the toner cartridge from a malfunctioning photocopier and slammed it so hard on the floor that it exploded." She stood back up and shrugged. "There weren't any witnesses, but I did ruin a really nice DKNY dress."

I felt a real smile slide over my face.

Lisa smiled back. "Would you like to have coffee sometime?"

"How about now?" I said.

I rewarded myself on the way home with a stop at the nursery. I'd already added a fiery-red begonia to the hollyhock and sweet alyssum that Marsha had given me, and the courtyard really was beginning to look like something. Today I picked jasmine.

I dropped the plant off in the courtyard and went in to change, snapping the TV news on as I walked by. There were rumors of Barry Bonds using steroids (the shock!), California avocado growers were concerned about an influx of Mexican avocados, and researchers had developed a new vaccine against the West Nile virus that unfortunately worked only on horses. My suit was back in my closet where it belonged and I was back in stretch denim and cotton where I belonged. I reached out to snap off the TV before I headed out to repot my new purchase, but stopped when the picture flashed to an angry man waving a directional at the camera.

"And she just snapped it off! Just like that!" he said.

The reporter—a young Latino man in a white shirt and a thin tie—stepped into the picture. "Mr. Darryl Miller of Sunnyvale was just pulling into the strip mall at Henderson and El Camino to drop off his dry cleaning when he was assaulted by a young woman who ripped the directional off his steering column."

Miller shoved his face up next to the reporter's. "She said I wasn't using it anyway, then she just dropped it in my lap."

"Your description of the young lady?" the reporter asked, angling the microphone toward Miller.

Miller blushed. "She had a butterfly tattoo on her hip and she had . . . well . . . she was . . . " Miller's hands cupped in front of his chest in the universal guy sign language for a girl with a nice rack. "She was blond."

I snapped it back off and went out to the courtyard with a sick feeling in my stomach. Maybe planting the jasmine would make me feel better.

Maybe pigs would fly.

*   *   *

The next day Mom and Marsha took me out for lunch to celebrate winning my first case in Santa Clara County. They're very liberal with their praise; they counted Machete Man not doing time as both a moral and a legal victory.

"Acchhh," my mother said after we'd been seated at our table.

"What's wrong, Mom?"

"That woman that just walked past us."

I turned to look. "What's wrong with her?"

"Can you imagine dressing so fancy every day? The expense!"

Marsha and I had already been treated to a speech on the evils of belly-button exposure while we waited for our table. Other fellow diners had been critiqued for having bellies that were too large (they should be ashamed); now we were on to breasts that were too large.

"Am I as heavy-bosomed as that woman over there?" Mom asked, in a highly nonwhispery whisper.

"I'm not going to check out some stranger's breasts to see if they're bigger or smaller than yours," I hissed, knowing full well that the chance of them being larger was slim to none. You do not have a figure like mine by coming from a flat-chested mother.

My mother looked hurt. "I'd just hate to think that I looked like that."

"What would you do about it if you did?" I asked. I don't know many nearly seventy-year-olds who are in the market for breast-reduction surgery, but maybe Mom was interested in some kind of plastic surgery. It's the latest thing. Breasts tend to be a little like Mount Rushmore out here in California: big, rock-hard, and lifelike without actually being real.

Marsha hissed at me to shush. I crossed my eyes at her and checked out the fancy woman instead. It seemed marginally more socially acceptable than staring at the chesty woman. "Maybe she just has a few good pieces that she wears all the time," I suggested.

My mother nodded. I knew the idea of a few good pieces that you rotated through your wardrobe would appease her. It sounded classy. Mom's "Still, she must spend a fortune on clothes" didn't have much bite.

"So, Mom, how did the computer class go?" Marsha asked.

"Not so good," Mom said. "I don't think computers are going to be my thing."

"It takes time to adjust to something new," I said. "Give yourself a chance."

Mom waved my words away. "I already dropped out of the class."

Marsha and I looked at each other. "But you only went once," Marsha said, blinking.

"That's right and I'm not going back." A flush began to creep up my mother's cheeks. Not good.

"Mom, what happened?"

She pressed her lips together in a tight little line. "The teacher kept telling us to hit buttons. I hit them, but nothing happened. Everybody else seemed fine and I didn't want to make a fuss, so I didn't say anything. I just kept hitting the buttons she said and waiting for something to happen. Finally she walked around and saw my screen was blank."

"Did she fix it?"

Mom nodded. "She plugged the computer in. I guess I knocked the plug loose when I tried to park my walker by the table."

Don't laugh. Don't even snicker. With nary a lip twitch, I said, "So then everything worked, right?"

"Yes, but . . ."

"But what?"

"But then everyone laughed at me," she wailed. "I was the dummy in the back of the class who didn't even know her computer wasn't plugged in. I can't go back. I can't face it."

I considered pointing out to her that she made me go back to Sunday School and face it after I threw up during a Purim Carnival in first grade and was known as Queen Barfy until my bat mitzvah. I also considered pointing out that she'd made Marsha go back to piano lessons even after the unfortunate recital where her page turner had spaced out and Marsha became forever known as the girl who played the first two pages of "Beautiful Dreamer" for ten solid minutes until the piano teacher came and led her away in tears. Then I saw how embarrassed and ashamed Mom really was and decided to hold my tongue. For once.

My mother complains so little—about losing my dad, about the years she spent nursing him, about her own health problems, about how her world has changed so much and without her permission—that I sometimes forget how hard some things are for her. Not wanting to be reminded that there's a whole level of technology that most of us take for granted, but that she can't even make sure is plugged in properly, really isn't that much to ask.

"So Terry said he asked Smashley to the junior prom," I said, looking for a good conversational gambit.

"Mmm-hmm," Marsha murmured.

"He said she got her tongue pierced, too," I said.

And she was off! Nothing like a rousing discussion on why Ashley's mother would have allowed her to pierce her tongue and even a partial list of the kinds of infections you could get with a hole in your tongue to spur my mother into a full gallop. Once I got both Marsha and Mom to ponder whether or not Ashley would change the tongue stud to go with her dress, I'd really made Mom's day.

When lunch was over, I told Marsha I'd give Mom a ride home so she could get back to her office. We were on our way out of the strip mall when Mom stopped me.

"Pull the car over, Alissa."

"Why?" There was nothing on the corner. No store. No mailbox. No newspaper kiosk. Just a woman wearing a shapeless plaid shirt over turquoise stretch pants and holding a sign that said she was homeless and needed money. But I am nothing if not obedient these days, so I pulled over.

Mom rolled down the window. "Miss!" she called.

Homeless Woman pointed to her chest with a questioning look at my mother. A car pulled up behind us. It could have gone around me, but no, it just sat there. Some people are complete morons.

Mom beckoned the woman over and thrust the Styrofoam box that held what was left of her lunch out the window. "Here. Take this. It'll just rot in my refrigerator. You look like you could use a meal."

"Thank you," the woman mumbled.

Another car pulled up behind the first one and honked.

"Listen," my mother said. "Don't wait too long to eat this. It was a chicken salad. You leave it until tonight, you're liable to get food poisoning."

And, after making sure that at least one homeless woman in San Jose knew proper storage techniques for chicken salad and at least two other drivers were thoroughly enraged, we drove off.

I dropped my mother at home and went back to the courthouse, where my purse thief was due to be sentenced. (Some people are just guilty, okay? Accept it.) On the way home I stopped at the nursery again and bought some herbs, and at the grocery store where I bought everything I needed to make an omelette for dinner.

I liked what I saw when I dumped it all on the counter in the condo. Snowball apparently did, too, since he jumped up on the counter and started to nibble at the parsley plant. My food. My plants. My fuzzy neutered man. Well, maybe it was time to change that last item.

So I called Kirk.

I remembered the way he looked walking away from me all too well. Plus, I hate to be chicken.

We made a date to see a movie on Thursday.

CHAPTER EIGHT

From *The Angry No More Manual and Workbook*

by Dr. Gail Peterson

WHAT CAN YOU ACCOMPLISH?

You can't always get what you want with anger. Think back to where anger has led you before. Do you have a history of putting your hand through windows and kicking walls? What about slapping family members and punching friends? Have any of these things accomplished anything except landing you in the hospital emergency room, police station, or unemployment line? If you really want to change something, often anger isn't the best approach.

Alissa's Anger Workbook:

Exercise #8

List other ways of expressing your anger that might accomplish something good instead of something negative.

1. Make America's parking lots better places to be.
2. Make best friend stop whining.
3. Make insurance company pay up.
4. Make mother hand over little black book.

shook the newspaper open.

CAPTIVATING CRIME WAVE
by Joel Shapiro

The car of San Jose businessman and resident Jack Hellner was damaged by grocery carts at the Albertson's Grocery on Lawrence Expressway last night at approximately six o'clock.

According to Hellner, approximately eight women wearing French Maid outfits and fuzzy stiletto mules leaped out of a late-model tan Suburban that had been idling nearby, grabbed nearly fifteen shopping carts, and surrounded his Lexus with them after he left a cart in a parking space rather than return it to the Cart Corral several spaces away even though the parking lot was nearly full.

Hellner says the women yelled something regarding "common courtesy," slapped a butterfly decal on his car, shoved the carts toward his Lexus, returned to the Suburban, and then drove away.

Whether this event is related to the two men claiming to be accosted by half-dressed women with butterfly tattoos remains to be seen, according to the San Jose Police Department. According to Detective Emmett Rodriguez, however, "This kind of vigilantism could get out of control. We can't have women in their underwear taking things into their own hands."

Despite police concern, Rodriguez sees no evidence that this is some sort of organized "Butterfly Brigade."

I threw the newspaper across the room. I couldn't believe what I was reading. Had I not told Sheila to cool it? Had she not looked at me with those big blue eyes and nodded her pretty blond head?

I picked up the phone and jabbed the numbers of her cell phone as hard as I could. At least the phone would know how pissed I was.

"Goddammit, Sheila!" I shouted as soon as she answered. "I told you guys to knock it off. Keep this up and I won't be able to keep you out of jail. Trust me, you won't like it there."

"Honest to God, Alissa, I don't know what you're talking about." Sheila's breathy voice had a frantic tinge to it.

"You damn well do. What the hell do you guys think you're doing? Why on earth would you dent some poor schmo's car with grocery carts, and who owns the Suburban?"

"Alissa, we didn't do anything. I don't know anything about a Suburban or about any grocery carts. I don't even know anyone who drives a Suburban. Do you know what kind of gas mileage those things get? Gas is expensive."

"Well, it says here in the *The San Jose Daily News* that eight women in lingerie blocked some guy's car in his space with grocery carts after he left his cart in a parking space at Albertson's at six o'clock yesterday evening."

"I hate people who do that. It's hard enough to get a space at that time of day, without somebody blocking one off with a cart they were too lazy to take back. Then once one person does it, it seems like everybody starts leaving their carts all over the place, and the mess just keeps getting bigger."

"Sheila, that's not the point."

"I don't know, Alissa. Maybe it is, because we didn't do it."

"What about the other women at the club? Could any of them be involved?"

"I can't imagine any of them even grocery shopping, much less caring that much about the carts. I mean, do you have any idea how little we actually eat? I could ask, but I kind of doubt anybody I know was there."

"Then who?"

"I don't know. Ask Helena. Maybe she's got some other friends involved. But I think maybe . . ." Her words trailed off.

"You think maybe what, Sheila?"

"Well, maybe some other people saw those newspaper articles or the TV thing or something, and it gave them an idea."

That worried me. It really did; I believed Sheila, now that I'd calmed down. First of all, the article put the number of women at eight, not three, and the women of the Crescent Moon had bigger fish to fry than grocery-cart etiquette.

"I don't know, Sheila. How likely is it that a group of women would suddenly decide to run around town in their skivvies, punishing people for their misbehavior?"

"Considering what I see every day, the big surprise to me is that it took this long."

I snorted. She had a point.

"Come on, Alissa. You know how it feels. You know how satisfying it is to see someone punished for the things they do wrong. How often do you get to see it?" Sheila asked.

Not often; even working in the judicial system. *Especially* working in the judicial system. "That doesn't mean that it's okay to do property damage to someone's car. You either have to work through the right channels or just let it go."

"Oh, yeah, that reminds me. Could you meet Lily and me down at the hospital? There's something I want to show you."

"I'm really busy today. Can it wait?"

"Not really. It's important, Alissa, or I wouldn't ask."

I sighed and mentally listed what absolutely needed to happen today before I went to my mother's for dinner. "Okay. I'll meet you there at about two. Okay?"

"Thanks, Alissa. It's super-cool of you to do this."

Yeah, yeah, yeah.

The next person I called was Detective Rodriguez. I expected to get his voice mail (cops are *never* at their desks), but got that honey-covered voice pouring over me instead. "A Butterfly Brigade?" I asked. "You realize that's going to stick, don't you?"

He chuckled. "It does have a ring to it, doesn't it?"

"If you like alliteration," I conceded.

"I've been a fan since I was a young boy. I think I only like onomatopoeia better."

I smiled. "Any other parts of speech you're particularly attracted to?"

"Well, the dangling participle always catches my attention."

I was bantering with the police detective trying to put my

client in jail. Kath was right. I did need to get out and get laid. "Seriously, Detective Rodriguez, what is the point of giving an interview like that?"

"The point is that what your client started is getting out of hand."

"You can't possibly think Sheila Montrose had anything to do with the incident at Albertson's."

"I don't." He paused. "That is, I don't think she was there. But I think she and her friends had everything to do with it. They started something. They got away with something, and now everyone else wants to try and get away with it, too."

We said good-bye and hung up. I stared at the phone for a while, worrying about the fact that both Sheila and Rodriguez seemed to be thinking the same thing.

Then I headed out the door for my powerwalking date with Kathleen. I stopped at Peet's and got a large nonfat latte with an extra shot. It's important to hydrate before exercising, after all. Add in all that calcium from the frothy milk, and before you know it, espresso really is a health food.

As the espresso surged through my bloodstream, I whistled along with the *Morning Edition* theme on the radio. Have I mentioned that caffeine is my all-time favorite drug? It's cheap. It's plentiful. It's legal. I love it.

I nearly skipped up to Kath's door, raring to discuss whether to plant lobelia or sweet william on the east wall of my court-yard as I jabbed my thumb in the doorbell and waited an inordinately long time for her to answer.

The door swung open slowly, kind of like when the Scooby-Doo gang has to knock on a door at a creepy mansion. There were no lights on in the house, and Kath must have drawn the curtains. It was dark as a cave.

"You look like shit," I observed.

It's not easy for Kath to look like shit. The worst she usually manages is looking like Callista Flockhart during that super-icky period that made everyone say she was anorexic. Sort of lank-haired and drawn, but not actually like shit. I develop these dark circles under my eyes that make me look like someone's punched me and a puffiness around my lower jaw that makes me look a little like Andre the Giant.

"Thanks. It's great to see you, too." She walked away from the door. I assumed I was supposed to follow. She went directly to the couch in her living room, crawled under the big floral quilt that was knotted up in a nest, and started picking at a tissue she had in her hand.

"Kath, what's wrong?"

She waved her hand as if to brush my question off and emitted a little strangled sob.

"Kath, what is it? Are you sick? Is it Rob? The kids? What's going on?" I was scared. I had never seen her quite like this. Sure, she'd had down and desperate moments, but not like this.

"It's stupid. I know I'm overreacting. I can't help it, though." She sniffled.

"So no one's dying? No one has a terminal illness or some kind of horrible chronic anything?" Okay. I know I'm morbid, but those are the first places my mind goes when I find a friend sobbing helplessly into damp Kleenex at ten o'clock on a Tuesday morning. You can't grow up with a mother like mine and not have that be the way you think.

"Not unless you count being a chronic loser." She blew her nose.

"You're not a chronic loser, Kath. Trust me, I know a lot of chronic losers. Most of my clients are chronic losers. You're just having a rough patch."

She sat up fast. "Then how come you knew I was talking about me? Huh? I didn't say who was a chronic loser. You just assumed I was the loser in question. Why'd you do that, Little Miss Lawyer?"

"Because you're the one curled up under a quilt on the couch in a dark room when it's seventy degrees and sunny outside. Come on. Put on your walking shoes and we'll get some exercise. It's cheaper than Prozac and you don't need a prescription."

I dragged her out with promises of postwalk muffins. I also had to drag the cause of this morning's misery-fest out of her. Apparently, the night before, Kath and Rob and the kids had watched the movie *Mystery Men*. That's the movie about the wannabe super-heroes. If you haven't seen it, it's worth it just to see Janeane Garafalo as the Bowler.

Anyway, as the movie rewound everybody started talking about what their superpower would be if they were super-heroes. Hayley would be Animal Girl, able to swim like a fish and climb like a cat. Jason would be able to shoot lightning bolts from his fingertips and run really really really fast. Rob wanted to be more like Batman and have really cool gadgets (he is such a geek). Then Kathleen asked what they thought her superpower should be.

"They all just sat there and stared at me like it hadn't even occurred to them that I could be a superhero, too!" She was doing that power-walking thing again with her elbows. Fuel that girl with a little rage and the promise of baked goods, and she could be on an Olympic team. "And then . . . then . . . Jason suggested dishes!"

"Dishes?"

"That's right. That is what my family thinks my superpower should be. Doing the dishes is all I'm good for. That is how my kids see me."

"Kath, he's just a little boy. He doesn't know everything else you do and everything else you are."

"Tell me this, Alissa. What else *am* I these days? A good laundress? I don't even do that very well; I almost never pretreat. And forget about vacuuming—I don't even know where that edge-tool attachment is anymore."

Maybe Kathleen could be the Whiner: she could let out high-pitched whines that burst the eardrums of the bad guys.

"Forget it," she said. "It's my own fault. I made the choices that put me here, after all."

"Do you really think they were such bad choices, Kathleen?"

"Not if you want your cape to have a big *L* on the back for *Loser*."

"I thought it would have a *D* for Dishwasher."

I was rewarded with a glare. "It's just . . . " she said, arms pumping harder and harder. "I look in the mirror sometimes and I don't recognize the person I see there."

We marched along in silence for a moment. Then she said, "When did I turn beige, Alissa? When did I become this person who looks askance at the woman down the street who doesn't keep her hedges trimmed? Or judges somebody for forgetting when it's their turn to bring snacks for the soccer team? When did I become the kind of person who yells at her kids for not using their napkins? I mean, what have I really dedicated my life to at this point *besides* dishes?"

"You've dedicated it to your kids, Kathleen. Your happy, healthy, well-adjusted kids. Surely that counts for something."

"And I love them. You know I do. Nobody wanted kids more than me, but for Christ's sake, why do they have to be such pains in the ass sometimes? Do you know that Hayley insisted on wearing shoes from two different pairs this morning? And I actually have to sniff Jason's mouth before we leave for school to make sure he's brushed his teeth. It's not like they come with instruction manuals. How am I supposed to know if I'm doing this right?"

"They're just kids, Kath. They're going to do stuff like that. We did, too."

"Yeah, well, I thought I did stuff like that because my mother was such a lousy parent."

This was not entirely fair. Kathleen's mother was distant, unavailable, and a little chilly, but there were no wire-hanger scenes in Kathleen's childhood. Mine, either.

"You're not a lousy parent, Kathleen. You're a terrific mom."

"How can you be so sure?"

"Because I know," I said firmly.

"Thank you," she sniffed. We walked the rest of the lap with my arm around her shoulder.

*   *   *

I went home and got to work. After all, there were no automatic paychecks for me anymore. Also no one to answer the phone, do the accounting, and make sense of the piles of notes I left for myself which had begun to pile up everywhere and on everything. I kept thinking that at some point the accounting elves would come and sort things out while I slept. Maybe Snowball was scaring them away.

My newest client was an enterprising young man who'd broken into a RadioShack, stolen a buttload of batteries, and then set up a stand near the train station, selling cheap batteries to commuters who needed them for CD players and Game Boys.

The State of California unfortunately frowned upon my client's entrepreneurial spirit, but he was (gasp!) neither a repeat offender nor a drug addict so I thought I could get probation for him. That is, I thought I could if I could just get Lisa Ferguson on the phone. Lisa had turned out to be a very reasonable woman, easy to work with and a complete pleasure to be around.

I left her a voice mail and put Battery Boy's file in the pile by my feet that I'd reserved for active cases. After five minutes or so of panicked searching, I found Mr. Chardlin's file and worked on his case until it was time to meet Sheila and Lily at the hospital.

I met Sheila and Lily at the front doors of the San Jose Community Hospital. I almost didn't recognize Lily with her hair pulled back in a ponytail, no makeup, and wearing scrubs. The top was covered with a design of interlocking tropical fish. Even Sheila didn't look like her usual self. She had on black pants that came up almost to her belly button and a peasant blouse that came down to her hips. She even had a camisole on under the blouse so you couldn't see right through it.

"Come on, there's someone I want you to meet," Lily said. "This is my day job," she explained as we walked through the hospital corridors. "I'm a phlebotomist."

"That means she draws people's blood," Sheila explained.

I nodded.

"She's really really good at it, too," Sheila went on.

Lily waved the compliment away and blushed.

"No, really. Lily's the one they call when nobody else can draw a patient's blood or start an IV. She has a special touch. Everybody here says so."

We got in an elevator. Lily punched the button for the fourth floor.

"She's especially good with kids."

I wasn't sure if the little person in the room we walked into could really be referred to as a kid. She was tiny, especially her arm and legs, which looked like toothpicks. But the rest of her looked so old. Maybe it was the bald head, but I really think it was her eyes. They were huge in her swollen, moonlike face. She winced a little when she saw Lily.

"Is it time again, Lily?" she asked in a small voice.

Lily nodded, her face serious and calm.

"Okay. Which arm do you want to try?" the little girl said. Her voice shook a little bit.

"I think we did the left yesterday. Let's look at the right,"

Lily said. She began tapping on the girl's inner elbow. She shook her head and started examining her hand. "By the way, Stephanie, these are my friends, Alissa and Sheila. I hope it's okay with you that they're here."

Stephanie nodded. Her left hand convulsively grabbed and released the bedcovers.

Lily straightened up. "I think this one will work."

Stephanie gulped.

We watched as Lily swabbed an area on the side of Stephanie's hand and readied a syringe. Stephanie's left hand grabbed and released faster and faster at the threadbare blanket that covered her. Her breath came faster and faster. Lily bit her lip as she worked the syringe into Stephanie's hand. Stephanie twisted and let out a strangled little cry.

All the air left the room. I couldn't get a breath into my lungs. My knees wobbled. I grabbed hold of the wall and inched my way out of the room.

I listened to Lily and Sheila make soothing noises to the hurt, frightened child while I waited for them in the corridor outside. "How often do you have to do that?" I asked as Lily came out. She seemed calm. Sheila's face had no color left in it; I imagined mine didn't look much better. To her credit, Sheila could still stand up without holding on to the wall.

"At least once a day. Sometimes more often," Lily said. "It depends."

"Isn't there another way? Some way that doesn't torture that child?" We can put a man on the moon, make low-fat reasonable-tasting microwave popcorn, and even my mother can program a VCR. Surely, someone must have worked out a way to draw blood from sick little girls without causing them excruciating pain.

Lily nodded. "Yep. Several."

I shut my eyes, but the vision of Stephanie twisting away from the needle sprang up. I opened my eyes again, fast. I never wanted to see anything like that again. "Then why aren't you using any of them?"

Sheila started examining her split ends. "Her insurance won't pay."

I was shocked. Beyond shocked, I was incensed. "Her insurance company turned her down? I can appeal the decision." I'd gotten damn good at dealing with insurance companies when my dad was sick. How could they ignore a child's suffering like that? I was glad there was something I could do. I hate feeling helpless. I hate it when it feels like the walls are crashing in around you and there's nothing you can do to stop it.

"They didn't exactly turn her down," Lily explained. "Her claim is pending. That means they haven't said yes and they haven't said no. You can't appeal a decision that hasn't been made."

I chewed my lip. "How long until they make a decision?"

"Lily thinks they're waiting her out," Sheila broke in.

"What do you mean?"

Lily shrugged. "I think they're waiting until it's kind of a moot point."

I stared at her. I didn't want to understand what she was saying, but I was afraid I did. "They're waiting for that little girl to die? Is that what you're telling me?"

Lily focused those beautiful almond eyes on me. "I have no

proof of that; it's just a feeling I have. Stephanie doesn't have much longer. Everything we're doing for her is just palliative care. If the insurance company waits a little while longer to put a port in for Stephanie, well, she probably won't be around to need it. Or she'll be on a steady morphine drip and be so snowed under that she won't care. They don't have to feel guilty for denying her claim, but they don't have to pay for it, either."

I could hear the breath begin to whistle in and out of my nose as my breathing quickened. My jaw clenched. I swallowed hard. I felt a cold block of ice form in the pit of my stomach. I was angry. Really angry. Fax-machine-stompin' plastic-chair-throwin' angry.

Wait. Time out. Step back and assess.

A big red stop sign flashed in my head. It didn't work. I switched to an image of a police officer blowing a whistle. His face changed to Rodriguez's. No good; now I was angry *and* horny. Try again.

I asked myself the Anger Management Four Questions.

Question One: Is this truly important to me?

I thought of Stephanie's hands spastically working the bedsheet. The real question was what kind of monster would I have to be, for this not to matter?

Question Two: Is my anger appropriate?

Let's see. Small children in pain so an insurance company can save money. Yep. Sounds like appropriate anger to me.

Question Three: Can I change the situation?

I was pretty sure that a way to change the situation was precisely what Lily and Sheila had in mind.

Question Four: Is it worth it to take action?

See answers to Anger Management Questions One and Two.

"You said our way isn't the right way. We thought we'd give you a chance to prove it." Lily's gaze stayed on my face.

"I'm on it," I said. "I need some information from you, and I'll start on it right now."

I faxed my first letter to Stephanie's insurance company before I left for my mother's that evening. I felt good about that. Another smart step in the right direction.

Then, in the car on the way over, the radio announcer chimed in with "Reports of Butterfly Brigade attacks are popping up all over the Valley. According to Detective Emmett Rodriguez of the San Jose Police Department, we have a case of copycat butterflies."

Emmett's voice flooded into my car, and I thought I might stop breathing. "There is no way that these actions are being committed by the same group of people. Descriptions vary too widely, even given the vagaries of all eye-witness accounts, to ascribe responsibility to one set of perpetrators."

The radio announcer came back. "So what do we have here, people? Is it a trend? A movement? A bunch of pissed-off chicks with too much access to Victoria's Secret? Let's hear what you think."

I snapped the radio off and drove the rest of the way in silence.

I thought I was prepared this time when I rang my mother's doorbell. She'd said there was someone she wanted me to meet.

She also said to bring dessert, so I was prepared with a half gallon of chocolate chip cookie dough ice cream and the best brownies Betty Crocker can make.

I was not ready for the small gnome in mauve Sansabelt pants and a light blue polo shirt that answered my mother's door. It stuck its hand out and said, "Hi. I'm Mort. Who are you?"

I shook the offered hand with some trepidation. "Hi, Mort. I'm Alissa. Who are you?" I asked.

"Ha! Ha! Ha!" the gnome barked. Okay, I don't know if gnomes bark or cackle or honk, but it sounded like a bark. "Your mother told me you were a card."

What was *that* supposed to mean? And when had my mother told him that? Where was she, anyway? And who the hell *was* this guy?

"Come in. Come in." Mort beckoned me down the hall. I kept expecting him to do the Marty Feldman "walk this way" bit from *Young Frankenstein*. In fact, he looked a little like Marty Feldman. An old Marty Feldman in Sansabelt pants. He grabbed the brownies and ice cream from me. "Let me take those."

I followed him to the dining room. Marsha, Terry, Andrew, and David were all ranged around the table with shell-shocked looks on their faces.

"Who's Mort?" I whispered to Marsha after I kissed my nephews.

"I think he's our new daddy," she whispered back.

"But I don't want a new daddy," I whispered in alarm. "I especially don't want Mort to be my daddy."

"I don't think we get to choose."

"Fine, but he's not taking me to the father-daughter dance." I thought for a second. "Do you think we should buy her some condoms?"

David snorted. Terry started to laugh, and Marsha kicked him.

"Mom! That hurt!"

"How's Smashley?" I whispered to him.

He grimaced and rubbed his shin where his mother had kicked him. "Her tongue got infected when she had to pull the stud to play water polo, and she might not be able to go to the prom," he whispered back.

"Rachel!" Mort bellowed in the kitchen. "How the hell am I supposed to get this damned ice cream in the freezer? Damned thing's stuffed tighter'n a Mexican virgin."

Marsha and I looked at each other wide-eyed. David laughed and Marsha kicked him, too. It would be a miracle if any of us were walking by the end of the evening. I poured a glass of iced tea from the pitcher on the table and added a packet of Equal from the stash that my mother keeps full by stealing packets from restaurants who are foolish enough to allow her uncontrolled access to their sugar-free sweeteners. Individually wrapped butter pats are not safe around her, either.

Mort was right about the freezer, though. Mom occasionally still shops like she's feeding a family of four and all four of them are sumo wrestlers. This happens mainly when things are on sale. It happens particularly often when turkeys are on sale.

When Marsha moved my mother out of the ranch-style

house we'd lived in since I was seven, she'd called me to report that Mom had four turkeys stashed in her freezer.

"Why?" I'd asked. I hadn't really cared at the time, being caught up in my own personal drama, but I'd felt guilty about Marsha shouldering the whole burden of moving my mother, so I thought I should at least act interested.

"Who knows? Maybe it's a security thing. That's why people hoard, isn't it?"

"You tell me, you're the psychologist," I'd said.

Marsha had started to cry. "That's so sad. She misses Daddy so much, she's hoarding food to bridge the gap."

Security poultry? That wasn't sad; that was an invitation to food poisoning. "Are you sure she bought them recently? Since Daddy died?"

Marsha had thought for a moment. "Well, no, I guess I'm not sure. Come to think of it, one of them was under a packet marked 'Enchiladas 1977.'"

Freezer overcrowding is not a new story for my mother.

"Take the ice cream to the freezer in my bedroom, Mort. There's space in there."

Yes, my mother has a chest freezer in her bedroom. The noise would have driven me nuts at night. Cycling on. Cycling off. Cycling on again. Mom says she doesn't notice it. I guess there are some advantages to losing your hearing.

After the anti-Latino Mexican Virgin remark, Mort went on, over a nice piece of fish, to make disparaging remarks about African-Americans, Asians, welfare recipients, and federal government employees. Either he ran out of time to insult Native Americans or he just hadn't encountered any he'd noticed enough to piss him off. He then actually swatted my mother on the ass as she lurched past him with her walker, belched, and said, "Good dinner, Rache."

Marsha alternated between trying to change the topic from whatever ethnic group Mort was insulting and looking so dumbfounded that deer in headlights had smaller eyes.

While Mort was off seeing a man about a horse (his words, not mine) and the boys and David had gone to the second bedroom to check baseball scores on the TV in there, I seized the moment to ask my mom about Mort. "Who the hell is he?" I asked.

My mother pursed her lips together in a little line. "He's my boyfriend."

I couldn't decide whether I was more upset by the fact that my mother had a boyfriend and I didn't, or the fact that she had such crappy taste in men. Apparently the look on my face told her precisely what I thought of him.

"What! You think you girls are the only ones with needs and urges? That just because I'm an old lady, I don't need love in my life anymore? Is that what you think?"

Eewwww! I didn't want to know about my mother's needs and urges. I wanted to run to the other room and watch baseball with the boys.

"Mom," Marsha said, sounding way more reasonable than seemed reasonable to me. "No one is denying your sexuality."

I thought about sticking my fingers in my ears and chanting "I can't hear you" over and over again. "Yeah, Mom," I chimed in. "It's not that we don't think that love should be part of your life. It's more that Mort is kind of a grumpy little gnome."

"And what do you think I am?" she asked. "Miss America?"

"Compared to Mort? Absolutely," I said.

"Take a harder look, Alissa. My hair is gray. I'm fifteen pounds over what even the doctor thinks is acceptable for me, and everything sags and droops. Some days I can barely find my eyes in all the wrinkles. I'm no bargain, either." She started to cry.

I mean really cry. Not a we-just-watched-a-sad-movie cry. Not a your-grandfather-died cry. Not even the shocked and shocking your-father-is-gone cry. A sorrowful cry. A heartbroken, soul-smashed cry. A cry that had been a long time coming and might not end anytime soon. My heart twisted and ripped just watching her.

"I'm so lonely," she sobbed. "Some nights I just can't stand it. The quiet of it. And the days are even worse."

It's surprising how much noise even a quiet person makes. Coughs, rustling papers, footsteps, and water running. It's all part of the background noise when you live with someone else. It's amazing how silent a house can be without another person there. The silence in my house after Thomas and I split was startling, and I'd only lived with him for five years. My mother had had forty to get accustomed to my father's noises.

"You know, every Sunday morning I'd sit in the kitchen and dole out those little pills. The pink ones, the brown ones, the big blue ones, and the little blue ones, all in their right spots in that pill organizer so he wouldn't forget. Though half the time he'd forget them anyway, if I didn't remind him."

"He hated all those pills," Marsha said. "I think he felt like needing them was a symbol of weakness." Sometimes she says stuff like that, and I just want to smack her. Unfortunately, she also makes sense. It doesn't make me want to smack her any less, though.

"Well, I suspected that he was forgetting about them on purpose. You know, just to spite me." Mom's shoulders began to shake. "I'd get so mad at him. Here I'd spent all this time, reading all those instructions and putting all those little pills in all the right places, and he'd just go and forget to take them. How could he forget? They were right here on the kitchen counter, for God's sake." Her shoulders started to heave.

Marsha left the table and went and put her arms around Mom. "It's all right, Mom," she said softly.

Mom shook her head violently. "No, no, it's not. I'd be so angry and it was such a stupid little thing. It's just that I hated putting those pills out so much. All that little print. All those little notes about what to take when and what not to take when and then he'd go and just leave them anyway. It made me so mad. And now . . . now . . . " Mom took a tissue out of her sleeve and blew her nose with a honk. "Now I miss him so damn much that I'd give anything to still be putting those pills out for him."

Marsha touched Mom's face. "I think he probably knows that."

Mom shoved the tissue back up her sleeve. Never, ever take a tissue from my mother unless you see it come from the box with your own eyes.

"Do you think so?" Mom looked at her through tear-filled eyes. "It's kind of comforting to think so, but I'm not so sure I can believe it. Do you think he knows that I miss him so much that I even miss doing that for him?"

My heart twisted harder.

On the bright side, when Mort finally came out of the

bathroom, we were able to hustle him out the door without having to share our ice cream and brownies with him.

Terry and Andrew came out of the second bedroom long enough to inhale the half gallon of ice cream and most of the brownies. No wonder Marsha is so thin. As they galloped back away to check the score, Marsha watched them go with a thoughtful eye.

"I caught Terry with Ashley," she said.

"What do you mean by 'caught'"?" I asked.

"You know, caught. Together. Without all their clothes on."

I gasped and my eyes just about popped out of my head. Mom sat up a little straighter. "I hadn't thought of that."

"Well, start thinking. They're clearly thinking a lot about it. In fact, based on the amount of time Terry spends in the shower, I think it might be all he thinks about."

Eewww. "Were they, you know, actually, well . . . you know . . . ?"

Marsha rolled her eyes. "Are you trying to ask if they were actually having sex?"

I nodded.

"No. I think I got home with the groceries before actual penetration was achieved."

"What are you going to do?"

Marsha put her head in her hands. "I'm not sure."

"Buy a lot of condoms and leave them in conspicuous places," Mom said.

Marsha and I whipped our heads around. "What?"

"Rubbers," Mom said, cutting another brownie for herself. "You know."

Yes, we knew. But we didn't know that she knew. Nor did we want to know that she knew. "You want Marsha to buy them condoms?" I asked, feeling my eyebrows creep up to my hairline.

Mom stacked up the dessert plates and headed toward the kitchen with them. "There's so much to worry about. Disease. Death. Pregnancy."

All in all, a pretty comprehensive list of worries. We watched her go. "Mom never bought us condoms. She just lectured us on how boys only really liked the good girls," I said under my breath.

Marsha snorted. "Mom didn't have boys. Speaking of Mom, we need to get her out more. She needs to get involved in something, get interested in something."

I wasn't used to talking about Mom as if she was some kind of project. She was just Mom. One of those immutable, inarguable constants, like gravity. Or the way thigh-highs never really stay up satisfactorily without being tight enough to make unattractive flesh bulges above and below their elastic and leaving giant red marks on your legs.

"Why? Isn't she pretty capable of doing that herself?"

"Let me put it to you this way: How many more Morts do you want to meet?"

Now *there* was a question I knew the answer to.

CHAPTER NINE

From *The Angry No More Manual and Workbook*
by Dr. Gail Peterson

NOT ALL ANGERS ARE CREATED EQUAL

Anger isn't necessarily a bad emotion. Anger can stir us to right wrongs, to protect ourselves and our loved ones, and to react appropriately in threatening situations. What you must decide is when is your anger good and when is it poisonous to you?

Alissa's Anger Workbook:

Exercise #9

Name three times anger is the right emotion.

1. When clerks at shoe stores are stupid.
2. When someone makes fun of your desk.
3. When you've been shushed in a movie.

My sneakers had started wearing blisters on my heels. Kathleen had looked at them, asked when I'd gotten them and if they were made for walking. Then she wanted to know if they were for walking on a track, for walking on a dirt track, and what kind of pronation I had, and so many other questions that I realized, finally, that I needed new shoes. Mine were clearly hopelessly low-tech. After my shower I pulled on a pair of jeans, a stretchy blue shirt, a hoodie, and my beloved

Urban Angel Fluevogs and headed off to Valley Fair Mall. I thought about calling my mom and asking her if she wanted to come with me, but I didn't have the time for that today. I needed to get in, get my shoes, get out—shop like a man, not like a sixty-seven-year-old retired woman with a walker.

I walked in through Macy's and willed myself not to even notice the clearance racks. I had two closets full of clothes, and my credit cards were starting to squeak a little. I needed to stick to the stuff that I actually needed. I hit the mall proper and steered myself away from Cinnabon (do they pipe that scent in through the ventilation system or something?) and didn't even glance at Victoria's Secret. I mean, really, why bother? It was then that I noticed a familiar-looking redhead coming toward me.

"Helena!" It was a shock to see her in a mall. Dressed in jeans with her hair pulled back in a ponytail, she looked like nearly every other pretty young woman walking by stores at Valley Fair Mall. You wouldn't have taken her for the leader of a movement that she'd become. "What are you doing here?"

A shrug. "Sometimes a girl's gotta shop."

She changed direction to walk with me. "Looking for something in particular?"

"Shoes," I said.

"Dress?"

"Walking."

She nodded and followed me into Lady Foot Locker. I picked up the new Nike Women's Air Swoops. Very exciting. Very red. Very on sale. Like half off, which still meant they cost about sixty bucks. I put them back on the shelf since I don't play basketball. White men can't jump; white women jump even less. Jewish white women don't even hop.

"How's the Stephanie Kendall thing going?" she asked.

I didn't like Helena's smile. It was too cat with a canary-ish for my taste.

"It's going." I checked out the Nike Women's Shox Walx shoes. I loved the springs under the heel but I didn't love them enough to shell out close to a hundred bucks for them.

Helena picked up a pair of Puma Women's California Walking Shoes. They were pink. Maybe she was thinking about some kind of stripper cheerleader outfit; I really can't think of another reason to buy those. "Got it all resolved, do you?"

"Not yet, but we're making progress." I grabbed something called Pure Simplicity (I'm a sucker for a good product name) and a pair of Reeboks. I gestured to the ponytailed, referee-shirted salesgirl who had been watching us with no interest whatsoever from behind the cash register even though we were the only customers in the store. "I'd like to try these both on in a size six."

Helena and I sat down. "And nothing I've done could land me in jail," I continued.

"They'd have to make something stick against us. Have you been watching the news, Alissa? More and more women are taking the plunge with us and the water out there is getting very muddy." She turned the Pure Simplicity around in her hands a few times. "A butterfly tattoo isn't much to go on especially if more and more people have them."

I sighed. "Look, the 'I am Spartacus' routine is cute, but

when push comes to shove, I don't think it'll keep any of you out of jail." Ponytail came back and handed me two boxes, one of which had some writing scrawled across the top. I tried on the Pure Simplicity first and nixed it immediately. Too flimsy.

"But you could make a lot more progress and do it a lot faster," Helena pushed.

"Yes, so it would be faster. That's not the point." The Reeboks fit the bill, so I handed them to the salesgirl. "I'll take these."

She bent to put them back in the box. "Oh, man. I can't sell you these." She seemed honestly distressed.

"Why?"

"They're f.d." Ponytail said, pointing at the scribble.

"And that means . . . ?"

"That I can't sell them." Ponytail had big liquid brown eyes that looked like they might just pool over with tears.

I searched for a way to get the information I needed. "Can you not sell this type of shoe at all? Or can you not sell this particular pair? Or can you just not sell them to me?"

"Just this particular pair. They're f.d."

"Do you have another pair of these in this size?" I decided that the exact meaning of "f.d." really didn't matter, knowing the definition probably wouldn't change the situation at all. I have some very pragmatic moments.

Ponytail brightened. "I might." Then she just sat there.

We stared at each other for a moment or two. Finally I said, "Could you check?"

"Sure." She leaped up as if I had released a spring.

I looked at Helena and arched my brow in my very best Leonard Nimoy.

Helena shook her head. "We can't punish someone just for being stupid, Alissa. There has to be deliberate malice there."

Ponytail did have a pair that were not f.d. I bought them. "So there are some rules after all," I said to Helena as we left the store.

"Of course there are. I thought you knew that."

"It just seems like you're breaking a lot more than you're keeping."

Helena smiled that cat-with-a-canary smile again. "I keep the ones I think are important."

When I got home, there were still no calls from Stephanie's insurance company. I had made it very clear in my letter that it was a matter of great urgency. Apparently I needed to follow that up with a phone call to make my point. Regardless of what I'd told Helena about making progress, all I could think was that every day that passed was another day that Stephanie would have to writhe as someone drew her blood.

I put my feet up on a little patch of desk that I'd cleared and dialed.

Forty-five minutes later I was still in the same position. I also was still on hold. Finally I got a human being who regretfully informed me that I'd called the wrong 800 number. They were the 800 number for medical professionals; I had to call a different one to make inquiries about claims. Before I could dial again, my phone rang.

"Alissa, it's Kathleen. I need a favor." She sounded terrible. The child wailing in the background sounded worse.

"Sure. What is it?"

"Can you pick Hayley up at preschool by one o'clock?"

"Of course. What's going on?"

"Jason stuck an eraser up his nose."

I could have sworn she'd said that Jason had stuck an eraser up his nose; her cell phone connection must be terrible. "What did you say? Jason stuck what up where?"

"An eraser. Up his nose." She enunciated each syllable so there could be no misunderstanding. "So far up his nose, in fact, that he can't get it out. Neither could his teacher. Neither could I. Not even with a tweezer. I just couldn't get a grip on the damn thing. I think the snot made it more slippery or something."

Eewww. "Enough detail."

"Sorry. Anyway, I'm on the way to the pediatrician's office to see if she can get it out. If she can't, I'll have to take him to the emergency room."

She sounded like she was about to cry. In the background, Jason's wails sounded like an air raid siren.

I bit my lip to keep from laughing. "Why on earth did he shove an eraser up his nose?"

"Apparently Kevin Xu put his eraser up his nose first. Then Ben Cohen said he could get a bigger eraser farther up his nose than Kevin had gotten his. So of course Jason said he could shove an even bigger eraser even farther up his nose than Ben had. He's so damn competitive."

"And he did it?" Jason had one of those little round noses

covered with freckles and ridiculously full and pouty lips. Remember Mikey from the Life cereal ads?

"We're going to the pediatrician's office, aren't we? Ben Cohen's mother is blissfully ignorant still and so is Kevin Xu's, although apparently they'll both be receiving notes from the teacher this afternoon about wasting valuable resources. Can you believe she lectured me about squandering school supplies while my child has an eraser so far up his nose it might damage his brain?"

I hoped that was a rhetorical question, because I simply did not have an answer. "Tell me what to do."

"Go to Li'l Dudes 'n Dudettes at about twelve forty-five and then take Hayley to your house."

"Li'l Dudes 'n Dudettes? You're kidding." I couldn't believe my ears. Wasn't that where Sheila worked when she wasn't bumping and grinding?

"I know. The name is idiotic, but it's the best preschool I could find nearby. It's private so it's a little expensive, but there's no church affiliation or anything like that. And why do you keep thinking I'm kidding? What in my voice right now would make you think I was kidding?"

Well, nothing. Her voice made me think she was wound so tight we could shove coal up her ass and get diamonds out in return.

Like any good friend, Kathleen accepted my apology, gave me directions, and told me not to forget my driver's license because they'd ask to see it before they released Hayley to me.

I closed my Stephanie file, checked my wallet to make sure I had my ID, and headed off to Li'l Dudes 'n Dudettes, hoping it was Sheila's day off.

I spotted her Tracker the second I pulled into the driveway.

A nice lady at the front desk checked my driver's license and then pointed me toward the four-year-olds.

Sheila spotted me from across the room before Hayley did. "Alissa, what are you doing here? Is something wrong?"

"No. I mean, yes. But not with you."

The other teacher, a round-faced young woman with curly hair, came over to the door. "Can we help you?" she asked with a faint Irish lilt.

"I'm here to pick up Hayley McAllister," I answered.

"Hayley?" Sheila gave me a funny look. "You know Hayley?"

"Since she was born," I said.

Hayley turned away from the picture she was coloring and dropped everything. "Auntie Lissa!" she squealed as she streaked across the room.

"Hi, sweetie." I picked her up in my arms. She smelled of grape Kool-Aid, watermelon shampoo, and little girl. The perfume nearly made me swoon.

"What are you doing here? Where's Mommy?" she demanded.

I decided to go with the truth. "Your brother has stuck an eraser so far up his nose that a doctor is going to have to remove it. Your mommy asked me to come pick you up while she took him to the doctor's office."

Hayley regarded me gravely. "Why would he do that?"

"Apparently he did it to prove that he could jam a bigger eraser farther up his nose than any other boy in his class. He was quite successful."

Hayley thought about that for a second. "Auntie Lissa, boys are weird."

"Yes, they are, dear. It's probably best that you learn that early."

Hayley and I had a lovely trip to Baskin-Robbins before heading home. Strawberry ice cream with strawberry syrup and whipped cream for her. She said it was a Princess Sundae. Daiquiri ice on a sugar cone for me. I had read the posted nutritional information and calculated how many laps around the track it would take to burn off a Princess Sundae, and decided that being able to button my jeans and still breathe was better than whipped cream. It was close to four o'clock by the time Kathleen arrived at my house with a teary-eyed but eraser-free Jason. Hayley's sugar buzz had worn off and she was crashed on the living-room floor in a heap of pillows watching *Hello, Kitty*. How a cat with no mouth could achieve such stardom is a question I will ponder for the rest of my days. Jason was so entirely demoralized by his eraser experience that he cuddled into the couch and didn't even argue with Hayley to change the channel.

Kathleen looked at the stack of unhung prints against the wall. "Are you ever going to hang those up?"

"They do that now in all the magazine ads. It's trendy to leave them against the wall," I said, heading toward the kitchen.

"It's trendy when it's a design choice. It's pathetic when you're just lazy." She followed me into the kitchen, went immediately to the refrigerator, pulled out an open bottle of white wine, and removed the cork with her teeth.

I grabbed two glasses from the cupboard. "I'm not pathetic. I just have other priorities."

"This place is a mess," she said, looking at my desk.

"I wasn't expecting company," I said stiffly, although it was hard to argue with that one. My office area looked like one of those scenes you see on the news when people's homes have been hit by tornadoes. I'd never quite finished unpacking all the boxes, and now I'd begun to use them as places to keep the stacks and stacks of paper I generated. I suspected that the papers were mating and reproducing while I slept, because every morning there seemed to be more of them. All I needed was some standing water and I could probably be declared a national emergency site, or at least be interviewed on TV with curlers in my hair. Maybe if they looked under my sink, I could be a Superfund site. On the other hand, if the papers were reproducing, it meant that at least something in the house was having sex. It sure wasn't me.

I looked around, and taking in the overwhelming chaos left me thunderstruck. "I know. I can't seem to get it organized."

"Have you heard of filing?" Kathleen moved the stack of files on the bar stool to the floor.

"Of course I have." It was just that during most of my professional life, there were secretaries, assistants, and clerks to take care of that. Unfortunately, at the Law Offices of Alissa Lindley, I was the clerk, secretary, and assistant. I was also the billing office, accounts payable, and a few other people.

"I just haven't been able to get to it." I picked up the stack she'd moved and tried to figure out why I'd made that particular pile. Ah, yes, a burglary case I'd been assigned to yesterday.

I looked around for a place to set it down, but there were no clear spots on my desk.

Kathleen began making stacks of the sliding mounds of papers.

"Don't touch those!" I squealed, nearly knocking over my wine as I tried to grab them from her.

"These?" She pointed to a bunch of scraps of envelopes, torn-off sheets of legal pads, and stickie notes. "Or those?" She pointed to some manila folders and books.

"Either. Both. I don't know." I sank back in my chair and covered my face with my hands.

"What are they?" Kathleen asked.

"The papers are billing information. You know, who and how much and when. The folders and books are research stuff."

"Alissa, have you billed those people yet?" She kept her voice low and gentle, like you would with a frightened child.

I shook my head, feeling a little like a spooked horse. You know, the ones who have to have their heads covered to be led out of the burning barn because if they saw the fire, they'd be too scared to save themselves. If I saw the pile of things that needed to be filed, I'd be too frightened to ever leave my chair and would end up drowning in a sea of paper.

"Have you billed anybody?"

I shook my head again. Maybe they could make special hoods for solo practice lawyers to wear in their offices, so their unfinished paperwork wouldn't scare them.

"There are more papers in my purse and my briefcase, and I think there are some in my coat pocket, too."

"Alissa, what are you living on?"

"I'm not sure. Money from the house in L.A.? None of the envelopes from the bank look like they have anything pink inside them, so I think I'm still okay." My father would have been horrified. His bank account always balanced to the penny.

Kathleen put her head down on the desk. "I'll come tomorrow. We'll start sorting through all this. Tonight you're coming home with me and I'll make you dinner."

I wanted to protest that a trip to the Organized Living store would fix this all up. Instead, I put my head on her shoulder and said, "Thanks. I think I might be in over my head. But I can't come to dinner; I have a date."

She nearly pierced my eardrum with her squeal. She is *such* a screamer. "With who?"

"With Kirk."

"He asked you for a Thursday night date and you said yes?" She stared at me, aghast.

"You're the one who said I should be going out more. You're the one who fixed me up with him."

"Yeah, but not on a Thursday. Thursday is not Date Night."

"Kathleen, we're thirty years old. There is no Date Night anymore."

"Not if you say yes when they ask you out for Thursday."

"Mooooommm," Hayley wailed from the living room. Jason had recovered enough to wrest control of the remote from Hayley and had changed the channel.

"So what are you wearing?" Kath asked over her shoulder as she headed into the other room to referee.

After Kathleen had negotiated a truce between Hayley and Jason, we chose the black cross-over shirt and the beige palazzo pants. We decided that the shirt was neither too low-cut nor not-low-cut enough and that the pants with the wide, swishy legs did not make my ass look like the size of Montana, because the fact that they've become a little loose is tremendously slimming. I felt very Katherine Hepburn in my outfit—or at least as Katherine Hepburn-ish as I *could* feel, considering that she never had a short, semitic phase.

The credits rolled for *In the Bedroom*. Tom Wilkinson lay on his side in his bed as the sun rose and stared with no expression as Sissy Spacek made coffee downstairs.

"What do you think that means?" I whispered. "Do you think that means he's going to be tormented forever, now that he's a murderer, too?"

Kirk gave me a weird look. At least he'd stopped shushing me. Apparently Kirk hates people who talk in movies almost as much as I hate being shushed. He hates people who talk in movies even if that person is whispering pithy remarks in the quietest voice imaginable. I hate being shushed even if it's just a look and not an actual shush.

By the end of the movie I was making remarks just to bait him. Probably a sign that the date wasn't going well. I should have known it wouldn't since it wasn't even Date Night.

Kirk whispered his answer back to me. "No. I think it means he's tired after spending the entire night out dragging bodies through the woods."

He had a point, just not a very satisfying one. "It was only one body, and if he was tired, why wouldn't he just go to sleep?"

"I don't know. Maybe he drank too much coffee."

"It didn't show him drinking coffee." Coffee? Had there been coffee? I remembered a diner scene, but surely that had been earlier in the movie. I wanted to talk about Wilkenson's motivations for killing his son's murderer. Had he done it for himself? Had he been quietly praying for a way to avenge his son? Or had he done it to shut Sissy Spacek up and get away from her nasty judgmental ways?

"Why should it show him drinking coffee?" Kirk yawned.

"Because if they want us to think that he's staying awake like that because of too much coffee, they should have shown us a scene or two of him drinking lots of coffee." I twisted around in my seat to face him. He was nice looking. He dressed well. I doubted he had a favorite part of speech. I wondered why that mattered.

"Alissa, it's just a damn movie."

The lights came up and I turned my cell phone back on. Three new messages. I dialed my voice mail and listened. All three were from Detective Rodriguez. He needed to speak to me. Urgently. I bet he wasn't neutered, either.

"I need to talk to you off the record," Rodriguez said when we finally got connected.

We were in the courtyard in front of my house. He'd wanted someplace we wouldn't be seen together, and since my office was here, it had seemed like a reasonable choice. Funny how things never work out the way they should. Sitting outside in my courtyard next to him with the sweet smell of jasmine wafting over us and the moon shining down was not a reasonable choice at all. I felt tingly and nervous.

"So talk," I said.

"You've got to talk to your girls." He leaned back on the bench and stretched his arm out along the back.

"My girls?" I was way too aware of that arm behind me; I could feel the energy emanating from it along the back of my neck.

"You know what I mean." He shifted toward me. "Can we please not play games here?"

I took a deep breath in. "Okay. No games. I assume you mean Sheila and her friends."

"I do." He brought one knee up and crossed his leg. "I'm getting nervous. Someone is going to get hurt. There are too many people out there just looking for an excuse to blow up. This Butterfly Brigade thing is going to be just the ticket for some psycho who won't know when to stop."

"Emmett," I said.

"Call me E.J. I only use Emmett at work. I don't want this to be work, Alissa. For one thing, neither of us should be having this conversation."

Oooh, I love a man with initials. I've never been able to figure out why. "Fine, E.J. Sheila and her friends aren't doing anything. I told you the grocery cart thing wasn't them. You said you believed me."

"I do. But it's not just the grocery carts anymore. Stuff is happening all over the place, and I can barely keep up with the Butterfly Brigade calls. Some guy got his legs duct-taped together by a bunch of women in masks, wigs, and teddies after he straddled two lines at the post office. A woman over by the university had a foot-high pile of dog shit dropped on her doorstep after not cleaning up after her dog. She just caught a glimpse of a bunch of women in camisoles and tap pants running away from her house. They all look different. They all dress different. They're different sizes, different shapes, and different colors. They all have butterfly tattoos, though."

I hesitated. "What do you want Sheila to do?"

"I don't know." He shook his head. "I just know they started this thing, and they should help stop it before it gets out of hand."

"I can't guarantee anything, but I'll talk to them."

He smiled. "Thanks. I had a good feeling about you from the first time I laid eyes on you."

"You did?" That sounded nice.

"Yeah, I did." The hand that had been across the back of the bench dropped to my shoulder. His thumb caressed the back of my neck. "I still do."

He leaned forward and our lips met.

Within five seconds he'd pulled me into his lap and we were playing some serious tonsil hockey. His lips went to my neck and hit that sweet spot that turns me into Jell-O. Just for a moment I thought I heard the voices of angels.

This was not good. Seriously not good.

I'd meant to have just a taste of him, but it was like when you take that one spoonful of ice cream, meaning to put the container back right away, and suddenly find your spoon scraping the bottom.

He kissed his way up my neck and my knees went rubbery. That dizzy, heady sensation of losing myself in a whirl of answered need made my heart pound. Then I heard that little angel voice again. Where was it coming from?

Oh, who cared? This felt soooo good!

The angel voice really started squeaking now, and I finally realized it came from Emmett's pocket. "E.J.," I said.

He didn't answer. He just kept kissing me.

I tried to push him away again, but he seemed intent on discovering exactly how many shivers he could get to run down my spine without taking off my clothes.

The angel sounded like it might be getting cranky.

"E.J.," I repeated. "Your pants are talking."

"I know, baby, they've got a message just for you."

He shifted beneath me so I knew just what he meant.

"Seriously, E.J.," I panted. How had I gotten so out of breath? "I hear a voice and I think it's coming from your pants pocket."

His tongue stopped its exploration of the hollow at the base of my throat, and I felt bereft. "Oh, shit." He slid me off his lap, reached into his pocket, and pulled out his cell phone. "Hello," he said into it.

Judging by the piercing notes emanating from the tiny phone, the angel was royally pissed off.

"Ma?" He ran his free hand over his face, and I couldn't help noticing how his fingers tapered into beautifully rounded pinkish fingernails. I turned away and straightened my top. The stars stopped swirling overhead and stood still.

"Uh, no, Ma," I heard him say. "A colleague. A lawyer working on a case."

I pulled my knees to my chest and wrapped my arms around myself. The temperature seemed to have dropped a couple degrees.

"Of course that's not how I work all my cases, Ma." I could tell E.J. was getting annoyed. The air around him bristled. "Ma, was there a reason you called?"

His eyebrows creased. "No, Ma. No, I didn't."

He listened again and then leaned back inch by inch to bang his head on the wall with soft thuds. "No," he said. "I didn't mean to. It was an accident."

He listened a while longer, his head now resting on the wall. "No. I'm sorry. I'm fine. Yes. I'll be there." He looked up at me and then away again. "I don't know. I'll ask."

He paused. "No. Not now. Bye, Ma." He clicked off the phone, but didn't move.

"Forget something?" The back of his neck had a little fold just above his collar. I wanted desperately to nibble it, but the timing didn't seem good.

"Yeah," he said, straightening up and giving me a grin that sent my heart a little jolt. "I forgot to lock the keys of my cell phone."

"Excuse me?"

"My parents' number is programmed into my speed dial. The phone was in my pocket. When I pulled you into my lap, we must have bumped the button to call them."

I felt like thudding my head gently against the wall, too. "Your mother was listening to us make out?"

He nodded. "And you're invited for dinner on Friday."

I covered my face with my hands. Complete humiliation

cleared the last of the fog of lust from my brain. "You've got to go."

He looked surprised. "You've got a date?"

"Not exactly, but you've got to go anyway." I started toward the door of my condo.

"Alissa, wait."

"What is it?" Damn. My hands were shaking, making it hard to get the key into the lock.

"Can we talk?" He leaned against the wall of the courtyard, arms crossed over his chest. I wanted to go lean my head right between the second and third button of his shirt. It had felt nice there.

"We're not on the same side," I said.

He shrugged. "It's superficial. It's the way the system's designed. It's supposed to be adversarial."

"That's my point exactly. You are trying to arrest my client."

"I'm not trying. I did it. I'm just trying to make it stick next time."

"That's my point exactly." I went into my house, shutting the door on him and the moon and the jasmine and everything else that was making my head whirl.

CHAPTER TEN

From *The Angry No More Manual and Workbook*
by Dr. Gail Peterson

OBJECTS OF ANGER

Stop to examine what has actually made you angry. Did your boss make you work overtime? Did your spouse forget to run that important errand for you? Are your children being loud and disruptive?

If these are the things that made you angry, why have you just kicked the dog?

Alissa's Anger Workbook:

Exercise #10

What has made you angry? List three things that have started your Anger Train in motion.

1. Lying spouse.
2. Cheating spouse.
3. Oh, who cares anymore?

Lisa Ferguson and I were walking out of the courthouse to the parking lot together. "How'd it go?" she asked.

I'd finally argued a case against a different ADA than her. It was Battery Boy's day in court. I shrugged. "Not bad. He's going to have to do some time, but not much."

"You okay with that?" she asked.

I smiled. "Don't tell anyone, but sometimes my clients actually are guilty."

She laughed. "Coffee?"

I hesitated, then shook my head. "Can I have a rain check? I'm beat. I just want to go home and vegetate."

"Hot date last night?"

"More lukewarm, turning to chilly after the movie. The guy actually expected me to sit there and not talk through the whole movie."

Lisa stopped walking. "Alissa, you talk during movies? In the theater? That's . . . that's . . . well, morally reprehensible!"

I stopped, too. "That's just what he said. Lisa, would you like to meet a really cute triathlete named Kirk?"

"Not if he's going to try and take me out on a Thursday. I, for one, have the self-respect to hold out for Saturday night," she said, grinning over her shoulder as she walked away.

I was glad to get home. I was so beat, I'd had to take Dido off the car stereo before she lulled me into a total stupor. I'd finally resorted to a Korn CD to keep myself from running off the road. When I walked in, I felt like I'd been punched in the gut. In the few hours I'd been gone, something terrible had happened to my office.

Everywhere I looked there was . . . nothing. No stacks of papers. No file folders lying on the floor. No bits and pieces of scrap paper floating around. No binders slipping off the shelves. Just Kathleen, sitting at my kitchen counter sipping a Diet Coke.

I looked at Kathleen, feeling seriously panicked. "What have you done? Where's my stuff?"

"It's all here," she said, smiling. "I just organized it."

"But where is it? Where did you organize it to?" I should never have let her do this. I wouldn't be able to find the research from half my cases and would never be able to bill those clients. Oh, God, weeks of work gone undone just because I thought Kathleen needed a project.

"Sit down. I'll show you where everything is."

I collapsed in my office chair; my knees were about to give out in shock. "Okay. Show me."

"See, this file holder here has the cases you're working on this week. I've put them in alphabetically by last name; I just thought it would be the easiest way to find them."

Certainly easier than sifting through the pile I kept by my feet. "Okay."

"That was easy. Your billing stuff is a nightmare, though."

"Tell me about it." I'd never dreamed it would be so complicated to bill people. Not only was it a hassle to keep track of all the expenses and minutes, but I felt kind of queasy making up the bill. The numbers seemed so big. Of course, so was the number on my monthly mortgage coupon, but actually asking people for what I was pretty sure I was worth felt somehow like I was bragging.

"Your system of keeping all those little scraps of paper all over your desk may not have been the most efficient." A smile quirked at the corner of her mouth.

"Don't patronize me, Kath, just cut to the chase."

She shrugged. "You can still do the little scraps of paper.

Just put them all in this box." She held up a cute little chrome box. "But you have to put them in the computer at some point. I set up a program where you just enter in the amount and what it was for, and it will generate bills. I'll come help, but you're going to have to meet me halfway on this one."

I wanted to meet her halfway right now in a great big hug. "And my research stuff? Where's that?"

"Turn around, Alissa."

There, in neat stacks on the sideboard, were my books and files. I took a deep breath and didn't even have to count the inhale or the exhale. I felt great. I felt calm. I felt in control. I felt . . .

. . . like me.

"I didn't want to change the way things were stacked in case it meant something to you; I just sort of straightened up the piles."

I almost cried.

Kathleen laughed. "You know what? This was fun. I'd forgotten how satisfying it can be to take a mess like this and whip it into shape. Even better, the papers go where I put them and stay there. I like being around things that mind."

"Your kids mind, Kathleen. They're good kids."

She smiled at me with a bit of wistfulness. "Yeah, they do. Maybe I'd appreciate it more if I was away from them a little bit. Hey, by the way, I took Goldie to the pet store to see if they could figure out what to do about her swimming upside down."

"What'd they say?"

"They said there was something wrong 'with her swim

bladder. They told me to put her in a Ziploc bag in the freezer."

"The freezer? That would fix it? How?"

Kathleen shook her head. "No, it wouldn't fix it. It would kill her. Then they said I should throw her out and get a new fish."

"Are you going to?"

She looked as horrified as if I'd suggested she put Jason in the freezer and get a new son. "No! I'm not going to kill Goldie just because she doesn't swim like the other goldfish. At my house she can swim around upside down all she likes."

I stood up and gave her a high five. "Right on, sister!"

After Kathleen left, I thought I should check in on my mother. She hadn't called me in days.

"Hello." CNN blared in the background over the phone. My mother keeps *Headline News* on pretty much twenty-four hours a day. Not much happens in the world these days without Rachel Jacobs being right on top of it.

"Hi, Mom. It's Alissa."

"Oh." That was it. Just "oh." No overly personal questions. No comments that set my teeth on edge. Nothing to even make me roll my eyes. Just nothing. Just "oh."

"How are you, Mom?"

"Fine." Again. Nothing more. I waited for the *Twilight Zone* music to start, but all I could hear was Lou Dobbs giving the latest Dow Jones statistics.

"I was wondering if you wanted to go out to lunch next week some time."

She sighed one of those heavy sighs that only older Jewish

women truly have mastered. I've heard some Italian women come close, but they never quite attain the same nuances as the best Jewish sighers. "Not next week, dear."

"You have big plans?"

"No."

"Well, if not lunch, how about coffee? Or maybe a little shopping? Tuesday is Senior Citizen's Day at T. J. Maxx."

"No, thank you, dear. I've started that new biography of President Kennedy."

My mother does love to read about the Kennedys. I scored more brownie points than I had since passing the bar by bringing her the article in the *Atlantic* where they detailed his recently released medical records, including information on a number of lower gastrointestinal tests. Still, to pass up lunch or a shopping trip wasn't like her. Especially with special discounts.

On the other hand, she was a grown-up, and if she didn't feel like having lunch with me, she didn't have to. I hung up and called Marsha right away. "Have you talked to Mom recently?"

"You mean since the Mort thing?" she asked. "Of course. I call every day on my lunch hour."

I tried to remember if I'd managed to call our mother after her heartbreaking confession of crushing loneliness. Surely I had, hadn't I? There goes that Daughter of the Year Award again. "Well, I just talked to her and she sounds like shit."

"She's depressed, Alissa. People don't usually sound their best when they're depressed."

After I got off the phone with Marsha, I called the new 800

number for Stephanie's insurance company. After about fifteen minutes on hold, I finally got to a person. "Hello," I said. "My name is Alissa Lindley. I'm the attorney for the family of Stephanie Kendall."

"Oh," the young woman said. "I'll have to transfer you to my supervisor."

I heard some funny clicks and then after a minute or so I got the "beep-beep-beep. The call you've made blah, blah blah." I dialed the 800 number again.

This time I got through to the supervisor after only being on hold for ten minutes. "What you need is a Certificate of Medical Necessity," she told me.

"Great. How do I get one of those? Can you express mail it directly to me?"

"I can't mail it to you at all."

I took a deep breath. "Then how do I get one?"

"Strictly speaking, you don't. Stephanie's physician has to request one from us."

I took her information and hung up. I called Stephanie's doctor's office and I got a voice-mail system that once again would not allow me to talk to a person. I left a message and hung up with a bang. My head answered with a throb in my right temple. Five-thirty. It seemed a reasonable time to throw in the towel.

Snowball and I had big plans that involved sweatpants, popcorn, alcohol, and mindless TV. One of the fabulous things about living alone is that you don't actually have to make meals and sit down at a table for them. I don't know why the addition of one more person means that you suddenly have to eat at a table every night, but apparently it does. As I looked at what I'd assembled for dinner, though, I wondered if I was just trying to avoid my mother's extra-plate syndrome. If you don't set the table, you can't wind up with an extra plate.

I'd just settled in on the couch when the doorbell rang. I looked at Snowball. "Are you expecting someone?" I asked. He opened one blue eye and then shut it again. I guess he didn't have any Friday night appointments.

I thought about not answering the door. I had a bottle of chilled sauvignon blanc, popcorn with Land O' Lakes butter, and the second four episodes of season three of *Sex and the City* ready to pop into the DVD player.

On the other hand, what if it was the next-door neighbor with fresh-baked cookies to welcome me to the neighborhood? Chocolate chip cookies go so well with popcorn and hope springs eternal, doesn't it?

Detective Rodriguez, in a clean white shirt with little tuxedo details and faded blue jeans, stood on my doorstep.

I blinked a few times. It didn't help. He was still there. "Can I help you?"

He shifted from foot to foot. "Is that what you're wearing?"

I looked down at my tank top and sweats. "Yep. What's it to you?"

"I guess it's okay. A little casual for my mother's taste, but it looks good on you."

"What does your mother have to do with what I'm wearing?"

"We're having dinner at her house tonight. Remember?"

"E.J., I never said I'd go to dinner at your mother's."

"You never said you wouldn't, either." He just stood there, shifting back and forth like a little boy. "Look, it was your inner thigh that called her."

"As I recall, your lap was doing more than its fair share at the time."

He held up his hand. "You're right. I'm sorry. Finger-pointing will not get us there on time. Now let's go." He grabbed my hand and started toward the street.

"I'm not going." I dug my heels in. Literally. Interesting sensation.

He froze. "But my mother's expecting you!"

Well, it just wouldn't be right to disappoint someone's mother, would it? Plus there was that little boy shifting from foot to foot, which was somehow very appealing, and the tuxedo shirt unbuttoned just enough . . .

I went to my bedroom to change. What exactly did you wear to meet the mother of a man you were emphatically not dating? I pulled a slinky black number with spaghetti straps and short skirt from the closet of Kathleen-approved clothes. In the pro column, It would probably make his mother hate me on sight. On the con side, it would probably also cling to the lumpiness that still afflicted my rear end. It's not that I'm all that vain, but I'm not a masochist, either.

Next up: a flowery A-line dress that buttoned up the front from the unapproved closet. Simple. Sweet. Probably a real mom-pleaser, but patently false advertising. I'm not simple and sweet; I'm complicated and a little bitter.

I pulled choice three from the approved closet. It still had the tags on it. Polka dots? How had I allowed Kathleen to talk me into buying a dress with polka dots? I looked like a Semitic Minnie Mouse. All I needed were gigantic red pumps, a huge hair bow, and an enormous Star of David hanging around my neck. Plus, exactly how many times did that polka dot pattern have to repeat to get all the way across my ass?

Aargh! What was I doing up here? Who was I trying to please? I grabbed black slacks and a gray cotton sweater and threw them on. Simple, but not definitely not sweet. More kind of bitter in a boring, monochrome way. I left my hair in its low ponytail, slid my feet into black slides, and headed for the stairs.

E.J. rose from his chair with a big smile on his face. "You look nice."

What was he crazy or just color-blind? "I look boring."

He shook his head. "I've seen you look many things in our short acquaintance, but boring has never been one of them."

Did his voice always have to make me need to press my knees together? I followed him out and locked the door behind me.

"So why are you doing this, anyway?" I asked.

"I like you. If we were in second grade, I'd pull your hair and make fun of you."

"Fine. But why?"

"Because in second grade I couldn't drive, which made it hard to pick up chicks for dates."

"Be serious," I said, stopping next to the car.

"That is the most blatant fishing for a compliment I have ever heard." He clucked his tongue as he unlocked my car door.

"That's not what I meant. I just . . . I haven't . . . I don't . . . " He was just looking at me, waiting patiently. I covered my face with my hands.

He peeled my hands away and looked down into my eyes. "Get in the car," he said softly.

He muscled the car through the Friday evening traffic, and after a few minutes of jamming on my imaginary brakes, I relaxed and let him pilot on his own. Besides, every time I'd slammed my foot into the floorboard, I'd seen his lips twitch with a suppressed smile. It's bad enough to be a frustrated control freak without being a comical frustrated control freak. He'd had enough amusement at my expense for the day.

I leaned back in my seat, closed my eyes, breathed in deeply, and began to imagine myself in a tropical garden.

"Whatcha' doin'?"

"Relaxing." I tried to stay in my happy place and still answer. Interstate 280 was definitely *not* my happy place.

"Does it take that much effort?"

"Generally." The garden faded a little more. I still had hold of a scarlet hibiscus flower, but keeping my mental hold on it was making me grind my teeth.

"Anybody ever tell you you're wound a little tight?"

The tooth grinding seemed at odds with my relaxation goal. I let the garden go and opened my eyes. "Yesterday I got a forehead cramp from overfurrowing my brow. What do you think?"

He chuckled. I shifted in my seat to look at him better. The sun had set and it was getting dark. Red taillights stretched in front of us in an unending parade. The glare of headlights flashed in our rearview mirrors. For a second I thought I saw words reflected on E.J.'s face, but they were gone in an instant as we rounded the curves by Stanford's Linear Accelerator.

He smiled. "I think you need to get out more."

"I get out plenty. Maybe too much. I think I need to stay in." Another car zoomed up behind us, its headlights sweeping into the mirrors. The words appeared again on E.J.'s cheek and I squinted to make them out. They were hard to read since they were distorted, backward, and small across E.J.'s cheek. It took me a second then I realized I knew what they were before I could even read them: Objects in Mirror May Be Closer Than They Appear.

We walked in and E.J.'s mother walked up to me, then around me, then looked me up and down without saying anything. I expected her to check my teeth. I don't know if I passed inspection or not, but she did let me help make the salad, which in my family meant a certain level of acceptance had been achieved.

His dad, his sister, his brother-in-law, and their children (a painfully shy three-year-old girl whose fingers never left her mouth even when she was eating, and a one-year-old boy who could fling a handful of peas across the dining room with the force of a major league fast pitch) were there, plus two aunts and one uncle. It made for a tight fit in the one hundred square foot dining room, but nobody seemed to mind rubbing shoulders or practically reaching into each other's plates as they tried to eat *carnitas* and talk.

These people clearly regarded food just like my family did. Dinner together was about sustenance, certainly, but only on the surface. Beneath the roasted meat and fat-laden side dishes was the need to congregate over food, to make the ritual dishes and offer them up to the gods that kept families whole and together. I tried to remember if my mother had made a brisket—her specialty—since my father died. I remembered spaghetti and stew and many of the ninety-seven different ways my mother knows how to prepare boneless, skinless chicken breasts, but no brisket. Perhaps the inability of our sacred meal to keep my father at the table was too great a disappointment for her.

I looked at E.J.'s dad, a quiet man with a pleasant smile and E.J.'s enormous shoulders, and wondered if *carnitas* would still be on the menu when his place held the extra plate.

E.J.'s aunt launched into a description of an encounter she'd had in the grocery store that week. I almost choked on my tortilla, and E.J. got a little pale.

"Aunt Rosa, you can't just stab a person with a shishkebab," E.J. said, sounding eminently reasonable to me.

"Don't tell me what I can or cannot do, Emmett Joseph Rodriguez. I changed your diapers." His aunt spit each word of that last sentence at him as if it gave her sway over him for the rest of his life.

Maybe it did. I certainly felt that way about Terry and Andrew and I know Marsha felt that way about me.

"I know you did. And I'm grateful, Rosa. It doesn't mean you can stab Mrs. Klassen with a chicken kebab." He pointed at her with his fork.

Aunt Rosa drew herself up. "She was in the express lane and she had fourteen items. I counted."

"Fourteen," E.J.'s mother chimed in.

"That's two over, E.J.," Rosa said with great seriousness. "Even so, I wouldn't have said anything. I'm not a petty woman."

"Two items. How much longer could that have taken to ring up?" he asked.

"The two items are not the point, *angelito*." Rosa grabbed his arm. "The point is that she then stopped to argue the price."

"She did?" I asked. That *did* take some nerve.

Rosa released E.J.'s arm and leaned back in her doily-protected chair, nodding. "Yes!"

"And me, with chicken kebabs. You can't leave chicken out. It's not safe. It gets that fish disease."

"Fish disease?" He rubbed the furrow between his brows with his thumb.

Rosa nodded. "The salmon thing. You know."

I stared at her and then it came to me. "Salmonella?"

"You're such a smart girl. No wonder he brought you home. You know, you're the first one he's brought here since the dental hygienist, and that's been what?" She turned to her sister.

"Two years," Mrs. Rodriguez said sadly. "Nice girl. Beautiful smile. No sense of humor."

Rosa smiled. I beamed back. It's nice to be appreciated. "So you see why I wanted to do it," she said.

I turned my attention back to my *carnitas*. Not a hard

thing to do. They were delicious, and like a lot of nice Jewish girls, I find it hard to pass up really good pork when I can get it.

E.J. started to turn purple. "You're lucky she didn't press charges."

Rosa waved her hand dismissively. "Pah! It was just a poke, a scratch. The woman's just a pantywaist. I know pain. Have I ever told you about the time I nearly severed my finger making the tamales for Christmas back in 1997?"

"Ilsa Klassen is a seventy-eight-year-old grandmother. I'm sure she's had her share of pain, too, Aunt Rosa," E.J. said.

"Weenie," Rosa muttered under her breath.

"You have to keep your temper."

"No, Emmett, I don't. I'm a Butterfly now," Rosa said.

He stopped eating. "You're what?"

"A Butterfly. Like those women on TV. The ones that run around in their underwear. I'm thinking of getting a tattoo, too."

"We knew it was happening," I told him, hoping to avoid a total meltdown.

E.J. kept staring at his aunt. "But not like this. Not this bad. They seem like they're everywhere."

"We are," Rosa said.

After dessert (flan!) E.J. drove me home and walked me to my door. "So I suppose I ruined any chance that you'll go out with me, by letting you meet my family."

I laughed. "They're no worse than anybody else's family. My own is much crazier. Or maybe it's just me that's crazy."

"How so?" He leaned against the gate.

"Well, I moved back here so they could take care of me, and every time they try to, they drive me wild."

"Isn't that what families are for?"

"The crazy thing or the taking care-thing?"

"Both, I think."

He leaned down, brushed his lips against mine, and then walked back to his car whistling, with his hands jammed in his trouser pockets.

This morning Kathleen was ready to walk when I got there. I should have known something was wrong when she let me drive without even a token protest.

"What's that stain?" I asked, pointing to a patch on her beige carpet.

"It's from the WD-40 I had to use to get the Silly Putty out of the carpet. Now I have to get on the Internet this afternoon and figure out how to get WD-40 out of carpet. It did get the Silly Putty out right away, though."

At the track she burst out the door of my Volvo like I'd shot her from a cannon. "So how are things going?" I asked when I caught up with her.

"Shitty" was her reply. "I rear-ended somebody."

Ouch. "What happened?"

"Hayley and Jason were playing Punch Buggy. Hayley started whining about Jason punching her too hard, but I know she whacked him good about three blocks earlier, so I guessed it was just payback. I turned to look at them, then I turned back and I saw . . . I saw . . ." She started to sob and her thin little shoulders shook. "I tried to stop. I really did, but the damn minivan is just so heavy. . . ."

"Was anyone hurt?"

She pushed back the sleeves of her long-sleeved T-shirt. The insides of both wrists were scraped. "Fucking airbag," she said. "Everybody else was fine."

"That's good, right?"

"I suppose so. I just keep thinking about why it happened. I was distracted by the kids because they weren't behaving, and why weren't they behaving, Alissa? Why?"

"Because they're kids stuck in the backseat of a car and they're bored?"

"No. Because I'm a rotten mother who allows her children to play games that involve them punching each other. Damn that woman!"

"What woman?"

"The one that was driving the yellow Punch Buggy. What did she think she was doing, driving around in her little Nazi car, getting little kids to punch each other? Does she even know what she started?"

"I'm sure she was just driving, Kath," I said.

I shouldn't have wasted my breath. As she just kept ranting on I wondered why everyone was so angry these days and felt so impotent to do anything about it. Wasn't that at the heart of all these Butterfly Brigade attacks? Were we all at our boiling points, ready to explode over the least little thing?

"Oh, forget it," Kath said. "There's nothing I can do about it, anyway. Tell me about your date with Kirk."

I told her about Tom Wilkenson and the coffee.

"Well, it is just a movie, isn't it?"

"Yeah, but it's a movie that's about something," I said. "What's the point of going to see a movie like that if you're not going to talk about it afterward?"

"Or during it?" She knows me too well. She smiled and shook her head at me. "I don't know. Maybe the point is a couple hours of entertainment."

"So why not extend the entertainment further by talking about what it actually had to say?"

"Some people don't find that kind of analysis enjoyable, Alissa. They just want to watch the story and walk out. You're being too picky."

"Don't you think I'm worth it?"

Kathleen rolled her eyes. "Of course I do. I just think you're using it as an excuse not to try too hard."

"How am I not trying?"

"Because you're just going through the motions. You're not letting anybody past this wall you've put up."

"The wall is there for a reason, Kathleen."

"I know you put it up for a reason, Alissa, but I think it's time you lowered it a little bit."

Ah, kind of like "sharing" in anger-management class. I knew all about lowering things a little. "You don't know. You weren't there."

"I know you were alone down there in L.A., Alissa, and I'm sorry about that. But I also think that if you can't lower that wall or your standards or something, you're going to wind up being alone for a lot longer."

I thought about E.J. and how it felt to sit next to him on my bench or beside him in his car. "Maybe I don't have to lower anything. Maybe I just have to meet the right person."

She came to a dead stop in the middle of the track. "You met someone and you didn't tell me? What kind of friend are you? How am I supposed to live vicariously through you if you won't tell me what we're doing? Now, spill it! All of it."

I did.

CHAPTER ELEVEN

From *The Angry No More Manual and Workbook*
by Dr. Gail Peterson

CHOOSING YOUR BATTLES

There are lots of battles out there waiting to be won. If you try to fight them all, you will exhaust yourself and you may never get to the ones you actually care about. Pick your battles carefully so you don't end up tilting at windmills.

Alissa's Anger Workbook:

Exercise #11

Choose three battles in your life right now that are worth fighting.

1. Giant insurance companies who play bureaucratic games with people's lives.
2. Getting Kathleen to realize how good she's got it.
3. Keeping my mother out of jail.

"Why the hell should I plead 'not guilty'? I am guilty, goddammit! I put the rock right through the goddamn window."

Mr. Chardlin was proving to be a rather difficult client. He couldn't get over the fact that I wanted him to plead "not guilty" when he had indeed put the rock through his brother's window and would do so again, given half a chance.

"I know that, Mr. Chardlin. Probably the judge is going to know that, too. What I don't want to have happen is for you to go to jail for assault. I want to make sure you plead 'not guilty' to that."

"Oh," he said, settling back a little into his chair. "Okay."

"Now, your brother is asking for seventy-five dollars to replace the glass on the door that you broke."

Chardlin came right back up out of his chair. He was a big guy, blond and burly, but he'd done this so many times now that I didn't even flinch when he loomed over me. "Sit down, Mr. Chardlin," I said, feeling tired.

He sat, but slowly. "Is my piece-of-shit brother gonna pay for my new engine?"

"No, he's not, Mr. Chardlin."

"Then why do I have to pay for the window?"

Fair question. "Because you broke the law, Mr. Chardlin. Your brother was just stupid. The law won't punish him for being stupid."

I thought I saw true understanding dawn in Mr. Chardlin's eyes.

Besides Mr. Chardlin, I'd added another case. A truly terrifying identity-theft case with a sociopath who'd stolen her sister's identity while the sister went through chemotherapy for breast cancer. Then she'd stolen the identity of the third sister who was taking care of the cancer sister. Thank God, the sociopath was going directly to jail without passing Go. I'd gotten her some psychiatric counseling, but I made sure she never saw any ID of mine, all the same. She was running out of sisters fast and probably looking for a new mark.

Then Stephanie Kendall's doctor finally called me back. He would be happy to request the Certificate of Medical Necessity form from her insurance company today and would, of course, let me know when it came in. I hung up feeling happy to have made some progress. I was all too well aware that while I had been enjoying puttering around in my courtyard garden this weekend, Stephanie Kendall had gotten two more needle jabs that left her twisting in agony. I hoped the insurance company would send the form quickly.

I was at Kathleen's for dinner again. To give Rob his due, he never seemed surprised or alarmed or upset to come home and find me in his kitchen helping with dinner, or in his living room helping Kathleen fold clothes, or just sitting at the table drinking Diet Coke.

We'd finished eating and I carried a stack of dishes into the kitchen. Rob called Jason to come back to the dining room, now that the table had been cleared. The kids needed to start their homework. Yes, four-year-old Hayley had homework. In Silicon Valley even unborn fetuses have homework.

"What's thirty-six plus seven?" Jason called from the other room.

Kathleen said, "You're supposed to do your own homework." It sounded like Rob was shaking open a newspaper.

"I am. I just want a little help."

"Jason, just do your work." Kathleen scraped the majority of the vegetables that she'd put on Hayley's plate into the sink. Hayley had picked out all the little kernels of corn and carrots and left the peas. "And stop tipping your chair back like that. I want all four legs on the floor," Kathleen called to Jason.

"Daddy's tipping his chair back," Jason complained, bringing his chair down with a thump.

"Daddy makes the money to repair or replace the chair, but it would be nice if he set a good example anyway." Then she asked me, "So do you think your mother is going to see this Mort guy again?"

"I don't think so. We hustled him out of there in a way that didn't leave much room for compromise."

"You know, your mother does have a right to have someone in her life."

"My mom is not your mom," I said. Kathleen's mom has been through enough husbands that we refer to her current single state as being between husbands. Kathleen finally made a policy that new men had to be around for at least three consecutive Christmases before she embroidered them their own stocking. "And my mom's fine the way she is," I continued. "Why can't she just be happy with how things are?"

"Because," Kathleen said as she slid a salad plate into the rack in the dishwasher, "even when you're relatively happy, don't you ever wonder, what if this is as good as it gets? This moment. Right now. With the kids doing homework and Rob reading the newspaper and me doing the dishes, this is as perfect as my life will ever be? What if everything else from here on out is downhill? What if this is it?"

"What if it is? This is a good life, isn't it?"

Kathleen stared at me as if she was looking right through me. "Yeah. I suppose." She didn't sound convinced.

"Alissa, I've been fired," Sheila's breathy voice said.

I can't say I was terribly surprised. I'd guessed that the proprietors of Li'l Dudes 'n Dudettes wouldn't be too thrilled if they ever found out about Sheila's night job. "How did it happen?"

"Bridget. The one with the freckles. You met her when you came to pick up Hayley."

"She ratted on you?" That did surprise me.

"She didn't mean to. She saw that article in the paper. You know, the one you yelled at me about?"

I did know.

"She asked if that was me. I said no, but one of the supervisors overheard and she started asking questions and Bridget told her everything and now I'm fired." Her voice rose with each syllable until the last word nearly squeaked. I was surprised she wasn't shattering glass.

"Sheila, how did Bridget know to ask anything?"

"The day you picked up Hayley, you know?"

I knew.

"She asked, you know, how I knew you and I told her. It didn't seem like it would matter so much."

"Oh, Sheila."

"What do I do? Tell me what to do, Alissa. Help me."

"Where are you?"

"Home. I didn't know where else to go."

"I'll be there in less than an hour. Just sit tight."

On the way there I heard a report claiming that stores all

over Silicon Valley were selling out of rub-on butterfly tattoos. Local henna artists were also experiencing a boom in butterfly-tattoo business.

I have to admit I was more than a little surprised when I pulled up in front of Sheila's house. It's not like it was huge or grand or anything, but in this neighborhood, even her little two-bedroom job would easily run over six hundred thousand. I wondered just how much she made in tips at the Crescent Moon.

Sheila answered the door with puffy, swollen eyes. Her nose was red and she had a crumpled piece of tissue in her hand. She threw herself into my arms. "I can't believe they fired me," she sobbed onto my shoulder, which was very awkward since she's a good five inches taller than me.

"I can," I said as I maneuvered her back in the door.

It took fifteen minutes and a promise to let her give me a manicure to get Sheila to calm down. It sounded bizarre to me, but she claimed that she used to give her mom manicures, and it always calmed her down to file someone else's nails.

I held her employment contract with my right hand while Sheila worked on my left. "Sheila, it's a private preschool. They can make whatever rules they want about their employees. It is certainly within their rights to have a morals clause in your contract and to claim that being a stripper violates it. That hurts, by the way." I tried to snatch my hand away, but she held on too tightly.

"When was the last time you trimmed your cuticles?" she asked.

"Probably the last time I had a manicure."

"When was that?"

I looked away from the contract for a second. "Probably for my wedding."

"That explains that, I guess." Her voice cracked a little. "I'm just going to miss those kids so much."

"You can get another job with other kids," I said, knowing full well that I might not be telling the truth.

Sheila kept working on my nails without looking up. She'd separated her hair into six strands and clipped each with a different-colored plastic butterfly.

"How?" she asked. "They'll ask why I left my last job and I'll have to tell them that I'm a stripper and that'll be it." Sheila rubbed lotion into my fingers. It felt so good, I almost drooled.

"Have you thought about doing something else?" I asked.

"But I love teaching kids," she protested.

"I meant something other than stripping, Sheila."

"Oh." She let go of my hand. "Doesn't that look better?"

It did. It didn't even look like my hand. It looked like the hand of a fairy princess who could ride around on a unicorn dispensing truth and happiness. I wish that was me, but it clearly wasn't: the truth hurt, and happiness usually just meant you hadn't noticed the problems looming up behind you. But at least my hands looked good.

Sheila leaned in very close to me and whispered, "Would you like some ice cream?"

"Yes," I whispered back, wondering from whom we were keeping it a secret. Sheila didn't even have a cat.

She fished two cartons of Ben & Jerry's from the back of the freezer out from under a box of unsweetened fruit juice Popsicles. Chubby Hubby and New York Super Fudge Chunk—the girl definitely knew her ice cream. She grabbed two spoons and plunked it all on the table between us.

Deep in the Fudge Chunk we discussed what else Sheila could do that was legal and made as much money as stripping in as little time. The answer to that is pretty much nothing. Sheila regaled me with stories of jobs she'd already tried and the hassles she'd been through. Sometimes, it's not so easy to be the prettiest girl in the office.

"Let's see, I tried the office manager thing a couple of times. One place, the guy tried to make me take dirty dictation."

"Dirty dictation?" I swirled my spoon around the edge of the carton where the ice cream was just a little bit melty. Mmmmm.

"You know, he'd ask me to work late and then he'd dictate letters about how hot he made me and how much I wanted him and then try to get me to read them back to him."

"Ewww."

Sheila giggled. "Sometimes the women are worse. The next place I started as a secretary and got promoted up to office manager. One of the secretaries left knee pads on my desk with a note about how I'd need them to keep moving up the corporate ladder."

I didn't hear the truck pull up and the door slam, but Sheila sure did. The noises didn't even register on me until she started scrambling to get the ice cream jammed back into the freezer behind some frozen spinach and a package of Boca burgers.

Gregory Velosovitch walked in like he owned the place, and it occurred to me that he might.

"Hey, baby." Sheila shoved the freezer door shut and gave him a big smile.

Without speaking, he walked over to the refrigerator, brushing Sheila aside like an annoying fly. It took him about two seconds to find the ice cream. He took both containers to the sink, shaking his head as he ran hot water over them. "Sheila, these are just going to make you fat. You want to lose your job at the club, too? Nobody wants to see a fat girl take off her clothes. If you gain any more weight, they'll be yelling for you to put it back on."

Sheila blushed crimson. "Greg, it's only like two pounds that I gained, and I think it's just that my period's starting. Really, I'll take it off."

"Not eating this crap, you won't." He looked over at me. "Did she bring it here?"

"Yes," I said before Sheila could get a word in. "I thought it would cheer her up."

Sheila gave me a look of wordless gratitude that chilled me.

"Figures." He threw the soggy cartons into the trash and sauntered out of the kitchen.

Sheila followed right after him. From the sounds I heard, Greg was waiting for her in the hallway. I heard a thud and then Sheila said, "Stop it, Greg. That hurts."

"What's she doing here?" he hissed.

"She just came over to look at my employment contract

with Li'l Dudes 'n Dudettes. You know, to see if there was any-thing I could do."

"I don't like her. She's trying to make you fat with that ice cream."

"Don't be ridiculous, Greg. She just wanted to be friendly."

"Don't call me ridiculous."

I heard Sheila give a whimper, and I cringed at what might be happening in the hallway. Part of me wanted to race into that hallway and bean him over the head with a frying pan. Unfortunately, it was overruled by the other parts that sat frozen and fearful in a wooden chair at the table.

"She's jealous. She wants what you have and she can't have it, so she's trying to ruin it for you," he said.

"Greg, she's my lawyer and my friend. She's not jealous of me or trying to ruin anything for me. Let me go. She's waiting and she can probably hear everything you're saying."

"So what? I'm not embarrassed by what I think. I'm not the one who's trying to ruin your body and your career."

"Greg, dancing is not my career. It's just something I'm doing on the side. I've told you that."

He laughed. "Yeah, and breathing is just something I do on the side. Face it, Sheila. You're just a stripper. Forget all that other crap." He must have let her go then. "So go on. What's keeping you from your precious new friend?"

I breathed a sigh of relief as Sheila came in apparently un-damaged. I stood shifting from foot to foot, feeling like an awkward fool and a terrible coward. "Maybe I should go." All I wanted was to get out of there, to be removed from all that naked aggression.

"Don't be silly!" she protested. "Don't mind Greg. He's just cranky. Sit down. We can still talk."

"I really should get going, Sheila. I've got a court date in the morning." It wasn't until ten, but I couldn't stay in that little house for another minute. I was choking on the very air that swirled through it.

It wasn't like I hadn't known that Sheila's relationship with Gregory Velosovitch probably wasn't healthy for her. It wasn't like I didn't have a clue about how vulnerable she was. I just hadn't had my nose rubbed in it before.

I wanted to treat Gregory Velosovitch like a faulty fax machine. I wanted to take Sheila by the hair and drag her out of that poisoned place. I wanted to find out what would make a beautiful young woman like Sheila allow someone to treat her like that, and fix that, too.

What did I do instead?

Exactly what I'd been doing about everything lately: nothing.

Nothing in Gail's anger-management toolbox seemed to address this situation, and I was so afraid of doing the wrong thing that I did nothing. Kathleen was right; I *was* chicken. And the thing I was most afraid of was myself.

I sidled out the door and nearly ran to my car. I slid behind the wheel of the Volvo, and I looked back at the house. What was happening in there? Was he hurting her? Or just belittling her? Was he telling her she was nothing more than a pretty piece of meat for men to look at?

I knew what that felt like. Thomas had had a real knack for making me feel small, of pointing out how much smarter and slicker he was than me. He had made a point of making sure I knew how lucky I was to be with him. I hadn't felt so terribly lucky when the emergency room doctor explained about my scarred fallopian tube.

Then again, maybe that was why Thomas had chosen Bethany over me. Maybe he didn't have to work so hard to convince her how much better he was than her, how lucky she was.

Looking at Velosovitch's house took me back to a place I didn't really want to be, so I turned on my engine and left.

The next morning I woke up stiff and sore. I'd dreamed all night that I'd been up on the high wire. I couldn't make a misstep because I couldn't see what was below me. All I could make out were swirling mists. I couldn't go back to safety because something was back there, chasing me. All night I tensed and jerked and twisted, trying to stay on the wire.

I got back from my walk with Kathleen a little looser, and showered. At breakfast I took a pile of the lower dosage pills Dr. Kinder had prescribed, cut them in half, and put one in every other day of my pill organizer. Then I pulled out the jacket on my newest client. Car theft. It was a bit of a wobbler since it was more of a joyride situation and had the possibility of my talking it down to a misdemeanor instead of a felony. Within a couple hours I was deeply absorbed in writing the motion I needed to file to get the kid off with a lighter sentence. Then the phone rang.

"Alissa, it's your mother," she said as if I might not recognize her voice.

"Hi, Mom, what's up?"

"Actually, I need your help, dear."

"Sure. What do you need?"

"Bail." I swear I could hear glee in her voice. "I'm at the police station and I need someone to come bail me out of the hoosegow."

"The what?"

"You know, Alissa. The joint. The big house. Jail."

"Mom, have you been watching old Barbara Stanwyk movies again?" My mother is plagued by insomnia and has been known to watch entire film marathons on AMC through the night.

"No. Barbara Stan-week isn't until next month. Besides, I've been sleeping just fine. I'm here because I bashed in Carl Finkus's car window with my cane, and he called the pigs on me."

"Mom?"

"Yes, Alissa?"

"Did you just call the police 'pigs,' and is there a police officer there with you now?"

"Yes, there's one nearby. Why?"

"Because I want you to stop talking. I'll be there in fifteen minutes."

I could not believe I was at a police station bailing out my sixty-seven-year-old mother. I could believe, however, that my mother was seated at an officer's desk giving her the family brisket recipe.

"It's important that you sear the meat first, dear," Mom

said. "It seals in the juices. And if you do it on the grill, it adds to the flavor."

"And you really use onion soup mix?" The officer was writing quickly in her pad.

"Oh, yes," Mom laughed. "My older daughter hates to use mixes for anything. She makes such a big deal about making everything fresh, but she's never been able to duplicate my brisket. It's always better with the Lipton's."

Too true. I can't count the pieces of meat Marsha has ruined in an attempt to make Mom's brisket without making it Mom's way. And everyone thinks that she's the pragmatic one.

"Did she tell you how to make the couscous to go with it?" I asked and leaned against the desk. There was a period of time when my mother rarely seemed to leave the house without a brisket and a box of couscous to go with it. I missed those days. At the very least, her hands would have been too full to smash up Carl Finkus's car.

Sergeant Dixon smiled at me. "She tried, but I don't think my kids would go for it." She gestured with her head toward the hallway. "Could we talk for a second?"

"I'd love that." As I followed her out of the room, my mother was straightening the stacks of paperwork on the sergeant's desk.

"Look," Sergeant Dixon said. "Nobody wanted to book your mom. She's a sweet old lady."

"She has her moments."

"But we couldn't just let her bash that man's window in with her cane."

"Of course not."

"Besides, we were worried she might have a heart attack or something. She was really going at it." Sergeant Dixon chewed her lip. "This Finkus guy is pretty angry. I don't think we can get him to drop the charges, and it might get a little ugly. She did a surprising amount of damage for such a little thing."

"Like I said, she has her moments."

I collected my mother, thanked the sergeant, and we were on our way out the door when my mother stopped and turned. For most people this would take just a second. With the bulky walker my mother had to use, it was more like watching a student driver try to parallel park.

"Sergeant Patty," Ma called.

"Yes?" The sergeant looked up from her desk, pleasant smile in place.

"Make sure not to buy an el-cheapo piece of meat. Start with quality. You'll be happier in the end." Then my mother stuck a thumb in the elastic waistband of her slacks and slid the side down to display the butterfly tattoo on her wrinkled hip. "And put this down as one for the Butterflies!"

I grabbed her arm to drag her, walker and all, out of the police station and ran directly into Detective Rodriguez.

I was hard pressed to decide which was more horrifying—the incredulity on E.J.'s face or the dismay on my mother's as I introduced them.

"Your mother?" E.J. repeated, looking from her to me.

"My mother," I said, not budging.

"Did I hear something about the Butterflies?" he asked.

"I bashed Carl Finkus's car window in with my cane, and I did it for the Butterflies," Mom said proudly.

I shut my eyes. "Mom, what did I tell you about talking to the police?"

"Not to?" she said brightly.

"That's right, Mom. Good-bye, E.J." I pushed past him and dragged Mom to the parking lot.

"Mom, did you change your medications?" I asked once I got her loaded into the car.

"No." She clicked her seat belt together. "Why?"

"I'm hoping for a pharmaceutical explanation of why you've lost your mind."

"You're making a big deal out of nothing," she informed me.

"So are you," I replied.

"You're dating a black man."

My mother is a closet racist. I know it doesn't jibe with her classic Jewish liberalism, but not everybody can act according to their own stereotypes all the time. She earnestly believes that the whole Bill Clinton–Monica Lewinsky thing was a Republican set-up, that the Israelis are always right, and that JFK was the closest thing to God to walk the earth in the twentieth century. She also believes that people of color should have the right to equal opportunities, equal pay, and equal treatment, except when it comes to dating her daughters.

"I believe the correct term is African-American, and he's not even one hundred percent that. His father is Latino."

"You're still dating him. Your father is probably turning over in his grave. Your grandfather certainly is."

I'd believe it of my grandfather, but not my father. He was amazingly tolerant and open-minded. "And you think they'd like your tattoo any better?"

"It's just a temporary rub-on one. It'll be gone in a week. They were on sale at the checkout at Safeway and you're over-reacting. You're always so dramatic. This is just like the time you stopped speaking to your cousin Daniel because you thought he'd keyed your car."

"This is nothing like that." I still think Daniel keyed my car. He was always a jealous little shit and I'd gotten into a much better law school than he had. "I'm not dating E.J. and it's not your tattoo I'm objecting to. You premeditatedly stalk Carl Finkus until he parks in a disabled zone, smash up his car, get arrested, then pull your pants down in a police station, and *I* am somehow overreacting?"

"You make it sound so nasty. You know, no white boy will want you after you date a black man."

"I'm ignoring that, Mom. You can keep your ugly racial slurs to yourself. What I'm doing is my private personal life, and I'm not doing anything anyway!"

"Saying someone is black is not a racial slur and I didn't stalk Finkus."

"No? Then how come you're all prepared with your little butterfly tattoo and everything?"

"Luck. I've always been lucky. Besides, Alissa," my mother protested, "he had no right to park in that spot."

"Ma, he has a disabled license plate. He has every legal right to park in that space."

"Legal shmegal." My mother snorted. "The only reason

Finkus has that plate is because his wife needs it. She's the one who's handicapped. He didn't have back surgery. He doesn't have arthritis. He's just fine."

"So? Their car has the plate. He can park there to make it easier to take his wife places."

"But she wasn't with him. She's *never* with him; she's virtually a shut-in. He won't take her anywhere because it's too much trouble to shlep her in and out of the car, but he uses the handicapped space just the same."

I rested my head on the steering wheel. "I understand that his parking in the disabled spot when his wife wasn't with him wasn't right in an ethical sense or a moral sense, Ma, but that doesn't make any difference. He still had a legal right to park there."

"Well, he shouldn't have. He should have taken Shirley with him to the store. And maybe for a little coffee or something, too."

"Yes, he should. But even if he doesn't, he *has* the right to park there. He doesn't have to take Shirley with him. *You,* however, did not have a legal right to bash his window in with your cane."

"I didn't bash his window in. I just left a few dents."

"The police officer said you did a surprising amount of damage for someone your size."

"She did?" My mother brightened. "That Patty is a smart girl. Pretty, too."

Maybe Sergeant Patty would like to take over dealing with my mother for a while. I made a conscious effort to unwrinkle my brow. If Mom kept this up, Marsha and I would both need face-lifts before we were fifty.

And speaking of Marsha, I pulled out my cell phone and speed-dialed her. "Can you guys come to my house for dinner tonight?"

"You're cooking?"

"Yeah. I'm cooking."

"Are the White Sox and the Cubs both in the World Series? Has the Seventh Seal been broken? Are there actually snowballs in Hell?"

"Very funny. Look. I just had to bail Mom out of jail—"

"Jail!" Marsha interrupted. "What was Mom doing in jail?"

"I'll explain if you come for dinner."

Mom leaned over in her seat to get closer to the cell phone and yelled, "And I'll tell you about Alissa's new black boyfriend."

My shoulders tensed nearly up to my ears. "Are you coming or not?"

"Oh, we're coming. If you're cooking, we're coming."

I snapped on the radio to avoid talking any more to my mother. The announcer listed traffic snarl-ups over a background of helicopter noise. I wondered if they really had a helicopter or if they just played a recording of one. Then came the news report and then the announcer said, "Tattoo parlors in Silicon Valley are swamped with female patrons these days. Body art has become increasingly popular in recent years, but area tattoo artists say this is something new. We spoke to Chas Taylor of Taylor's Tattoo and Piercing."

"Yeah," another male voice said. "Tons of chicks have come in the last few days asking for butterflies. Like way more than we usually get. And they're not all young chicks, either. There've been some righteous older babes asking for butterflies. Not all of them on their hips, either. Some of them on shoulders and some on ankles and stuff. I think it's because of that one group of chicks that are running around in their underwear, man."

I shoved the first CD that came to my hand into the player, and Bonnie Raitt suggested we give them something to talk about.

I think we already had.

I drove home, slamming my car from gear to gear as if grinding my clutch to death would help somehow.

CHAPTER TWELVE

From *The Angry No More Manual and Workbook*
by Dr. Gail Peterson

KNOWING WHEN TO TAKE A TIME OUT

Sometimes you're too angry to process your feelings. You need to temporarily stall your Anger Train until you can figure out what to do.

Alissa's Anger Workbook:

Exercise #12

Name three things you can do to stall your Anger Train.

1. Take a walk.
2. Buy a new plant for the courtyard.
3. Have amazing sex.

I have one fail-safe meal. Everyone should have at least one. You know, the one that always turns out, that is utterly predictable in its timing from refrigerator to table. The one you can practically do in your sleep. Marsha has at least fifteen that she rotates through. Mine is roasted chicken with mashed potatoes.

My mother was occupying herself by standing in front of whatever utensil I would need next, and constantly trying to do things that I either didn't want done then or wanted to do myself. For instance, I had just put the chickens in the oven, and she was already trying to check their temperatures.

"Mom, I'm fine. I don't need you to help." Since roasted chicken is the only dish I can reliably make, I don't like anybody trying to steal my thunder.

She threw the meat thermometer down on the counter. "Of course you don't; nobody does these days. You don't need me, Marsha doesn't need me, your father certainly doesn't need me. Who needs some slow old lady? I'm just in the way. A burden!"

I stared at her, stunned that we'd been so blind, so unaware.

Before she got married, my mother had been a nurse. She'd had Marsha within a year of her honeymoon. Nearly nine years after that, I came along. Then there were grandchildren. I'd only been out of law school for a couple of years when my father's health began to fail. She'd been taking care of other people most of her life, and now there wasn't anybody to take care of anymore. Even her grandchildren were past the stage of needing someone to tend them. They only let her put ointment on their scrapes to humor her and she knew it.

"You're not in the way," I said. "I just don't need to check the chicken's temperature yet. It's barely been in for half an hour. I do need someone to clean the green beans so I can make the salad, though."

Mom appraised me through narrowed eyes as if she was trying to assess whether I really needed help with the green beans or not. Truthfully, I had time to do them and make the salad, but who really likes cleaning green beans anyway?

"Fine," she said. "Where's your colander? They need to be washed."

By the time Marsha got there, Mom and I were peeling potatoes. It's hard to convince my nephews to eat my cooking without promising some kind of comfort food. They still talk about the time they came to visit me in L.A. and found nothing in my fridge except Diet Coke, two yogurts sweetened with NutraSweet, and some olives. In all fairness I was only twenty-four and fresh out of law school and working eighty-hour weeks.

I am actually pretty good with mashed potatoes. I don't stint on the butter, milk, sour cream, or salt, except for a brief period before my father died when he pretended to cut salt and fat from his diet. He snuck ice cream and french fries whenever my mother wasn't looking. She stuck to his diet and lost ten pounds.

"I brought you a verbena," Marsha said. "You should put it where you have that bougainvillea."

"Where would the bougainvillea go, then?"

"Where I told you to put it in the first place. By fall the place you have it won't get enough sun and it'll die. It's starting to drop leaves already. You need to move it."

"But if I put the bougainvillea there, I have to move the geraniums and the herbs," I argued.

"Only because you wouldn't put the bougainvillea where I told you to put it in the first place. Now you're going to have to shift everything else." She crossed her arms over her chest.

"Stop bossing me around. I'm perfectly capable of leading

my own life and that includes putting my plants where I want them."

Marsha lifted her hands in one of those "what am I to do with you?" kind of gestures. "What are you doing?" she asked.

I looked at the potatoes in front of us, the peelers in our hands. Then I looked at the discarded peels and the bowl of naked skinless potatoes and said, "Constructing a space shuttle."

"What does it look like, Marsha?" Mom asked and then, ever the pragmatist, said, "We're peeling potatoes."

"Why?" Marsha responded. "All the vitamins are in the peels. Just leave them on."

"First of all, your kids won't eat them that way. Secondly, David won't eat them that way, either." Why I was getting my nose out of joint over potato peelings is beyond me, but there you have it. Sometimes Marsha brings out the best in me. Those times are rare.

She grabbed a paring knife from the knife block and threw herself down into a chair. "I know. I like the peels, though."

"So leave them on." I grabbed another potato and handed it to her. "At *your* house. When *you* cook."

"Then everyone complains." She looked at the potato as if it might tell her how it preferred to be prepared.

"What bee flew up your butt?" I asked with sisterly concern. Sometimes sisterly concern just comes out sounding like annoyance.

She slumped down at the counter. "Two of the condoms are missing."

"Two of what condoms?"

"Terry's condoms. The ones I bought, which, let me tell you, is no walk in the park these days. Do you have any idea how many choices there are? I don't remember there being that many kinds."

That was enough to make Mom set down her paring knife. Me, too. "Do you think he used them for . . . you know . . . ?" I asked.

"No, Alissa. I think he and Smashley made water balloons out of them and then had a pillow fight."

She was right. Dumb question. "You did know it was coming," I said.

"I know I did. I just didn't expect to feel this . . . " Marsha's voice trailed off.

"This what?" Mom asked.

"This old. My child is a man. He's having sex. In two years he'll leave home and Andrew will be right behind him. They hardly need me anymore. Soon they won't need me at all."

"You always need your mother," I said. "Look at us. We can barely cross county lines without the umbilical cord snapping us back so fast, we almost get whiplash. Besides, who will buy them their condoms?"

Mom just patted Marsha's hand and passed her some unpeeled potatoes. "Here. Make some separately for yourself," Mom suggested.

"It's not worth it," she said.

A grin quirked the edge of my mother's lips. "These days I keep the skin on if want and I keep the peanut butter in the cupboard instead of the refrigerator. There are some advantages to being alone and not putting someone else's needs first."

"Peanut butter in the fridge?"

"Your father read some cockamamie article about some bacteria they found in peanuts, and was convinced that if we didn't keep the peanut butter in the refrigerator we'd die of some bizarre intestinal parasite. But peanut butter doesn't spread well when it's in the fridge. And the flavor doesn't come through the same." Mom's eyes misted over a little. "The day after his funeral I put it back in the cupboard. It spreads like a dream now. It's a wonderful thing."

I stared at my mother and wondered if I knew her at all.

I sent her off to set the table.

"So how dark is this new man of yours?" Marsha asked, glancing over her shoulder to make sure Mom couldn't hear.

I tried to fight back a smile, but wasn't completely successful. "Dark enough to give Mom the heebie-jeebies."

"C'mon. Give."

I thought about E.J.'s eyes and the way they stood out against the color of his skin. "Hot chocolate with a lot of milk."

"Ghirardelli or Hershey's?"

"Are we talking taste or color?"

"I'm still on color."

"Probably Hershey's," I said.

"Could we be any more politically incorrect?"

"Probably not. We're completely appalling. But as fun as this is, this is not what we're here to discuss. Mom is out of control."

Marsha looked over into the dining area where Mom shuffled along with her walker while putting dishes on the table. "Yeah, she's a wild woman."

"Seriously, Marsha, she thinks she's one of those Butterfly Brigade women," I said.

"And the problem with that is?"

I put my head in my hands. "The problem with that is that she can't go around bashing in car windows just because someone doesn't take his wife out enough."

Marsha shrugged. "Sounds like Finkus had it coming. Do you remember when he was president of the Temple? How mean he was to the kids at the Oneg Shabbat? One Cookie Finkus. That's what we called him."

"Marsha, this is not about Finkus. This is about our mother and whether she's going to end up with a police record."

"So she ends up with a police record. What's it going to do? Keep her from getting a job? Stop her from getting into the college of her choice? Look at her."

I did. She was humming. "So?"

"She's happy," Marsha said. "The last few times I've called her or stopped by, I could barely get her to turn CNN off to say hello. Now she's setting the table for us and she's humming."

She was right; Mom clearly felt great. On the other hand, I still felt like scum after running out on Sheila last night. "Fine. She needed a hobby. I'm just saying it can't be vandalism."

Marsha set down the knife she wasn't using anyway and asked, "How serious is it with this policeman?"

"I don't know."

"Because of the color thing? Mom'll get over it in time."

I shook my head. "Not the color thing. It's a job thing. He's a cop."

"So? Lots of cops date lawyers."

"On TV. It's more complicated in real life."

"Oh." Marsha appeared to be contemplating that one a little further. Then she asked, "Do you really think that this is all that much healthier, Alissa?"

"What is that supposed to mean?"

"Nothing, I suppose, if you want to be an ice queen."

"Ice queen?"

"Yeah. As in no feelings."

"I have plenty of feelings. I have so many feelings I barely have time in the day to feel all of them. Just because I don't think our mother should jump on some misguided vigilante-stripper bandwagon, doesn't mean I don't have feelings."

"Well, you clearly don't have time to show any of them. Have you even cried since Daddy died?"

That shut me up so fast and tight that I could almost hear my molars grind against each other. Of course I'd cried when my father died. Just not a lot. I'd put it down to the fact that his death had been so expected; he'd spent the last three years of his life in the process of dying. Plus, I'd cried so much over Thomas I thought I'd depleted my supply. My tear ducts were tapped out and dry and dusty. "Are you implying that I wasn't sad when our father died? That I don't miss him?"

Marsha gritted her own teeth now. "Of course not. That's precisely my point. I *know* you're sad. I *know* you miss him. I know you miss Thomas, too. You're just not expressing it. The point of all those anger-management classes wasn't to keep you from expressing your emotions, Alissa. The point was to learn to express them appropriately. You've taken all that fire that was burning inside you and turned it into ice."

"Well, it's better than burning down the house, isn't it?"

"Why are you so sure anything's going to burn?"

It's immeasurably annoying to have a psychologist for a sister. Every question you ask, she answers with another question. "Excuse me, but I believe it was you that Anger Management Gail spoke to on the phone. I think we both know what can happen."

"Alissa, your emotions were still so raw. You had barely filed your divorce papers and Daddy had just died. You felt lost and abandoned."

"Don't project your namby-pamby emotions on me, Marsha. I didn't feel lost and abandoned. I was pissed. I still *am* pissed. I'm just trying to get through my days without doing major property damage."

"You are so dramatic sometimes, Alissa. You destroyed one faulty fax machine and one plastic chair that had probably been around since the 1970s. That's hardly major property damage." She grinned. "You can't hold a candle to Mom. She took out an entire Buick."

I'd been calling Kathleen for twenty-five minutes by the time she finally answered her phone the next morning.

"Kathleen McAllister," Kathleen said briskly on the other end of the phone.

"Kath?" I asked.

"That's what I just said," she answered.

Well, yeah, but . . . Oh, hell. "Hey, I've been trying to call you forever. The line's been busy. I'm not even getting call waiting."

"It's been a madhouse here. I know. We're mobilizing."

Mobilizing? I hadn't heard anything on the news, but maybe San Jose was annexing Mountain View and they were calling out the Mommy Militia. "Who exactly are we invading?"

"Li'l Dudes 'n Dudettes."

"We're taking over Hayley's preschool?"

"Not exactly taking over. Just trying to influence policy."

My stomach did a flip. I had a very bad feeling. "What kind of policy?"

"Employment. They fired Miss Sheila."

"I know."

"Just because she has a job at night as an exotic dancer."

"I know."

"I mean, seriously, Alissa, if we paid the people who take care of our children a decent wage, she wouldn't have to . . . Hey, what a minute. Did you say you already knew?"

"Sheila Montrose is my client," I said slowly, trying to decide what I could and couldn't say.

"Alissa, that's fantastic! I had no idea she'd already gotten a lawyer. Wow, is that preschool ever going to be sorry they messed with her. You'll rip 'em to ribbons!"

I winced. I don't know which was worse—realizing that I'd become a lousy defense attorney or having to tell Kathleen that. It had been hard enough to accept myself as a failure; I wasn't ready to have everyone else accept yet. "Sheila didn't seek my representation in regard to her employment at Li'l Dudes 'n Dudettes."

"Then what did she need a lawyer for, if it wasn't that?"

"Kathleen, you know I can't tell you that."

She didn't say anything for a second. I could tell she wanted to press me, but she didn't. "So, would you help with her employment at Li'l Dudes 'n Dudettes?"

I sighed. "Maybe she'd be better off with someone who knows more employment law than I do. I've already looked at the contract, and it's pretty straightforward. They're well within their rights to terminate her."

She snorted in disgust. "They may have a right to fire her, but I have a right to let them know how I feel about it, too. I pay for my kid to go there, after all."

"Kathleen, what are you up to?"

"Not much yet. I just started calling people whose numbers I knew and asked them to call whoever they know. We're all calling, faxing, e-mailing, and writing Li'l Dudes 'n Dudettes to let them know that we want Miss Sheila back. She's one of their most popular teachers."

"How about a sit-in, Kath? We could all link arms and sing 'Give Peace a Chance' by candlelight. That always influences corporate policy."

"Go ahead and laugh, but people are sick of their opinions not mattering. Just look at those Butterfly Brigade women."

I put my head in my hands. Not them again. "What about the Butterfly Brigade?"

"They know what to do. They're mad as hell and they're not gonna take it anymore. They're doing something about it.

If I could figure out what they would do, I'd march right down to the daycare center in the teddy that Rob gave me for Valentine's Day and give them a piece of my mind."

I snorted at the mental picture that was forming. "Great, Kath. You're going to go from soccer mom to slut in ten seconds flat?"

"Why not? As a matter of fact, I think it's a pretty good idea. I bet that would certainly get some press."

Uh-oh. I knew that tone of voice. It was not dissimilar to the one she'd used on me when I'd expressed surprise at the Southern Belle bridesmaid dresses with the giant hoopskirts she'd wanted Andrea and me to wear at her wedding. I'd pissed her off then, and we'd had to wear the damn things. Now she'd really dig her heels in, and this would undoubtedly be even worse than having to figure out how to sit down in a hoopskirt. "Because the Butterfly Brigade isn't solving anything. Because there are right ways of going about these things. Ways that won't involve someone getting hurt."

"You already told me that the right ones aren't going to work. Besides, I'm not talking about kidnapping anyone or beating anyone up. I'm talking about expressing my opinion in a way that might get someone's attention. I'm talking about not being beige for once."

"This doesn't have anything to do with colors, Kathleen. You're not redecorating your living room or picking an outfit to wear to Rob's office Christmas party. You're messing with people's lives." I sighed. There really wasn't any point in arguing with her, but did I shut my big mouth? "You're living in a dreamworld, Kath. I just hope you're not the person who will get hurt."

"Don't patronize me, Alissa. Just because I stay home with my kids doesn't mean I don't know what goes on in the big, bad world. Do you have any idea of how gifted a teacher Sheila is?"

I didn't; I'd kind of pooh-poohed her daycare job. I guess, in truth, I'd kind of pooh-poohed Sheila in general. I'd labeled her an airhead, a ditz, a misguided do-gooder.

"Do you know, there's a little autistic boy in her class who wouldn't speak except in catchphrases from videos, wouldn't play with the other kids. He'd sit in the corner and rock so hard that he'd get blisters. He tried to poke another kid's eyes out with a pencil because the kid touched his drawing."

Joey, I thought. Joey of the long eyelashes and deadbeat dad.

"Well, three months with Miss Sheila, and that kid goes out on the playground and plays with the other children. He participates in Circle Time. He can tell you his name and shake your hand. Do you know what that means to that boy's mother? He's four years old, and last month he told his mother he loved her for the first time. Do you understand what kind of teacher it takes for a kid to make that kind of transformation?"

"Kathleen, this has nothing to do with Sheila's gifts as a teacher. It has nothing to do with Joey."

"Well, it should."

"Yeah, well, my Peeping Tom client shouldn't have been abused as a child. My stolen-goods purveyor should never have tried crack." Thomas should never have screwed around on me, and my father shouldn't have died before I had a chance to give him another grandchild.

"That's exactly my point!" she crowed.

"It can't be your point, Kathleen. It's mine and we're arguing."

"Then we're on the same side." She sounded so smug. "Doesn't it make you angry?"

"Does what make me angry? Being on the same side as you?"

"No, Alissa! Everything. All the stupid, unfair things that happen every day."

"Look who you're talking to? Of course it makes me angry. I'm the Queen of Anger."

"No, you're not," she said with a decidedly snotty tone to her voice. "I think you're the Queen of Misdirected Anger."

"What the hell is that supposed to mean?"

"Well, you got mad at Thomas and you beat up a fax machine. Does that make any sense? You're a bully."

"I am not."

"Are, too. You only pick on things that you know can't fight back. Chairs. Fax machines. Are you going to start kicking crippled dogs next?"

"I'm just trying to pick my battles."

"Yeah, like you do such a great job of that."

"What's *that* supposed to mean?"

"You never fight the battles that really matter. At least, not anymore. Why don't you, just once, take your anger out on the thing that actually made you angry? Maybe then you'd change something, and we wouldn't all have to spend six months watching you mope."

"I do not mope."

"Oh, please. You're the Queen of Mope."

"If I'm the Queen of Misdirected Anger, I don't see how I can also be the Queen of Mope."

"You have dual citizenship and we're definitely on the same side."

"I'm not on a side, Kathleen. I'm not for you or against you. I'm just pointing out that what you're doing is fruitless. There is a gaping maw out there between what is and what should be. Tormenting some self-righteous daycare center owners isn't going to change that, except in some kind of dreamworld."

"Yeah, well, doing nothing certainly isn't going to help. At least my dreamworld is trying to do something. In fact, my dreamworld is beeping on call-waiting right now. So good-bye." She slammed down the phone.

I almost didn't pick up the phone when it rang later, but as the only secretary I had, I didn't really have a lot of choice.

It was E.J. "Have dinner with me," he said.

"No."

He didn't even pause. "Why not?"

"Because we're not dating. We're on opposite sides." And I seriously doubted my ability to stay on opposite sides when in his physical presence, but he didn't need to know that. "Besides, I already told my mother we're not dating and I never lie to my mother."

"Oh, please. Everyone lies to their mother. Who is, by the way, pretty cute for a potential felon. In fact, you should go out with me tonight just so you would be lying to your mother. It's the natural order of things."

"No."

"I'll sit on the other side of the table to preserve our opposite sidedness."

I wanted to go. I knew I shouldn't, but I really wanted to. Really really wanted to. "Where would we go?"

"How about Thai?"

"No. I'm not sure there are opposite sides when you're sitting on the floor without your shoes."

"Italian?"

"Too Lady and the Tramp."

"Gordon Biersch?"

"Can we sit on the patio?"

"Whatever you want."

E.J. and I were going on a date. An actual date. Not bantering over the phone or in the courtroom hallways. Not canoodling in the courtyard. A real grown-up date.

It took me only five minutes to get dressed. Of course, I'd spent an hour and a half picking out what to wear. I ended up in a white sweater that buttoned up the front, a pink swirly skirt, and a pair of strappy sandals. As for what I had on underneath, well, maybe my lingerie choices had been influenced by hanging out with Sheila a little too much.

At dinner we covered the basics. Divorce. Family. Educational background. We were a total mismatch. Me: Jewish, liberal, white, white, white. Him: Baptist, Latino/African-American, and, unbelievably enough, Irish. Me: Berkeley undergrad, Stanford Law. Him: Sacramento State Criminal Justice program and the Police Academy. My divorce: a vile volcano of vituperation. His divorce: never married.

We did cover that horrible question that always gets asked eventually: What happened to your marriage?

The short answer—the easy answer—was that Thomas had screwed around on me. I'm perfectly willing to use the short-and-easy answer in public, but I still wonder about the real answer on the inside.

What *had* happened to Thomas and me? Why had he chosen Bethany over me? It wasn't just for the baby. I can do the math. I know he was still sleeping with Bethany after he and I had separated, but were still in counseling.

Thomas claimed that I'd left the marriage long before he did. I will admit that I did get overwhelmed by work now and then and had been known to come home without the energy to do more than watch *L.A. Law* reruns while drinking margaritas through a bendy straw. Maybe I had been looking for something more—but at least I'd had the decency not to look in someone else's pants.

E.J. followed me back to my condo after dinner. Just to make sure I got home safe.

I invited him in for a glass of wine. Turns out both of us had had enough at dinner, so we switched to tea, instead.

E.J. didn't say much as I put the water on to boil and got out tea bags and a package of Lorna Doones. Nothing says comfort quite like a butter cookie, except maybe chocolate. I settled myself down at the kitchen counter next to him to wait for the teakettle to whistle.

"I went on two Butterfly Brigade calls today," he observed.

"Two?"

"Yep. Two. I talked to the third person this week to have their cell phones ripped from their hands and smashed by some nearly naked woman. I have to admit that the one I liked the best was the woman who used a golf club to obliterate one. Tonight's lady apparently just stomped it with a stiletto." He took a bite of a Lorna Doone. "Hey. These are pretty good for not being chocolate."

I nodded, still wordless as I got the chocolate syrup out of the refrigerator and poured some in a dish so we could dip the cookies. "And the other call?"

He shrugged. "I'm still trying to make sense of that one. Seems like this guy pulled up in front of the video store and left his car idling while he dropped his movie in the slot. Somehow these women attached something to his rear bumper without him seeing them. Don't ask me how a bunch of women in garter belts could do something like that without a guy seeing it, because I can't figure it out, either." His lips twitched a little with that one. "Anyway, they attached this bungee cord to a concrete planter, so when he took off, he left his bumper behind. Apparently they're tired of people blocking traffic there, but they didn't stick around to say much besides pointing out that he was blocking a fire lane and that he was not the only patron of the shopping mall. There were five of them." He rubbed his face. It reminded me of the way Terry used to rub his eyes when he was a toddler.

I let out my breath. "You know, none of those things had anything to do with Sheila."

"Not in a literal sense, no. I know that." Frustration made his voice a little biting. I moved away from him, almost reflexively. He grabbed my arm and pulled me back. "But in another sense, yes. These women out there think they can get away with this because your client got away with this. They think there are no consequences to these actions, that they can do whatever they want because your client didn't face any consequences. It's not going to stay that way. Someone is going to get mad. Someone is going to do something about it."

"That's what this is really about. These women are angry about all the little injustices, all the little discourtesies that they see every day and now they're doing something about it. They're tired of seeing jerks get away with whatever they want and having no one do anything about it. And you know what? I'm tired of it, too. I don't blame them one bit."

E.J. turned to face me. We were nose to nose. "Is that so, Alissa? Do you condone what these women are doing?"

I swallowed hard. There it was: the issue in a nutshell. When the system is broken, do you take matters into your own hands? What's to stop people from abusing that power, once they had it? Our species doesn't exactly have a great track record when it comes to wielding power responsibly.

"It's not up to me to condone or condemn these people's actions, E.J. My job is to defend my client. It doesn't even matter if she's guilty or innocent. That's not my decision to make."

"Oh, so you're going to hide behind the 'just doin' my job' excuse?"

I grabbed his arm. "C'mon, E.J. Don't you get tired of seeing it every day? How many of the people who break the rules do you even get to arrest, much less put on trial and put away? And how often do you find yourself protecting something that you're not sure is worth protecting? Do you expect me to believe that the guy whose cell phone got smashed was behaving in a way that was considerate and polite? Haven't you ever wanted to teach someone a lesson after they'd blocked you in at a parking lot by parking illegally because they feel that somehow their time is intrinsically more valuable than yours?"

He freed his arm from my grasp. "Do you think this is what I meant to do, Alissa? Do you think I became a police officer to defend the rights of assholes and idiots?"

"No, E.J., I don't. No more than I became a defense attorney to do the same thing. But we're too old now to think that we can ride in on our white horses and fix everything. We've been around too long to pretend that we're knights in shining armor anymore."

"Actually, I had more of a sort of Shaft thing in mind when I was a kid," he mumbled.

"Well, mine was more of a fairy princess on a unicorn spreading joy and love kind of thing," I admitted.

He laughed. He had a great laugh. "You're kidding."

I grimaced. "Only a little. Are you kidding about the Shaft thing?"

"Only a little." He kissed me. His lips were soft on mine. His tongue slid between my lips. Somebody made a funny noise, between a squeak and a moan. Oops. It was me.

He pulled back and smiled. His fingertips traced my jaw. "Fairy princess, huh?" he asked.

"Uh-huh," was all I could think of to say.

He kissed me again.

It took E.J. about ten seconds to figure out where the bedroom was. It took him about another ninety to half-carry and half-kiss me up the stairs, then we got a little heated up in the hall, and I'm pretty sure that's where I lost track of time altogether.

He unbuttoned my blouse. There were only four buttons and he undid each one with such deliberation it felt like every button was a crossroads, a decision point—when really the decision had been made at the door, or maybe on the stairs, or maybe the first time I saw him in the courthouse, but certainly by the time we were in the hall.

He ran his fingertips over my collarbone, and I felt a rush of heat between my legs that made my knees weak.

His hands ran down my body in a caress so gentle I wouldn't have known he was touching me, if all the hairs on my neck hadn't stood at attention. I felt the blood rush to my face.

He smiled. The bastard.

"There's nothing to be embarrassed about." His voice had gone from its velvet smooth flow of honey to something raspier. "You're not alone in this, Alissa."

My skirt slid to the floor. He took a good look at what I was wearing and said, "Earlier tonight I was going to suggest you'd been hanging out with those strippers too much. Now I'm pretty sure you've been hanging out with them just enough."

He laid me down on the bed and kissed me some more. He kissed me until I thought I couldn't breathe, until I wasn't sure where his mouth ended and mine started, until I remembered why I loved kissing so much.

He stood up and all but tore his shirt off. He slid his jeans and boxers to the floor and stood before me, naked and erect and beautiful.

It took everything I had not to clap my hands and squeal with delight.

We woke up in a tangle of duvet and naked limbs. The morning air chilled the room, and being snuggled under the covers was delicious.

Then it suddenly occurred to me that I was naked. With E.J. In bed.

He opened one eye. "Does the anxiety switch flick on the second you wake up every day?"

I nodded, not wanting to open my mouth. I wasn't sure exactly how bad my breath would smell, but I knew it wasn't going to be good.

"Turn it back off." He rolled me onto my side, spooned up behind me, and landed a kiss on the back of my neck that made me tremble.

"Off," he growled again. This time the kiss landed on my shoulder and his hand moved up to my breast. I twitched.

"I mean it, Alissa." His hand skimmed my torso and slid between my legs.

"Oh," I said and pressed back against him.

"Oh, indeed," was all he said back.

That's all either of us said for a while.

"Look what you did to her." Gregory pointed at Sheila.

E.J. had left that morning, giving me a kiss and asking me to talk to Sheila again. I hadn't expected to do it quite so soon. Velosovitch had called me and demanded my presence. I'd thought about refusing, just on the basis of hating to be bossed around, but decided I should check in on her anyway.

She lay in bed and I'm guessing her hair hadn't been washed in at least three days. Based on the smell in the room, she might not have left it for that long, either.

"How did I do this to her?" I didn't recall forcing Sheila to stay in her room, not bathe, and eat nothing but Twinkies (that last I'm basing on the number of empty wrappers lying around the bed).

"You got her fired."

"I did no such thing. Sheila got herself fired. She knew she was in violation of Li'l Dudes' morals clause when she started dancing at the Crescent Moon." I turned to face Gregory, who was really starting to piss me off.

"Well, she's not going to have a job at the Crescent much longer, either, if she keeps this up. Look at her. She's disgusting."

He was right. Greasy-haired, dull-eyed, slack-mouthed. Not exactly every guy's wet dream. "She's depressed," I said.

He squared off and shoved his face in mine. "They never would have found out she was dancing there if you hadn't showed up to pick up your friend's snot-nose brat."

"You are fooling yourself if you think it wouldn't have come out some day in some way. Things like that have a way of making themselves known."

"That may be so, but it's because of you that it came out this time. So it's because of you that she's been lying in that damn bed shoving junk food down her throat for half the week, and it's going to be because of you that she gets up. Fix it, lawyer lady. Fix it now."

Under the best of circumstances, I do not respond well to being ordered around. This was not the best of circumstances.

I was sick to death of Sheila and Helena and Mom and the whole damn group of them running around town, making a mess, and then expecting me to clean it up. If Sheila's job at Li'l Dudes 'n Dudettes was so damn important to her, she should have kept her clothes on at night. It wasn't my fault that she was fired. It wasn't my responsibility to see that she got out of bed.

I clenched my fists and gritted my teeth together so hard that it was difficult to get words out. "You will not speak to me that way, Mr. Velosvitch."

He smiled. "What are you going to do to stop me?"

A dozen answers raced through my head. They ranged from spitting at him to clubbing him with something. I knew none of them were the right choice. I closed my eyes. I envisioned ocean waves and salt sea breezes. I forced myself to breathe. I coaxed the furrows on my forehead to smooth and I breathed some more. There were no right answers for the situation, but there was a right one for me.

"I'll leave," I said quietly. So quietly I could barely hear myself over the roaring in my ears.

Velosovitch's smile faded. "No," he said, grabbing his coat. "I'll go. You stay and help her."

I didn't move until I heard his truck start outside. Then I sat down on Sheila's bed. "Sheila, honey, what the hell are you doing?"

"I miss the kids," she whispered. "I miss Hayley and Joey and little Ryan, even if he's a total pain in the ass. What is so wrong about what I do? Why does it have to be this way?"

What was wrong with it? There was the exploitation of her body, the commercialization of sex, the dehumanization and objectification of women. And those didn't begin to scratch at the surface.

"It just is, Sheila. There's not much you can about it, either. All you can do is decide what you need and want most, and arrange your life so you're most likely to get it."

Her fingers stopped worrying the tassels on her bedspread. "That's it?"

I shrugged. "Yeah. I think it is." Why am I always so much better at fixing everyone else's lives than I am at dealing with my own?

Sheila knew what she wanted. "I want my job back, then. The one at Li'l Dudes."

"That ship's sailed, Sheila. You might be able to get a job at another child-care center, but not there."

"Okay. So what do I have to do to get a job at another day-care?" She sat up and her eyes began to lose some of their dull sheen.

I looked around the room. "I think the first step might be to get out of bed and take a shower. Then I think we need to work on a plan to move you out of here."

I went into the living room to wait for her. I tried to leaf through a copy of *Marie Claire* (those things are soooo raunchy these days!), but I kept thinking about what I'd said to Sheila.

Was it really that simple? Decide what you want, and try to arrange your life to get it?

So what did *I* want?

It takes no courage to throw a temper tantrum. Ranting and railing against injustice doesn't help. It takes no guts to shut down your emotions and try to pretend you don't feel them, either. Shrugging your shoulders and letting the system drag you along in its current will never get you where you want to be. What takes actual courage is to stare it in the face and act on it. To feel the anger, feel the rage, feel the sadness, the pain, and all the rest of the messy, nasty emotions, and do something with them. It takes courage to decide what your life—your world—should be, and try to make it that way.

Did I want to be a loveless, passionless woman? Or did I want to be the woman who could melt when her lover's lips hit her neck? Would I be the woman who shed a few solo bitter tears over her father's death, or the woman who would sense the depth of her mother's grief and walk through the darkness with her to the other side?

My life hadn't been working out the way I wanted it to lately. Not since the emergency room doctor had sadly shaken her head over my scarred fallopian tube.

What was I going to do about it?

I'd tried retreating. All that had gotten me was ten extra pounds on my hips and thighs. I'd tried acting like everything was normal. That had landed me on top of a fax machine in the middle of my office.

Starting over had been an appealing idea, and the move back to San Jose might not have been a bad one, but I still hadn't really confronted what brought me here.

I knew there was another choice. I just had to figure out what it was.

*   *   *

While I waited for Sheila to get out of the shower, I checked in with Stephanie Kendall's doctor. They'd gotten the form and submitted it back to the insurance company. No, they didn't know how long it would take to get an answer. I needed to be patient.

Sheila was out of the shower and blow-drying her hair when my cell phone rang.

"Alissa Lindley," I said.

It was Kathleen's husband, Rob. Weird. He never calls me. "Alissa, you need to talk to Kathleen."

"Okay, Rob. Put her on."

"She's not here. You'll have to go to Li'l Dudes 'n Dudettes."

"What for?"

"Turn on the Channel Five news."

I switched on Sheila's TV just in time to see Kathleen walk by in a lace teddy, thigh-highs, and fuzzy mules, carrying a sign that said: DON'T STRIP OUR SCHOOL OF A GREAT TEACHER. There were at least three other women there in lingerie, each with a sign protesting Sheila's firing. I know I'm not objective, but Kathleen was the only one who should have been parading around with that little on in front of a television camera. They really do add ten pounds.

"She looks great, Rob."

A heavy sigh traveled down the phone wires. "I know that. I didn't need her to parade around in front of Hayley's preschool in last year's Valentine's Day present to find that out. In fact, I really didn't need her to parade around in front of Hayley's preschool in her underwear at all. Can you do something?"

"What? Buy her a robe?"

"Alissa . . ."

"I'll talk to her, but I can't promise anything."

"Look, Alissa, it's not like I don't know that she's unhappy. I keep telling her to do whatever she needs to do to make herself happy. I don't care if she stays home with the kids or goes back to work or goes back to school. Hell, at this point I wouldn't care if she decided to run for governor. I just want her to be happy."

Wow. Hearing that conversation from the other perspective changed the whole meaning.

"I'm going," I said.

CHAPTER THIRTEEN

From *The Angry No More Manual and Workbook*
by Dr. Gail Peterson

DEALING WITH ANGRY PEOPLE

Don't feed coal into other people's Anger Train furnaces. You are not the only angry person out there. In fact, many of the conflicts you enter into each day are caused by two or more angry people coming in contact with each other.

Alissa's Anger Workbook:

Exercise #13

Name three things you can do to deal with conflict without escalating it.

1. Speak calmly
2. Breathe deeply and stay relaxed
3. Grind your teeth until your molars crack

Getting to Kathleen's picket line wasn't easy. I had to fight my way through gawking spectators, reporters, cameramen, and photographers. I finally broke through to where Kathleen and now seven other women, whose husbands all apparently gave them Valentine's Day gifts from Victoria's Secret, marched with signs.

I trotted along beside Kathleen because she refused to stop.

"I have an idea. An idea of how to help Sheila. Really help her. Please. Just give me a few minutes to explain," I said.

Kathleen didn't look like she wanted to leave the picket line. I can't completely blame her; I knew how she felt. That powerful feeling you get when you feel like you're finally doing something that matters, something that will make a difference, can be almost addictive. There are few things like it in the world. Luckily, under the flush of feeling her existence was justified, she was still my Kathleen and could be coaxed off the picket line with the promise of a Nonfat Mocha Latte No Whip from the closest drive-thru espresso stand. We didn't speak until she had her coffee in hand.

"So what's this big idea of yours?" Kathleen asked, pulling the seat belt over her lace teddy.

"I'm not sure I can even look at you right now, much less talk to you. How are you keeping that thing from showing your nipples?"

"Double-stick tape." Kathleen's eyes narrowed. "Rob sent you, didn't he?"

"Yes, he did. But I need you to stop this and come home anyway. Please, Kath, I really need you to make this work."

Something in my voice must have gotten through to her. "You're pretty serious about this, aren't you?"

"I have to be, Kathleen. I'm not playing dress-up here. I'm trying to help someone get their life back together."

Kathleen's face flushed. "Playing dress-up? Is that all you think I'm doing here?"

I bit my lip and put my head down on the steering wheel. "Kind of. Yes. None of this really touches you. After you're done parading around in the latest Victoria's Secret outfit, you'll go home to your house and your children and your husband."

"And because I made a happy life for myself, what I'm doing is meaningless?"

"Not meaningless, but certainly there's no risk for you. What's Rob going to do? Fire you?"

"Take me back to the daycare center." She turned her face to the window.

"Kathleen, listen to me. I'm talking about something that could really make a difference."

"I'm done listening to you preach. Take me back to the daycare center, or I swear to God I'll get out of this car and hitchhike back there."

I turned the car around. I may have been angry at her, but nobody should hitchhike in thigh-highs. "Please, Kath, meet me halfway on this one."

"No. Not this time. I'm not compromising on this. I'm sick of it. Every day I give up a little of myself here and a little more of myself there. And you know what? The whole thing's almost gone now."

"What whole thing?"

"The thing that's me, dammit! That little kernel of something underneath everything else that makes you who you are. I've given so much of myself up that there's hardly anything left at all. I need to feel like what's important to me actually matters. That I have some control over what happens around me."

I knew what she was talking about. I pulled into the parking lot of a dry cleaner and slammed on the brakes, sloshing Kathleen's latte onto her and making her squeal.

"Kathleen, this is *exactly* what I'm talking about. I've got something that I think will change all that. For both of us."

"Really?"

"God, I hope so, because I don't want to feel this way anymore."

"Me neither." She slumped down in her seat. "It's a really good idea?"

"An excellent idea."

"What do I have to do?"

"Go home. Put on some clothes. And then we have got to get Sheila out of Gregory's house."

"Who's Gregory?"

"Her boyfriend."

"Why?"

"I think he might be evil."

That got her attention. "Evil?"

She looked skeptical, so I told her about the night Sheila was fired. She looked uncomfortable. Then I told her about his tail.

"A real tail?"

"According to Lily, and Sheila didn't deny it. She said it was like a piggy tail."

"Sheila's dating a guy with a tail?"

"Actually a vestigial caudal appendage, but yeah, basically, a tail and there's always dead moths on his car. I think he might be some kind of instrument of Satan."

"Well, we can't let that go on."

"My sentiments exactly."

"So, Fearless Leader, do you have a plan?"

I grinned. "As a matter of fact, Natasha, I do." I explained

my plan, which mainly had Sheila providing child care in exchange for a room at Kathleen's until I figured out what to do
next.

"That's brilliant, Alissa," Kathleen said after I finished lay-
ing it out for her.

"You're sure you won't be uncomfortable having her in your
house all the time?"

"Having her in the house will mean that I don't have to be
in the house all the time."

"Yeah, but she'll be in the house with Rob all the time," I
prompted. "Looking the way she does. With him looking at
her looking the way she does."

Understanding dawned on Kathleen's face, then she shook
her head. "Alissa, I trust her with my children. Do you really
think I won't trust her with my husband? When is she coming?
Does she need help packing?"

"Let's just take this one step at a time."

She closed her eyes. "No, Alissa. That's not what we need to
do. What we need to do—what *you* need to do—is to step forward. Not step back."

"What if I'm wrong? What if I fail at this, too? And this
time I drag the rest of you down with me?"

"Fail again? What did you fail at before?"

I stared at her. "Umm. How about everything? Marriage.
Career. Family. You name it; I didn't manage to succeed at it."

"Alissa, I know things didn't work out the way you planned,
but that doesn't mean you failed."

"I believe not achieving your goals might be the definition
of failure."

"So what do you call it when you get everything you wanted, just to find out it doesn't make you happy?" Tears stood in Kathleen's eyes. "What do you call that, Alissa?"

"I don't know," I whispered.

"I'll tell you what it's called. It's called life. You don't always get to win. It doesn't always work out the way we plan, and we have to learn to live with it. Now, let's both grow up and tell Sheila what we're doing. For God's sakes, Alissa, a tail? Why didn't you tell me sooner?"

Kathleen and I double-teamed Sheila.

"That's not your house you're living in, is it, Sheila?" I asked.

She shook her head.

"You're not even paying rent, are you?" I pressed.

She shook her head again.

Kathleen patted her hand. "It would be nice to not have to worry about Greg and still not have to pay rent, wouldn't it, Sheila?"

She nodded.

We kept pressing, me from one side and Kathleen from the other, and with logic and compassion combined, Sheila never stood a chance. When she finally gave in, I had the sense she was relieved. As I walked past Kathleen to the kitchen to get some wine to toast Sheila's new living situation with, I whispered in her ear, "Next time I get to be the Good Cop."

"It's not really your style, sugar," she whispered back.

Over coffee the next morning I surveyed my Prozac situation. I still had a few pills left. Not many though. I looked at the schedule Dr. Kinder had given me and at the pill organizer and then threw the bottle out, pills and all, then went to work on a brief, trying to get my newest client, a check-kiter, a shot at probation.

I had told my mother to be ready at eleven-thirty. I rang her doorbell and then used my key and let myself in. "Ready to go, Mom?" I asked.

"Yes." She didn't look ready to go. She was sitting in the recliner chair—Daddy's chair—watching the Weather Channel. Storms were brewing in the Midwest.

"Okay, then. Let's go," I said with the kind of maddening brightness that people had used with me right after Thomas dumped me. I used to hate that false cheeriness, and I didn't like it any better coming out of my own mouth. It didn't work any better on my mother than it had on me. She was still sitting there. "Mom?"

"Coming," she said, not moving.

I waited. Nothing happened. "Mom?"

"Yes?"

"If we're going, you have to get out of the chair."

She rose slowly, using the walker to pull herself up.

"Is there anything I can do for you before we go?" I asked, just to make sure.

She just shrugged.

"Where are we going?" she asked after I'd loaded her and her walker into the car.

"You'll see."

As I drove from the comfortable flower-filled yards to the grittier streets of downtown San Jose, she barely said a word.

Her dander started to rise, however, as I pulled into the parking garage for the San Jose Community Hospital. First she drew her shoulders up. Then she started to scowl.

I didn't say a word.

"What are we doing here, Alissa? There's nothing wrong with me."

"I know that." I smiled at her. "Did you bring your disabled sticker, so we can park in the handicapped spot?"

She dug in her purse and handed it over.

"Thanks," I said, nabbing a spot right by the elevator.

I wouldn't say that convincing my mother to come into the hospital with me without telling her what we were doing there was easy. My "Trust Me" routine barely got us into the lobby, and the "But It's a Surprise" shtick barely got us to the elevator. I finally had to resort to the "Please Do It for Me, Mama" act to get her to the big double doors of the neonatal unit. That's when she balked for real.

"Alissa Marie Lindley, I am not taking another step until you tell me what's going on here." Her face creased into a glower, and if she'd drawn her shoulders up any higher, they would have been touching her ears.

I considered my options. I could call her bluff, leave her standing there as I marched on without her, but I wasn't entirely sure she was bluffing. There was a distinct possibility that she'd just stay there indefinitely until I did what she wanted. A mental picture formed unbidden in my mind: My mother—still in the hallway by the double doors—surrounded by TV news cameras. A hairsprayed manicured reporter thrusts a microphone into her face and asks, "Mrs. Jacobs, you've been standing in this hallway for six days. What does this mean?" My mother would reply, "It means my ungrateful daughter will never do what I ask."

"This is the neonatal unit, Mom. It's where the babies who are born early, or at such low birth weights that they might as well be preemies, have to stay."

"I know what a neonatal care unit is, Alissa. I was a nurse, you know."

I nodded. "I do know. It's one of the ways I got us this gig. Listen, Mom, there are five babies in there whose mothers abandoned them. At least three of the babies were born addicted to crack. One has HIV. Those babies are going to be there for weeks before social services can figure out what to do with them. The hospital is understaffed. The nurses are overworked. There's nobody with the time or the love for these babies to hold them and rock them while they're fed."

My mother's eyes had grown very round.

"Do you remember," I asked, "how we used to fight over holding Terry and Andrew when they were babies?"

Mom nodded. It's a miracle those boys ever learned to walk, with as little time as they spent out of our arms.

"Look at them now. They're confident, assured, wonderful young men. They know they're loved. Well, these babies might have that, if somewhere in the back of their brains there's a memory of being held and treasured, even if it's only for a little while."

"We're going to do that?" Mom asked.

"Yes. We are. We're going to come here once a week and rock those babies and feed them. I figure you and I have a little extra love that no one's using right now, and these babies need it."

Mom marched right through the double doors.

The nurses gave my mom a surgical mask and gown to drape over her clothes. She sat down in the rocking chair in the corner and they brought her a baby about the size of a dinner napkin. His diaper could have been an eye patch and even so, his skinny little legs stuck out like pencils.

They gave me a screaming little ball of fury named Samantha. I touched the nipple of the bottle to her lower lip, and she clamped her mouth around it like a trap cracking shut. Her legs stopped kicking and her arms stopped flailing. One of her incredibly tiny hands came up and clasped around my pinky finger.

Something welled up inside me. I'd expected to be touched. But a horrid combination of anger and hate and pity and sorrow and wonder and pain rose up in my throat until I thought I might choke. Why did some woman who didn't even care enough about her baby to stop doing drugs while she was pregnant get to carry this little human being in her womb for nine months and then give birth to her just to abandon her, when I, who would have even given up coffee, couldn't get an egg into the right spot? Why did this innocent and amazing tiny person have to be all alone in a world that was hard enough even with family to help? What kind of universe was this anyway, and wasn't there something we could do to change it?

Rocking this one tiny baby while she ate was just a drop of compassion in an ocean of cruelty. It probably wouldn't make one damn bit of difference, so I don't know why my heart practically sang when I looked at the tiny miracle in my arms.

"Are you okay?" one of the nurses asked.

I nodded, afraid to speak, not wanting the tears that pricked at the back of my eyelids to spill. I looked over at my mother and saw on her face a look that I knew mirrored the one on my own.

Maybe turning into my mom wasn't such a bad thing after all.

I showed up at Sheila's at about three o'clock. Jason was busy bouncing a red rubber ball off the garage door over and over. He grunted a hello.

"Hey, Jason, what's up?"

"Kevin Xu got an XBox." Bounce. Thud. Bounce. Bounce. Thud.

"That's nice."

"It's really cool." Bounce. Thud. Thud. Bounce. "Dad said he'd get me an XBox if I promised never to stick anything up my nose again. He said it would be cheaper than the medical bills."

"That's nice, too," I said.

"Yeah. I feel kind of bad, though." Thud. Bounce.

"Why?"

He caught the ball and turned to me. "I wasn't really planning on sticking anything else up there. That was nasty, Aunt Alissa."

"Good lad," I said and headed for the house.

Kathleen met me halfway there with an open box in her arms. "Alissa, you're here." She thrust the box at me. "Put this in the van and then come get some more."

"Is there a lot?"

She shook her head. "If we each take a load, I bet that'll do it. We should be out of here in half an hour."

The time limit was important. Velosovitch was due back here at five and I wanted Sheila out of here as long before that as we could manage. Statistically the most dangerous time for a battered woman is right when she leaves. I wanted that time period over before Velosovitch even knew it was happening.

The sound of Korn pounded from the house, nearly knocking me over as I walked in the door. Inside, Sheila twirled from room to room, grabbing items and wrapping them in newspaper. Then she'd hand the item to Hayley, who twirled along in Sheila's wake, and Hayley would drop whatever it was into one of four half-filled boxes that were ranged around the living room.

I felt like I'd stumbled into bedlam.

I walked over to the stereo and turned the volume down. Sheila stopped in mid-pirouette with a ceramic vase in her hand. "Alissa, you're here!"

I smiled. She bounced over, all jiggle and wiggle, and threw her arms around me. Hayley followed right after her and threw her arms around my leg. "How's it going, Sheila? You okay?" I asked.

"Great! Just great! I've got almost everything packed up. I can't wait to be out of here." Sheila's words tumbled from her, high-pitched and breathy even for her. Her eyes were unnaturally bright and a fine sheen of sweat covered her forehead.

I looked over her shoulder at Kathleen, who simply shrugged. "Super, Sheila. Hand me a box. I'll put it in my car."

"Can I help you, Auntie Alissa?" Hayley asked.

"Sure, sweetie. Take the other side of the box."

It took double Kathleen's original time estimate with me stumbling along taking tiny steps, stooped over so Hayley could hold the other end of whatever box I was carrying without actually supporting any of its weight. I almost wished she'd go bounce a ball with Jason, although my eye had begun to twitch to the rhythm of the *bounce thud bounce.* Somewhere in there I managed to switch the stereo from Korn to Susan Tedeschi, and Sheila's manic rampage through the house slowed.

"Sheila, we're going to take our loads over to Kathleen's. Are you almost ready?" She was sitting in the lotus position in the middle of the living room floor and rocking gently back and forth.

"Almost," she said with a catch in her voice.

I sat down beside her. "Do you need a minute?"

She nodded, eyes wet.

I looked at my watch. It was only four; we should be fine. I stood up. "Okay. Don't take too long, though, all right? We'll be waiting out front."

"Okay." She smiled up at me, looking even younger than she usually did.

It took more than fifteen minutes for a teary-eyed Sheila to finally emerge. I didn't want to rush her; I knew this was a big step for her. But I was pretty sure if she didn't come out soon I'd have to kill Jason—I couldn't take another bounce thud bounce—and I didn't think Kathleen would forgive me for murdering her firstborn.

We got our little caravan in gear. Kathleen went first, then me, and then Sheila. Within a few turns, we were all waiting in the left-hand turn lane at El Camino and Lawrence Expressway. It was getting close to five o'clock and traffic was already getting heavy. The wait for the green arrow seemed interminable.

Finally, it was our turn. The two cars in front of Kathleen went, then Kath. Just as I started into the intersection, the light turned yellow. I scooted through and then looked into my rearview expecting to see Sheila right on my tail. Damn. She'd decided to stop and wait for the next green. The girl certainly picked her moments to go all law-abiding.

I grabbed my cell phone and punched in her number as I maneuvered over to the left to run around. "Sheila," I said when she answered.

"Sorry, Alissa," she sighed.

"Not to worry. I'll circle around and get behind you. Just turn left onto Lawrence. You've got a few miles before the next turn. I should be able to catch up with you by then."

We hung up. I'd only just hit the End button on my cell when I heard the sickening crunch of metal on metal. Great. Just what we needed. A fender bender at this time of day in San Jose would snarl up traffic for hours. Maybe we could scoot out ahead of it.

I whipped the Volvo into the parking lot of one of the thirty bazillion strip malls that line Lawrence Expressway and headed back toward Sheila and El Camino. I heard the screeching brakes and shattering glass as I turned. Even once I was facing what had happened, though, it still didn't register.

Sheila's little blue Tracker was shoved out into Lawrence Expressway. A Toyota Camry was embedded in the passenger side. Gregory Velosovitch's red Avalance was smashed into its rear.

I pulled the Volvo into the next strip mall and was out of the car running toward the Tracker, while dialing 911 in what felt like slow motion. I'm sure it was only a matter of seconds, but the journey to that car felt interminable. Brakes continued to squeal all around as the fifty-mile-an-hour traffic attempted to avoid piling into the already smashed cars. A middle-aged woman stood on the sidewalk screaming, "He pushed her. He just drove up behind her and pushed her into traffic! Oh, my God. He pushed her." A man who had nearly laid his motorcycle down to avoid the Camry grabbed Velosovitch by the neck and forced him to the ground. I kept screaming at the 911 dispatcher, "Ambulances! Now! El Camino and Lawrence. Hurry, please!"

I steeled myself as I finally reached Sheila's Tracker and looked in the window. The air bag had deployed. Sheila slumped behind it, breathing shallowly. Her face was horribly pale, except where blood smeared it. I shut my eyes and breathed in slowly to quell the nausea that welled up, and took one of her hands.

"He must have come back early," she whispered. Her eyes opened just a little.

Why hadn't we been faster? Why had we let Sheila take so long to leave? I heard sirens. Thank God; they were coming. "Sheila, I'm so sorry. Help is coming. Just hang on."

"At the stoplight. I heard a thud. Then I was going forward. I couldn't stop it. I tried, Alissa. I tried."

"I know you did."

A ghost of a smile traced her lips and she shut her eyes again.

Seconds later, the paramedics were shouldering me aside. A twenty-something guy with fashionably messy hair and a young woman who could practically have been Sheila's double loaded Sheila onto a stretcher. They cut away some of her clothes and prodded here and there, asking what hurt and what didn't.

"How bad?" I asked them as they strapped her in.

"We won't know for sure until we get her to the hospital," Messy Hair said. He and his partner bumped the gurney into the ambulance. Another crew was working on the man in the Camry. A police officer was putting cuffs on Velosovitch.

The female paramedic waited until her partner had gotten into the ambulance, then beckoned me over. "It could be her spleen. It happens a lot with car accidents. The seat belt, you know."

I nodded, trying to process what she was telling me.

"We're going to San Jose Community. You can follow us there, but you probably won't be able to see her until she's out of surgery. We'll take the very best care of her." She slid her waistband down just enough so I could see the butterfly tattoo on her hip. She got in the ambulance and I ran to my car and followed.

Ah, waiting rooms. Is there any more miserable place on earth to wait than a waiting room? The chairs are uncomfortable, the magazines are old, and the TVs only seem to get CNN and ESPN. I'd called Kathleen and told her not to come. Now I was reduced to listening to *Larry King Live* while leafing through an *Entertainment Weekly* from 1998 that proclaimed David Letterman as king of late-night TV. In a way, it was okay. My brain wasn't really functioning. Every time I shut my eyes, I saw Sheila's bloody face. I kept hearing that woman scream, "He pushed her" over and over again. My heart felt like rock in my chest. How could I have let this happen?

A cop I recognized from the accident scene came in. "Oh, there you are," he said. "The investigating officer wanted to talk to you."

"Who's the IO?" I asked.

"I am." E.J. came in.

Of course. Why did I even ask? "Aren't there any other cops in San Jose?"

He shrugged. "You should have told me she was in trouble." His voice was flat. So were his eyes.

"If you'll recall, you were the trouble that made her my client," I said.

"That's not what I meant. I meant trouble with this asshole boyfriend of hers."

I looked away. "I didn't think it was that bad. I mean, I knew she needed to get out, but I had no idea . . ."

"Well, you were wrong."

"Don't you think I know that now?"

"You should have told me. We have systems set up to deal with just these kinds of situations."

I snorted. "Yeah. Real effective ones, I know. That's why so few women are killed by their husbands or boyfriends."

It was his turn to wince. "I know they're not perfect systems, but at least they're a start. We could have helped her. I could have helped her. At least through this first part. I don't want us to be on opposite sides here, Alissa. I wouldn't have to be if you'd trust me for a second."

I turned away. I'd thought I was helping Sheila. I don't know what misguided part of me thought I had the right to make those decisions for her. Stay or leave? Take it or fight back? Somehow, in my blind faith in my own intellect and disdain for her naïveté, I had decided it was okay for me to decide for Sheila to leave, to fight. And where had my big brain landed her?

Intensive Care.

My fault. Failed again, just when I thought I'd gotten it all back together again. My big start over turned into another personal and professional disaster.

The tears actually surprised me. First I made a few strangled whimpers while I tried to choke it all back, but I couldn't do it. So I let it loose and cried. It had been so long since I'd cried. I hadn't even realized that, either. So I ended up crying over *all* the things I hadn't cried over.

I cried because Thomas didn't love me anymore. I cried because I hadn't loved Thomas enough to notice when he'd stopped loving me. I cried because I missed my father. I cried for all the wonderful moments we'd had together and for those we'd never get to have. I cried because I was so unlucky that he'd never hold my children if I could have them, and because I was so lucky to have had him beside me through so many of the important moments of my life. I cried for my mother and her loneliness, and her worry that we didn't need her anymore. I cried for Sheila and whatever made her need to be loved so desperately that she was willing to strip herself bare in front of total strangers to get it. I cried for Helena and her need for power. I cried for Kathleen, whose dreams had all come true and yet didn't satisfy her.

When I finally stopped, I thought I would feel empty, drained, completely out of emotion. Instead, I felt an incredible buoyancy, a lightness that I hadn't had in years, if I'd ever had it at all.

Through it all, E.J. sat beside me and handed me tissues. He didn't try to stop me from crying. He didn't try to fix whatever was wrong. He let the storm pass over me and just kept the Kleenex coming.

When I was done and he was still there, I was so happy, I could almost have cried.

That's when he stood up and told me he had to leave. "Police stuff, Alissa," he said. "I need to make sure Velosovitch goes away, and I need to do it right. Sometimes that takes a little extra time."

It was so unfair. I'd done it right this time. I'd gotten angry at the right person and acted accordingly. And what had I accomplished? Nothing good.

And what about my other project, Stephanie Kendall? A week after I took her case, she was still getting stuck daily while she lay in her hospital bed in this very institution. I left the emergency room waiting area and headed up to Stephanie's room.

The TV was on in her room, but the sound was off. It didn't seem to make a difference to her. She looked like a baby bird that had fallen out of the nest too soon.

"Hey, Stephanie," I said.

Her head swiveled slowly on the pillow her mouth twitched into a little smile, but she couldn't hold it for long. "You're Lily's friend, right? The one who's going to try to make it so they don't have to stick me all the time?"

"Yep. That's me." I came the rest of the way into the room.

Stephanie sighed a little. "How's that going?"

"Slow," I said.

"Yeah, slow," she echoed, and her eyelids fluttered shut.

As I watched Stephanie sleep, the chasm in my heart opened wider and wider until I finally fell all the way in.

Where was the justice in this? What had doing things right done for me or for anybody else? Hadn't my mother and my sister and I invested huge portions of ourselves in doing things the right way? And where had it left us? Lonely, confused, and used up.

I went to the bathroom, washed my face, and called Helena.

"What do we do?" I asked. "Tell me. I'm sick of trying to do the right thing and getting nowhere. I'll do whatever it takes to help Stephanie."

There was a brief silence on the other end. "We go out tonight and take care of it," Helena said.

CHAPTER FOURTEEN

From *The Angry No More Manual and Workbook*
by Dr. Gail Peterson

WHAT HAS ANGER STOLEN FROM YOU?

Have you lost friends? Jobs? Lawsuits? What about your family? Do they all speak to you? If they do speak to you, are they constantly watching their words to make sure they don't upset you? Anger can take your money, your opportunities, and any chance you have at human relationships and throw them all out the window.

Alissa's Anger Workbook:

Exercise #14

List three things you've lost because of anger.

1. Self-respect.
2. Boyfriend.
3. Meaning of Life.

I met Lily and Helena in the Crescent Moon's parking lot. Helena's smile of welcome changed into a frown the minute I got out of my car.

"What are you wearing?" she asked, brows drawn together.

"I thought that was only a phone-sex question." I looked down at the skirt and blouse I was wearing. "The other stuff is underneath."

The stuff I was referring to had been scavenged from Sheila's suitcases at Kathleen's. Let's just say they weren't my mother's foundation garments.

Helena pointed to the trenchcoat over my arm. "Lose the Goody Two-Shoes stuff and put that on."

I dug my heel a little harder into the insurance agent's chest. He cried out, but amazingly still seemed to be doing his best to get a good look at my crotch.

This was wrong. Really wrong. As wrong as Stephanie in a hospital bed trying not to cry every time someone stuck her with a needle? No, not many things are that wrong. But this was still pretty darn wrong.

"Will you sign, Todd?" Helena asked sweetly behind me.

"Yes. Yes. I'll sign," he gasped. "Whatever it is."

"That's right, Todd. Good boy," Helena purred. She untied his right hand so he could sign the Explanation of Benefits that would get the insurance company to pay for a port for Stephanie. Of course, he didn't know exactly what he was signing. Helena had everything but the place where Todd had to sign to approve it covered up.

Todd hesitated. I twisted my heel just a little bit. He moaned.

In addition to being wrong, I was becoming increasingly aware of how stupid it was. I was risking everything here. Everything. I could be arrested and disbarred. Everything I'd worked for could be undone.

Residential burglary was a nonprobationable offense. Mandatory jail time. Of course, we weren't taking anything away except a signature.

On the other hand, it looked like Stephanie would be getting her port. How wrong could it be if it got the right results?

Helena stood up and backed away from Todd. "Now, was that so hard?"

"Yes," Todd panted. "It is. Was. Whatever."

She turned to the rest of us. "Ready, ladies? I think we have what we need." We headed for the door.

"Wait!" Todd yelled. "What about me? Aren't you going to let me go? Are you going to let me, you know . . . ? I mean, are you just going to leave me here like this?"

Helena walked back to him. She put one foot up on the edge of his chair and looked down at him. "No. We're not going to let you go. Yes. We are going to leave you like this." She checked her watch. "Your wife will be back from aerobics class in about an hour, and I'm pretty sure she'll untie you."

"But what about . . . well . . . could I . . . I mean, would you let me . . ." Sweat shone off Todd's forehead. His Adam's apple bobbed up and down a few times as he fought to swallow. "It'd only take a second."

"Not a pretty confession to make, Todd," Helena commented.

"Give me a lap dance and I won't say a word to anyone about this ever," Todd said.

Helena cocked her head to one side.

"You're not seriously considering that, are you?" I squeaked.

She shrugged. "Why not? The most I ever got for a lap dance was a hundred bucks and he was a big tipper."

"Because it's demeaning, no matter what you get for it." I couldn't believe she would even entertain the thought of getting this scumbag's rocks off with a lap dance.

She stared at me, right into my eyes. "Is it demeaning to us or to him?"

"Us," I said promptly.

"Are you sure? Who's in whose thrall during a lap dance? Who's in control? Who has the power?"

I had never considered it that way. The whole lap-dance phenomena had always seemed one step away from prostitution to me, and my views on who was the victim of that particular victimless crime were pretty well set.

Helena went on. "I've had men near tears begging me to come back after a lap dance. I feel nothing for them or from them, and they're willing to pay me just to stick my ass in their face. Who is being demeaned? The one begging to sniff my crotch or the one who walks away with a hundred dollars?"

It was a new way to think about it, and I needed time to consider.

"So what's the verdict?" Todd whined. "Do I get the lap dance or not?"

Helena looked at me. I shrugged.

"Who do you want, Todd?" she asked.

"The short brunette with the tits. The one who didn't want to do it," he said, licking his lips.

I looked down. Okay. The tanga covered the worst of the cellulite on my thighs and the push-up bra was doing its job admirably. I could practically rest my chin on my cleavage. Even given all that, though, this guy must be into some kind of head trip to pick me for this questionable honor. Even I'd pick Lily or Helena instead of me and I'm predisposed to like me.

"I like the idea that she doesn't like me, and I like women with a little meat on their bones." Todd was already breathing heavily.

"But I don't even know how . . ." I stammered.

Lily giggled. "It's not brain surgery. I'll give you some pointers." She whispered some directions in my ear.

"That's it?" I asked.

"Pretty much," Lily said with a shrug. "You can get fancier if you want, but it's mainly a lot of rubbing and grinding."

I walked over and straddled Todd. He was breathing like a bellows. I sound better after running three miles. To be honest, I think just being tied up kind of excited him. Being tied up and then teased by a woman who clearly didn't like him definitely excited him.

It occurred to me that Todd might have a lot bigger problems than having a bunch of strippers break into his house and demand he sign a few papers.

I leaned down and whispered in his ear, "No."

I have to admit I was a little excited myself. Not about Todd; Todd really disgusted me. But Helena had a point about the power. There was something exhilarating about knowing you could reduce a man to the sweating, shaking thing Todd had become in front of me while feeling nothing yourself.

As we got into the car, tucking our trenchcoats around ourselves with great discretion, Helena said, "You know, Alissa, you could probably make a lot of money being a dominatrix. You seem to have a knack for it, and I've heard it pays very well."

I shook my head. "Nah. It'd take all the fun out of it if I was getting paid for it."

Helena got one of the other girls from the club to drop by Moffat's office the next morning and slip Stephanie's paperwork into his out-box. By the end of the day, surgery to implant her port had been scheduled. I couldn't figure out why I still felt uneasy, though. Maybe it had been the dream I'd had the night before. I'd been on my moonlit tightwire over the mist, but this time I'd fallen. I'd woken right before I hit the jagged rocks that lay hidden in the fog.

The uneasy feeling couldn't be guilt. We'd done good, right? We hadn't done it the right way, but sometimes you had to act, not wait.

I had no court appointments that morning, so I spent a few hours sifting through the paperwork and dumping it into Kathleen's boxes and file trays. I'd been at it for a couple of hours when the doorbell rang.

A smile sprang to my lips when I looked through the peephole. It was E.J. I threw open the door.

"I thought we were on the same side on this one," E.J. said.

I laughed. I couldn't help it. "We were never on the same side. You're the one who pointed out that the system was designed to be adversarial."

"That's not what I mean. I mean that I thought you understood why all this Butterfly Brigade crap is wrong."

"What makes you think I don't?"

"I got called out to a crime scene today. Anything that smacks of that damn Butterfly Brigade comes up, they call me."

My stomach began to churn. Maybe I should have given Moffat that lap dance. "So? You're the investigating officer. That's what they're supposed to do."

"I know. So I'm at this guy's house. He's an insurance paper pusher. Three women broke in and duct-taped him to a chair. It fits the original M.O. They've lost the blonde and added a brunette, but I'm pretty sure it's the core group. They made him sign some papers approving some kind of medical care."

"Did he say for whom?" I asked, trying to sound nonchalant even though my heart was in my throat.

"He couldn't see the name on the top of the form and he couldn't be sure who it would be. From what the women were saying, he said it could have been any number of people."

Any number of people? How many terminally ill children was this insurance company stringing along? How many people were being denied medical access by this company? The temperature seemed to rise in my head. What kind of people pulled this kind of crap on unsuspecting subscribers who probably all paid their premiums every month like good little lambs?

I realized E.J. was still standing there, fingering something in his pocket.

"So what brings you here?"

"Where were you last night, Alissa?"

"Why, Dad, was I out past curfew?"

He pulled a Pepto Bismol–pink piece of paper out of his pocket and handed it to me. It was penis-shaped. It had my name on it. "It seems you dropped your dick on the way out of that guy's condo."

I stood frozen, staring at the pink paper penis in my hand. How had my name tag from Andrea Rappaport's bridal shower ended up on Todd Moffat's floor? I hadn't even realized I still had it. Where had it been lurking all that time?

Oh, dear God, I had shoved it in the pocket of my trench-coat as Kathleen had dragged me from the restaurant that night. The trenchcoat I hadn't worn again until I'd thrown it over my underwear when I headed out on my one and only Butterfly Brigade raid.

My thoughts hopped and skipped from the humiliation of being disbarred to how on earth I would explain this to my mother to that horrible little hard stone that formed in my heart as I watched E.J.'s broad shoulders disappear through my courtyard doors.

It's not like I hadn't known it was wrong. I couldn't even plead temporary insanity. I'd been well aware that our method of getting Stephanie the port was a bad way of going about it. I had just been equally sure that displaying our ends had justi-fied our means. Or something.

It had been more than six months since I tried to smack my anger-management counselor with a chair and nine since I de-stroyed the fax machine, and what exactly had I learned?

Nothing. Absolutely nothing. When faced with a problem I didn't know how to solve, I'd crashed my personal and professional lives right into the toilet again. What the hell was wrong with me?

Yes, I was frustrated. Yes, I was angry. Yes, trying to do everything through proper channels was time-consuming, didn't always work out, and, in Sheila's case, came damn close to destroying her.

On the other hand, doing things outside the proper channels might just destroy me. Then what good would I be to anyone? Even to myself?

There had to be a balancing point somewhere, between going through the motions of working within the system and flying off into the ruleless void. I had no doubt that, assuming I could find that balancing point, it would be a tightwire act of constant adjustments and accommodations, but certainly it had to be better than what I had been doing? Anything would have to be better than careening between shutting down and the soul-sweeping rage I felt looking at Stephanie's battered little body.

Well, it wouldn't matter now. My legal career wouldn't withstand accusations of duct-taping insurance company bureaucrats to their chairs and lap-dancing signatures from them.

Then it occurred to me that E.J. had just left the evidence in my hands. He had pulled it out of his pocket and dropped it in my hand.

What the hell did that mean?

My first instinct was to go to bed and stay there. Unfortunately it was only eleven o'clock in the morning, and the sheets still held a faint whiff of E.J.'s scent. I was not going to be able to sleep this one off.

I went downstairs and snapped on the TV. They were advertising a show called *Boiling Point* where some guy goes around and tries to piss people off. Whoever stays calmest the longest gets money. I felt my forehead start to ache as I watched clip after clip of people hitting their breaking points and physically attacking the man.

I headed out into the courtyard, where I swept the dead leaves and dust up and made sure everything was watered. A few foreign twiggy things had popped up in the pots. I snapped them off.

When you tend your garden, you don't always have a lot of choice about what grows. Weeds come up along with the flowers. You do have a choice at that point, though. You can let the tough and nasty weeds strangle whatever beauty you were trying to coax from the soil, or you can pull them out. Your hands will get dirty. They might even get cut or hurt. But if you let the weeds take over, the flowers will never have a chance to bloom.

I had close to twenty pots of various plants ranged around. I had jasmine and hollyhock, bougainvillea (which was dropping leaves like crazy) and hibiscus, geraniums and sweet alyssum. I had pots of herbs and even a dwarf potted palm. It had gone from a dry, dusty place of hard concrete to something living, growing, and blooming.

Kind of like my heart.

I'd come back to San Jose so beaten and confused that I'd been afraid to feel anything, lest my emotions knock me off the fragile balancing point I'd found. They nearly had, too. Then, when I'd watered the garden of my heart, a few weeds had sprouted, too, threatening to strangle everything else I had accomplished and grown in the dusty unused places inside me.

It was time to do some weeding.

Sheila was only in the hospital a scandalous three days.

The day before she was discharged, I stopped in to see her. She still looked wan and tired, but she was sitting up and chatting with Helena while Lily brushed her hair for her.

"Hi, guys." I set the balloon I'd brought to brighten the room next to the three other flower arrangements on one of the rolling carts.

"Alissa, I feel like so much better," Sheila enthused. "Lily helped me take a shower and Helena washed my hair."

Lily helping Sheila shower didn't surprise me, but I hadn't pegged Helena for a Florence Nightingale type. Of course, every time I thought I had these women pegged, they surprised me. "That was really nice of you," I said to Helena.

She smiled. "I just stopped by to say good-bye, but I don't have to hit the road right away."

"You're going somewhere?"

She nodded. "It's time. The Crescent Moon is closed, at least for a while, and I'm ready for a change of scenery."

"So that's it. You just pack up and leave?"

"Yes, Alissa. That's what I do. I'm done here."

"What about you, Lily? Are you leaving?" I asked.

She laughed. "Oh, no. I love working at this hospital. I was ready to quit the Crescent anyway. I have almost enough saved up for a down payment on a condo."

I left, shaking my head and promising to be back the next day to help Sheila get discharged. She was going home to Kathleen's house to recuperate.

We had all hoped it wouldn't be long until she was up and around but she surprised us all by practically bouncing out of bed on day two. Who needs a spleen anyway?

After our walk I'd gone home with Kathleen to see Sheila. She was drinking coffee and playing Hi Ho Cherry-O with Hayley.

"See," Kathleen said. "She's going to be fine."

"No thanks to me," I said, pouring myself a cup of coffee as Kathleen started to unload her dishwasher.

"What is that supposed to mean?"

I set the mug down. "Have you forgotten about the whole pesky car accident thing?"

Kathleen turned to face me. "You didn't do that, Lissa. Velosovitch did that."

"It was my bright idea to put her in a position for him to do it, Kathleen."

She shook her head in disbelief. "Are you trying to tell me that getting a woman to leave an abusive lover is somehow wrong?"

"It is if you don't do it the right way, Kathleen."

"Well, as far as I'm concerned, there is no wrong way to do it."

"I would have preferred a way that didn't almost get her killed." I gave Hayley a hug and left.

*　　*　　*

Part of keeping one's balance is knowing when you've made a wrong step. Turns out there's a fine line between courage in your convictions and pigheaded stubbornness.

The bougainvillea was in the wrong spot. That was why it was dropping leaves. I should have put it where Marsha said to put it in the first place. I called Marsha's house and invited Terry and Andrew over to help me rearrange the courtyard garden. When the boys were done rearranging, I'd send out for pizza. They'll do almost anything for pizza; they were at my condo in fifteen minutes.

My nephews are Greek gods. I'm not quite sure when it happened. The last time I looked they were still in that baby giraffe phase, the one where their legs and necks are way longer than they used to be and they kind of lope around like unsteady quadrapeds. That's all a thing of the past now. The boys picked up impossibly heavy pots and moved them with lazy grace and without even grunting.

"Are you sure you don't want to leave this one right here, Aunt Alissa?" Terry grinned at me. "It looks just fine to me."

"Heavy, is it?" I asked, grinning back. "Well, you're out of luck. Your mother told me to put it over on the east wall and I didn't listen. Now you're paying the price for my not listening to her."

"Tsk, tsk." He shook his head. "I could have told you resistance is futile."

"Especially about plants," Andrew chimed in. "There's no point in it."

"Yeah, but what would I be if I didn't try?" I asked.

They laughed even though they didn't get the musical reference. Why would they? I doubt any kids their age listen to Lyle Lovett. I'm barely old enough to listen to Lyle Lovett. Lyle did have a point, however.

Later, as I chewed my pizza and washed it down with a Diet Coke, I thought about what it would mean to try. And how to even go about starting to try.

Fortunately, I still had some clients that I hadn't almost killed. I'd spent a busy day at the courthouse, although I managed to squeeze in time to have coffee with Lisa Ferguson and find out how her first date with Kirk had gone. She doesn't talk during movies, and apparently owns both a road bike and a mountain bike—a match made in heaven.

I was heading into my condo when I was intercepted by a tall thin man with dark hair, glasses, and a little notebook. He held out his hand. "Ms. Lindley?"

"Yes," I said, not quite ready to shake his hand.

"My name is Joel Shapiro. I write for *The San Jose Daily News.* Do you have a minute to talk about Sheila Montrose and the Butterfly Brigade?"

After I got done choking, I invited him in.

Joel turned out to be a delightful man. Cute, too. Queer as a three-dollar bill, unless I miss my guess, which is entirely possible because generally speaking I have no gaydar, but cute.

He sat at my kitchen counter and sipped green tea. I went for my usual Diet Coke. "Have you seen these?" he asked, pushing some newspaper clippings across the counter.

The first one I picked up was about an incident in Minneapolis. A child on a bike had been chased by a dog whose owner had let it off its leash. Later that day a group of women in negligees with butterfly tattoos on various body parts had returned to the park and chased all the dogs out of it with baseball bats.

The second article was about a man who had left his car blocking access to some gas pumps at a Kwik-Mart in Atlanta. A group of women in bras and panties pushed his car out into a busy intersection. The gas station attendant was pretty sure that at least two of them had come in minutes before and purchased rub-on butterfly tattoos.

The third one I didn't think counted. It came from Iowa. A bunch of women in bikinis had used baseball bats to smash up a swimming pool vending machine that consistently stole their quarters. As near as I could tell, none of them even had butterfly tattoos.

There were at least seven more articles, though, from Rhode Island to Phoenix. Clearly the Butterfly Brigade had gone national.

"You know that Sheila Montrose had nothing to do with these incidents," I said, shoving the stack of articles back to Joel.

"I know she's been the only person to be arrested in conjunction with the incidents here in Silicon Valley," he said, pushing them back toward me.

"Arrested, but not charged." I didn't touch them this time.

"Still, I'd like to hear her opinion of these other incidents."

"I'm afraid that's not possible. Ms. Montrose is currently recuperating from—"

"A car accident. I know. I also know that it was her boyfriend who caused it. Will domestic abuse be part of what she tries to address with the brigade?"

I nearly shot Diet Coke out my nose. "Will *what* be part of which that she tries to do what with?" I asked, staring at him. What the hell was he talking about?

"Don't you see it, Ms. Lindley? You and your client have a nearly unprecedented opportunity here. This Butterfly Brigade thing is starting to sweep the nation, and it's doing it pretty much by itself. Are you really willing to let this kind of momentum just roll to a stop?"

How had we become a grassroots movement? And why the hell did Shapiro care? I asked him.

He smiled. "Because I'm the one who spotted it from the beginning. I'm the reporter who watched it all unfold. The farther you go, the farther I go."

Shapiro finished his tea and left. I sat down in the courtyard. Maybe all of this hadn't happened for nothing. Maybe something good could come out of it.

No.

What was I thinking?

I had already tried to turn it around into something positive. I'd tried it for Stephanie Kendall and it hadn't worked. I'd tried it for Sheila and it had damn near killed her. Who else was I willing to risk?

I thought about all that energy out there, all the swirling animosity directed at all the daily bullshit. That was part of the problem, too, wasn't it? The Butterfly Brigade incidents were all directed at annoying little things. Vending machines and lines at the gas station and people who wouldn't stand in line. Everyone was angry. Everyone was frustrated. There was too much out there for one person to take on. There was too much out there for an army of people to take on. But what if we could take just a tenth of that hostility and turn it into something positive? Wouldn't that count for something?

Look at what Sheila and Helena and Lily had started. They'd struck one little blow (okay, two blows if you counted the directional guy), and suddenly women all over the country were rising up. Problem was, the hostility wasn't always directed at the right person for the right reason in the right way.

The other stuff—the big stuff—was just too big, I suppose. Who had the hubris to think they could take on domestic abuse and win?

Well, I suppose I did.

I know—I'd tried and I'd failed. So I wasn't perfect. What else was new?

I could give up and crawl into a cave, away from the light and the garden, or I could get back up on the tightrope and try again. Even if it did always seem like I was trying to walk it in heels. Maybe with a few more resources behind me and a little help, I could do it. Maybe with somebody to help me keep my balance when the waves of anger threatened to wash me right off the rope, maybe then I could pull it off.

Let's face it, what other choice did I have? Go back into my cocoon? I'd barely moved into it before it had started to suffocate me. Try not to feel? That had worked real well, hadn't it? Throwing office equipment around had been sooooooo very helpful.

I called my mother. "Hi, Mom. What's up?"

"Nothing really. Paula Finkelstein's daughter had her baby. A little girl."

"Mom, would you like to help with an idea I have?"

"How?"

"Would you be willing to make a brisket?"

Then I called Joel Shapiro's cell phone number. He hadn't even made it to the freeway yet. "Could you come back?" I asked.

CHAPTER FIFTEEN

From *The Angry No More Manual and Workbook*
by Dr. Gail Peterson

LETTING GO OF YOUR ANGER

> You have to know when to leap off the Anger Train and let it go. There are things that will always make you angry that you cannot change. Letting go is perhaps the hardest Anger-Management skill to learn and also the most crucial.

> *Alissa's Anger Workbook:*

> *Exercise #15*

> What things have you had to let go of? Name three.

> 1. The idea that I'm always right.
> 2. That the ends justify the means.
> 3. That I can do it all myself.

My place looked so much better since Kathleen started working her magic on my office and the rest of the condo. She had come in twice this week already. I'd talked her into letting me pay her a little to help with the billing and the filing and all the other stuff. She'd even gotten me to hang a few of the prints in the living room. It was still pretty bare, but it could almost pass as a design choice rather than total apathy. It was definitely ready for company.

Everyone was coming for dinner tonight. Marsha, David, Terry, and Andrew. Kathleen, Rob, Hayley, and Jason. Mom. Sheila.

"Mom, I'd like you to meet someone," I'd said when Kathleen arrived with Sheila in tow, along with the rest of her entourage.

Sheila had peeked out from behind Kath. "Nice to meet you, Mrs. Jacobs."

"Oh, my," my mother said. "You're so pretty."

I sighed. Sheila sighed louder.

Marsha and David and the boys were already waiting in the living room. "Everyone, this is my client, Sheila Montrose. She is the original Butterfly Brigade woman."

There. I'd done it. Just put it out there, just like that.

"You're kidding me," Kathleen breathed. "That is so awesome."

"No, Kath. It's not awesome. It's dangerous. It brought her 'night' job to the attention of her employers and got her fired. She loved being a daycare teacher. It's who she really is."

Everybody just stood there and stared at me, so I did what any self-respecting Jewish girl would do in a time of stress: headed for the food. "How about we all sit down to eat?"

Everyone sat down except Mom and me. Mom had made her brisket. She grumbled a little about having to use my oven, but she did it. "Marsha, come help stir the gravy," she called. "Alissa, you toss the salad."

I smiled. Who'd have thought that having my mother boss me around would gladden my heart?

There was barely room for all of us around my dining-room table. We squoze in eleven places, with the plates practically touching. Jason begged to sit between Terry and Andrew, his little pink mouth hanging open as he gazed adoringly from one big boy to the other. Hayley twirled and spun so fast that she fell and missed hitting her head on the trunk that was serving as my coffee table by inches.

That launched my mother into a description of the time I fell while pirouetting down the hall and nearly split my face on the door latch. I was so happy watching them all together that I didn't even bother to remind Mom that the first words out of her mouth when I'd done that had been not to get blood on her new rug. She'd gotten to the part where blood was spurting from my nose and lip, before Andrew and Terry could get her to stop with a chorus of "Grandma, we're trying to eat."

I looked around at their faces, at their moving mouths and shining eyes, and thought my heart might burst. Five years ago the idea of moving back to San Jose and having my mother and sister and Kathleen around my dining-room table would have been the definition of failure for me.

True, I was only here because I'd made such a mess of everything in Los Angeles. Somehow, though, this wasn't so bad. Plans change and so must our definitions of who we want to be and where we want to be. We grow up and we make compromises, and sometimes we make them until we no longer recognize ourselves. Maybe that's okay. Maybe we just have to learn to look in the mirror and accept who's there, unless we want to wind up yelling religious slogans in the Albertson's parking lot.

Yes, I'd damn near blown it. In a moment of self-righteous indignation, I'd come close to throwing it all away. It broke my heart every time I thought about E.J. leaving my courtyard, that I had thrown what might have been with him away.

But at least I'd found where I needed to be. I still had this.

At my crowded dining-room table, there was no room for an extra plate. I would always miss my father. I might always miss Thomas, even if he didn't deserve it. This wasn't what I'd planned. It wasn't what I'd dreamed.

And I didn't give a damn.

"So why a butterfly on your hip, Sheila?" my mother asked as she ladled gravy over Sheila's couscous. Everyone was having couscous with their brisket except Marsha. We'd made her a special batch of mashed potatoes with the skins still on.

Sheila took a teensy tiny bite. "Stretch mark."

"You're kidding." I'd expected some discourse on butterflies being free or unicorns being too expensive, but not stretch marks.

"Nope," she said, blond hair gleaming in the glow of the overhead light. "My first year in college I gained a bunch of weight."

Marsha nodded. "Ah, the Freshman Ten."

"More like the Freshman Fifty," Sheila said.

"Fifty?" I asked. I couldn't imagine Sheila fifty pounds heavier. "How'd you manage that?"

She shrugged. "My mom always had this thing about food. No sugar, no bleached flour, weekly weigh-ins—that kind of stuff. My dad and my brother got to eat whatever they wanted, but my sister and I pretty much just had to watch. So when I walked into the school cafeteria for the first time and they asked me what I wanted and there wasn't anyone to tell me no, I kind of wigged out."

Marsha's eyes narrowed. "How did you wig out, Sheila?"

"I ate everything in sight and just blew up. It took me a couple years to get rid of it all. I was lucky. I really only had one bad stretch mark, but it was right there on my hip. I figured a tattoo would be just the thing to cover it up."

"Where did you go to college, dear?" Mom asked, bless her heart for changing the topic while I contemplated that Sheila's problems might go well beyond being drawn to an abusive boyfriend.

"San Jose State. My degree is in child development. I have a certificate in mild to moderate disabilities, too."

A certificate and a degree. What the hell was she dancing around without her clothes on for? Oh, yeah. Money.

Once we were all stupefied from stuffing ourselves and had sent the kids off to watch a video in the living room, I said, "Okay, everyone. I have an idea. An idea that actually makes some sense."

"Really?" Sheila said.

"Yeah, really." I took a deep breath. "I know this sounds crazy and maybe we'd never get the money we needed to get it going, but I think it's worth a try. What if we could provide the kind of legal service that people like Joey's mother and Stephanie's mother needed before their situation got that desperate? What if we could do it some way that wouldn't be so expensive?" What if I could really be that avenging fairy princess on a unicorn?

"I'm not sure. What do you mean?" Marsha asked.

"Well, let's say that I provided legal services, and Kathleen, you could run the office. You've got to be the most organized person I know. Sheila could either set up a daycare service herself or provide some kind of referral service for affordable daycare. Marsha could offer counseling services. Mom could help Kathleen and teach basic health-care classes, first-aid, and preventive care. It seems to me that if we pooled our resources, we'd have a huge amount to offer."

Sheila put her fork down. "You're the one who's always saying the need is too great, that it would swamp you."

"It would, if I had to do it alone. It still might if we let it. That's why I need you guys. To keep it from swamping me. Or you. What do you think?"

"Why now?" Marsha asked.

"I've been thinking about all the things I can't control. I can't do anything about giant insurance companies whose policy is to rook their clients, or all the deadbeat dads who don't pay child support. The only thing I really control is what I do. But even if there are twenty people out there that I can't help for every person I do, at least I helped that one person."

Kathleen chewed her lip. Sheila inspected her hair for split-ends. Marsha tapped her fork against her lower lip.

Mom slapped her fist down on the table and said, "I'm in."

Then the real planning began.

*   *   *

Later that night I called Joel Shapiro. "Run the story," I said.

BUTTERFLY BRIGADE GOES LEGIT
by Joel Shapiro

Local lawyer Alissa Lindley hasn't been able to ignore all the reports about semidressed women acting like vigilantes around Silicon Valley. That's partly because one of the first, and only, women arrested in conjunction with these acts of daring is Sheila Montrose, Ms. Lindley's client.

"There is no hard evidence connecting Sheila Montrose to any of these crimes, but watching the stories unfold started me thinking," said Lindley in an exclusive interview with the *Daily News*. What Lindley noticed at first was what all of us notice every day. People are tired of the rudeness and incivility that seems to infect our society. Everybody seems to be at their boiling points, ready to explode over the littlest detail.

"A few of the Butterfly Brigade incidents seemed to concentrate on some more important issues, though," Lindley observed. Deadbeat dads and crooked insurance companies were on the Butterflies short list.

"Those are the cases that I can do something about myself,". said Lindley, "and I can do something about them without stripping down to my underwear. Not that there's anything wrong with that."

What Lindley can do is set up her own legal-aid office, but she doesn't want to stop there. "There's so much more out there that we can all help each other with. Daycare services, physical and mental health-care services, the list goes on and on. We can all contribute to the solution, and I'd like to think we all can do without resorting to vigilantism."

Lindley admits that doing things the "right" way is often frustrating and time-consuming, but she feels it's worth trying anyway.

CHAPTER SIXTEEN

From *The Angry No More Manual and Workbook*
by Dr. Gail Peterson

CHANNELING YOUR ANGER FOR GOOD

So you're angry. Now what are you going to do? Try to seek a positive way to express that anger, one that might resolve the situation for the good of yourself or, even better, for the good of others.

It was months before all the bugs were worked out. Kathleen and I didn't know anything about writing grants or where else to go for money and support. We still run up against things every day that make me want to pull my hair out, but at least I feel like I'm going bald for a reason.

I'm not alone in that. Just the other morning Kathleen asked me, "By the way, do you know what Jason said should be on the back of my superhero's cape the other night?"

"No, Kath, I don't know," I said, feeling like her straight man.

"He said it should be a big *G* for the Giggler. He said my superpower would be a high-pitched giggle that would immobilize my enemies."

Was that good or not?

"My kid loves my laugh! Isn't that great? When he thinks of me, he thinks of someone with a great laugh! And that, my friend, is awesome." Kathleen glanced at her watch. "Hey, isn't it time for you to get out of here?"

She was right, I had a court date. I changed clothes and headed down 280 to Almaden. Again.

I still get the flutters going into a courtroom, but these days that's all they are: flutters. I don't have to wear my lucky suit, write everything down on index cards, or keep my hands behind my back to keep the trembling from distracting the judge. I just do it.

I think it must be part of the balance thing.

Today, though, the one thing that could knock me back off balance again happened. E.J. was standing outside the courtroom next to mine on the fourth floor. I had waited for him to call so I could explain. My calls to him had gone unreturned.

I suppose I could have swept past like I hadn't seen him, but it was inevitable that we'd cross paths again and again. San Jose is a big city, but the circles E.J. and I ran in were considerably smaller.

"Hey," I said, coming to a stop.

"Hey, yourself," he replied. Damn. That voice again.

I felt the color rise in my face and I didn't know what to say. There's something about running into someone in a professional environment who's seen you naked that just confuses a girl. Not that I regretted having E.J. see me naked, or any of the things we did while naked together. Given half a chance, I'd get naked with him again in a New York minute.

"You look good, Alissa," he said.

So did he. I would like to say that I'd slimmed down to supermodel proportions, but that would be a lie. First of all, there are no five-foot-four-inch supermodels, and second of all, I simply like ice cream, margaritas, and my mother's bundt cake way too much to ever be truly skinny. Still, I wasn't nearly as lumpy as I had been when I'd first moved back, and it was nice of him to notice.

I thanked him. We said our good-byes. Then I went into the courtroom and grabbed hold of the back of the first set of chairs until my knees stopped wobbling.

When I got back to the condo, Kathleen was gone. She'd left a newspaper clipping on my desk.

SPREADING THEIR WINGS
by Joel Shapiro

The Butterfly Brigade idea has taken flight. With offices opening in Los Angeles, San Antonio, Minneapolis, and Newark using that name, the idea of coalitions of people offering everything from legal advice to daycare referrals has clearly come.

The concept, which originated with San Jose lawyer Alissa Lindley, is literally flying across the country.

How cool was that?

There still wasn't enough money to do what we were doing

full-time and there was way more need out there than we could ever fill, but the work was exciting.

Well, maybe sorting through twelve inches' worth of files isn't exactly thrilling, but Lisa Ferguson had given me a tip about this particular case. The county was going after a young woman for defrauding the welfare system. The problem was, she was disabled, which meant the lifetime limit didn't apply to her. Lisa had told me to go through the prosecutor's files with a fine-tooth comb, and I would get everything I needed to prove that my client was innocent and the prosecutor was an idiot. I had the distinct impression that the prosecutor hadn't bothered to read his own files. I also got the impression that this guy had pissed Lisa off in the past.

The work was mind-numbingly tedious—reams of government red-tape paperwork, stacks of medical red-tape paperwork, case-worker reports, supporting documents from everybody except her second-grade piano teacher, but that little spark inside of me sang. This was it. This was the right path.

I felt like that spark was a homing beacon now, or I had found my new balancing point. I might stumble or fall, but I also now had a net. Kathleen, my mother, Marsha, and even Sheila would catch me if I fell, or even stop me from falling all the way off should I trip.

After weeks of waiting for E.J. to call, my caller ID finally lit up with his name that evening. I grabbed the phone.

"I'm about a block away," he said. "I wondered if I could stop by."

Ten minutes later we were sitting in my courtyard on the same bench where my inner thigh had called his mother. This time there was a stately eight or nine inches between my thigh and his phone.

"I've been meaning to call," he said. "I heard about your new venture."

I held my breath. "You did? What do you think?"

He smiled. "I think it's a better way of going about what you want to accomplish. And while I'm not saying that I haven't had certain thoughts that involve you, me, and a set of handcuffs, I'd prefer not to have to arrest you."

"You know I didn't have much to do with the other stuff, don't you?" I'd wanted to tell him a million times that he'd caught me in the only Butterfly Brigade raid I'd actually participated in, but it seemed like a pretty weak defense.

"Yeah, I figured." He leaned back on the bench.

I leaned against him. "Why'd you do it, E.J.? Why'd you give me back my name tag and not turn it in?"

He put his arm around me. The weight of it across my shoulders felt delicious. "I had this funny notion that you should know I could be trusted. That we could be on the same side if you had just been willing to give me a chance. You know I didn't totally disagree with what they were doing, don't you?"

"I kind of figured that out. Yeah." I looked up at the moon shining high above us.

"Don't get me wrong; I much prefer the way you're handling your Butterfly Brigade activities now."

"Are you sure?" I teased. "I think you might have liked the

Butterfly Brigade wardrobe a little better than plain street-clothes."

"Well, there's no reason you can't keep in practice—just in case you're called on some kind of emergency. And if you ever need someone to practice on, I know someone who could fill in."

"You do, do you?"

He reached for me. I felt the world tip around me. Then his lips met mine and everything came back into balance. I was pretty sure it wasn't just good technique.

"Yeah, I do," he said.

Up Close and Personal
with the Author

ARE YOU ANGRY?

Not as angry as Alissa, but certainly frustrated, and I see a lot of anger out there on a daily basis. It seems like people are ready to explode everywhere and over anything. I see it on the roads here in California a lot, but I also see it on the bike paths and in the grocery story and at PTA meetings and in letters to the local newspaper editor. There are so many huge things wrong in our world—poverty, cruelty, tyranny, bigotry—that seem impossible to do anything about, and we're all exploding over little things, like the guy who cuts us off at the intersection or the woman who shoves in front of us in the grocery store line. I guess Alissa's story is sort of a wish fulfillment or a dream of mine that we could channel all that daily frustration into a positive force.

HAVE YOU BEEN ABLE TO CHANNEL YOUR ANGER?

I try to stay involved and do some volunteer work when I can. I'd like to do more. I hope to do more as some of my commitments at home become less time consuming.

VIGILANTE STRIPPERS? WHERE ON EARTH DID THAT COME FROM?

I live in a college town in northern California. Our streets are populated with beautiful young women who don't seem to find it necessary to wear a lot of clothing. I was in a coffee shop in downtown Davis when a very beautiful young woman walked in wearing extremely low-cut jeans and a low-cut blouse that also bared her midriff. When she bent over at the waist to look at what was in the bakery case, I realized that I could probably have cleaned out the cash register without anyone noticing. All eyes were on her. Somehow, from there, the wheels started turning.

WITH KATHLEEN'S STORY LINE, ARE YOU TRYING TO IMPLY THAT STAY-AT-HOME-MOMS CAN'T BE HAPPY?

Absolutely not. I've been a stay-at-home-mom. I've also worked full-time outside the house. In fact, I think I've tried just about every combination of motherhood and job status out there. I was one of those women who really really wanted to have kids. The biological urge to reproduce was very strong for me and, to be honest, my kids are still pretty much the center of my universe. I did find, however, that I needed some kind of outside distraction—otherwise, like Kathleen, I got a little strange on occasion.

My point with Kathleen is that sometimes you get to the place to which you've been striving and find out that it somehow doesn't satisfy you. Then what do you do? Abandon ship? Add guilt to the equation, and you really have a problem.

HAS THIS EVER HAPPENED TO YOU? THAT YOU'VE WORKED HARD TO GET SOME PLACE AND FOUND YOU DIDN'T NECESSARILY WANT TO BE THERE?

Yes. Absolutely. Constantly, even. Like Kathleen, I've been lucky. It hasn't been that I necessarily didn't want to be there, but what I thought would be the be-all end-all turned out to be not quite enough or not quite what I expected. In some ways, it's a good thing. It forces you to continue to grow. In other ways, it can be a real pain.

YOUR LAST BOOK, *DO ME, DO MY ROOTS,* HAD QUITE A FEW AUTOBIOGRAPHICAL ELEMENTS IN IT. DOES *BALANCING IN HIGH HEELS* HAVE THE SAME KIND OF RELATIONSHIP TO YOUR REAL LIFE?

No, not really. I'm not a lawyer and never have been. Nor have I ever been a stripper. That said, the character of the mother is very similar to my real-life mother. Much of *Balancing* was written when my father was critically ill and we had to face the very real possibility of losing him. My parents had been married for more than fifty years. Needless to say, my mother was really struggling. I tried to imbue the character of Alissa's mother with the grit and determination I saw in my own mother during that awful time.

There are other elements that bear some similarity to things that have happened. The bridal shower, for instance, wasn't entirely made up. For the record, I can dangle a hot dog off the back of my skirt with the best of them!

Good books are like shoes...
You can never have too many.

American Girls About Town
Lauren Weisberger, Jennifer Weiner, Adriana Trigiani, and more!
Get ready to paint the town red, white, and blue!

Luscious Lemon
Heather Swain
In life, there's always a twist!

Why Not?
Shari Low
She should have looked before she leapt.

Don't Even Think About It
Lauren Henderson
Three's company... Four's a crowd.

Hit Reply
Rocki St. Claire
What's more exciting than an I.M. from the guy who got away...

Too Good to Be True
Sheila O'Flanagan
Sometimes all love needs is a wing and a prayer.

In One Year and Out the Other
Cara Lockwood, Pamela Redmond Satran, and more!
Out with the old, in with the new, and on with the party!

Do You Come Here Often?
Alexandra Potter
Welcome back to Singleville: Population 1

The Velvet Rope
Brenda L. Thomas
Life is a party. But be careful who you invite...

Great storytelling just got a new address.

downtown press

PUBLISHED BY POCKET BOOKS

11656

Try these Downtown Press bestsellers on for size!

11226

Be the Next Downtown Girl
Contest Rules

NO PURCHASE NECESSARY TO ENTER.

1) ENTRY REQUIREMENTS:

Register to enter the contest on www.simonsaysthespot.com. Enter by submitting your story as specified below.

2) CONTEST ELIGIBILITY:

This contest is open to nonprofessional writers who are legal residents of the United States and Canada (excluding Quebec) over the age of 18 as of December 7, 2004. Entrant must not have published any more than two short stories on a professional basis or in paid professional venues. Employees (or relatives of employees living in the same household) of Simon & Schuster, VIACOM, or any of their affiliates are not eligible. This contest is void in Puerto Rico, Quebec, and wherever prohibited or restricted by law.

3) FORMAT:

Entries must not be more than 7,500 words long and must not have been previously published. Entries must be typed or printed by word processor, double spaced, on one side of noncorrasable paper. Along with a cover letter, the author's name, address, email address, and phone number must appear on the first page of the entry. The author's name, the story title, and the page number should appear on every page. Electronic submissions will be accepted and must be sent to downtowngirl@simonandschuster.com. All electronic submissions must be sent as an attachment in a Microsoft Word document. All entries must be original and the sole work of the Entrant and the sole property of the Entrant.

All submissions must be in English. Entries are void if they are in whole or in part illegible, incomplete, or damaged or if they do not conform to any of the requirements specified herein. Sponsor reserves the right, in its absolute and sole discretion, to reject any entries for any reason, including but not limited to based on sexual content, vulgarity, and/or promotion of violence.

4) ADDRESS:

Entries submitted by mail must be postmarked by July 31, 2005 and sent to:

Be The Next Downtown Girl
Author Search

Downtown Press Editorial Department
Pocket Books
1230 Sixth Avenue, 13th floor
New York, NY 10020

Or Emailed By July 31, 2005 at 11:59 PM EST as a Microsoft Word document to:

downtowngirl@simonandschuster.com

Each entry may be submitted only once. Please retain a copy of your submission. You may submit more than one story, but each submission must be mailed or emailed, as applicable, separately. Entries must be received by July 31, 2005. Not responsible for lost, late, stolen, illegible, mutilated, postage due, garbled, or misdirected mail/entries.

5) PRIZES:

One Grand Prize winner will receive:

Simon & Schuster's Downtown Press Publishing Contract for Publication of Winning Entry in a future Downtown Press Anthology, Five Hundred U.S. Dollars ($500.00), and

Downtown Press Library (20 books valued at $260.00)

Grand Prize winner must sign the Publishing contract which contains additional terms and conditions in order to be published in the anthology.

Ten Second Prize winners will receive:

A Downtown Press Collection (10 books valued at $130.00)

No contestant can win more than one prize.

6) STORY THEME

We are not restricting stories to any specific topic, however they should embody what all of our Downtown Press authors encompass—they should be smart, savvy, sexy stories that any Downtown Girl can relate to. We all know what uptown girls are like, but girls of the new millennium prefer the Downtown Scene. That's where it happens. The music, the shopping, the sex, the dating, the heartbreak, the family squabbles, the marriage, and the divorce. You name it. Downtown Girls have done it. Twice. We encourage you to register for the contest at www.simonsaysthespot.com in order to receive our monthly emails and updates from our authors and read about our titles on www.downtownpress.com to give you a better idea of what types of books we publish.

7) JUDGING:

Submissions will be judged on the equally weighted criteria of (a) basis of writing ability and (b) the originality of the story (which can be set in any time frame or location). Judging will take place on or about October 1, 2005. The judges will include a freelance editor, the editor of the future Anthology, and 5 employees of Sponsor. The decisions of the judges shall be final.

8) NOTIFICATION:

The winners will be notified by mail or phone on or about October 1, 2005. The Grand Prize Winner must sign the publishing contract in order to be awarded the prize. All federal, local, and state taxes are the responsibility of the winner. A list of the winners will be available after October 20, 2005 on:

http://www.downtownpress.com

http://www.simonsaysthespot.com

The winners' list can also be obtained by sending a stamped self-addressed envelope to:

Be The Next Downtown Girl
Author Search
Downtown Press Editorial Department
Pocket Books
1230 Sixth Avenue, 13th floor
New York, NY 10020

9) PUBLICITY:

Each Winner grants to Sponsor the right to use his or her name, likeness, and entry for any advertising, promotion, and publicity purposes without further compensation to or permission from such winner, except where prohibited by law.

10) INTERNET:

If for any reason this Contest is not capable of running as planned due to an infection by a computer virus, bugs, tampering, unauthorized intervention, fraud, technical failures, or any other causes beyond the control of the Sponsor which corrupt or affect the administration, security, fairness, integrity, or proper conduct of this Contest, the Sponsor reserves the right in its sole discretion, to disqualify any individual who tampers with the entry process, and to cancel, terminate, modify, or suspend the Contest. The Sponsor assumes no responsibility for any error, omission, interruption, deletion, defect, delay in operation or transmission, communications line failure, theft or destruction or unauthorized access to, or alteration of, entries. The Sponsor is not responsible for any problems or technical malfunctions of any telephone network or telephone lines, computer on-line systems, servers, or providers, computer equipment, software, failure of any email or entry to be received by the Sponsor due to technical problems, human error or traffic congestion on the Internet or at any website, or any combination thereof, including any injury or damage to participant's or any other person's computer relating to or resulting from participating in this Contest or downloading any materials in this Contest. CAUTION: ANY ATTEMPT TO DELIBERATELY DAMAGE ANY WEBSITE OR UNDERMINE THE LEGITIMATE OPERATION OF THE CONTEST IS A VIOLATION OF CRIMINAL AND CIVIL LAWS AND SHOULD SUCH AN ATTEMPT BE MADE, THE SPONSOR RESERVES THE RIGHT TO SEEK DAMAGES OR OTHER REMEDIES FROM ANY SUCH PERSON(S) RESPONSIBLE FOR THE ATTEMPT TO THE FULLEST EXTENT PERMITTED BY LAW. In the event of a dispute as to the identity or eligibility of a winner based on an email address, the winning entry will be declared made by the "Authorized Account Holder" of the email address submitted at time of entry. "Authorized Account Holder" is defined as the natural person 18 years of age or older who is assigned to an email address by an Internet access provider, online service provider, or other organization (e.g., business, education institution, etc.) that is responsible for assigning email addresses for the domain associated with the submitted email address. Use of automated devices are not valid for entry.

11) LEGAL Information:

All submissions become sole property of Sponsor and will not be acknowledged or returned. By submitting an entry, all entrants grant Sponsor the absolute and unconditional right and authority to copy, edit, publish, promote, broadcast, or otherwise use, in whole or in part, their entries, in perpetuity, in any manner without further permission, notice or compensation. Entries that contain copyrighted material must include a release from the copyright holder. Prizes are nontransferable. No substitutions or cash redemptions, except by Sponsor in the event of prize unavailability. Sponsor reserves the right at its sole discretion to not publish the winning entry for any reason whatsoever.

In the event that there is an insufficient number of entries received that meet the minimum standards determined by the judges, all prizes will not be awarded. Void in Quebec, Puerto Rico, and wherever prohibited or restricted by law. Winners will be required to complete and return an affidavit of eligibility and a liability/publicity release, within 15 days of winning notification, or an alternate winner will be selected. In the event any winner is considered a minor in his/her state of residence, such winner's parent/legal guardian will be required to sign and return all necessary paperwork.

By entering, entrants release the judges and Sponsor, and its parent company, subsidiaries, affiliates, divisions, advertising, production, and promotion agencies from any and all liability for any loss, harm, damages, costs, or expenses, including without limitation property damages, personal injury, and/or death arising out of participation in this contest, the acceptance, possession, use or misuse of any prize, claims based on publicity rights, defamation or invasion of privacy, merchandise delivery, or the violation of any intellectual property rights, including but not limited to copyright infringement and/or trademark infringement.

Sponsor:
Pocket Books,
an imprint of Simon & Schuster, Inc.
1230 Avenue of the Americas,
New York, NY 10020

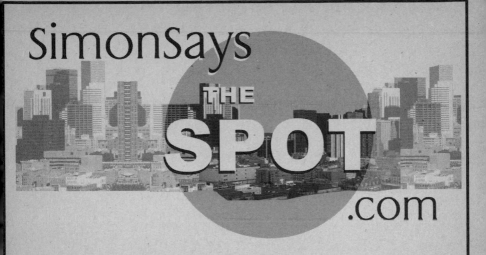